The Discretionist

GALE
CENGAGE Learning®

LIBRARY OF CONGRESS CATALOGING-IN-PUBLICATION DATA

Hawvermale, Lance, 1972–
The discretionist / Lance Hawvermale. — First edition.
pages cm
ISBN 978-1-4328-2866-0 (hardcover) — ISBN 1-4328-2866-5 (hardcover)
1. Limousine services—Employees—Fiction. 2. Young women—Abuse of—Fiction. 3. Assassins—Fiction. 4. Las Vegas (Nev.)—Fiction. I. Title.
PS3615.R585D57 2014
813'.6—dc23 2014006958

First Edition. First Printing: July 2014
Find us on Facebook– https://www.facebook.com/FiveStarCengage
Visit our website– http://www.gale.cengage.com/fivestar/
Contact Five Star™ Publishing at FiveStar@cengage.com

Printed in the United States of America
1 2 3 4 5 6 7 18 17 16 15 14

The Discretionist

Lance Hawvermale

FIVE STAR
A part of Gale, Cengage Learning

GALE
CENGAGE Learning

Farmington Hills, Mich • San Francisco • New York • Waterville, Maine
Meriden, Conn • Mason, Ohio • Chicago

To my dad, Dennis “Bag” Hawvermale, U.S.M.C.

"A gentleman is simply a patient wolf."

—Lana Turner

Chapter 1

"No matter what happens in the next few minutes, don't turn around."

The driver nodded and kept his eyes on the glittering street beyond the windshield because when a client wanted discretion you had, sensibly, two options: shut up and take the money, or shut up and take the money.

"This submarine of yours have one of those partition thingies?"

The driver didn't bother to nod this time—*partition thingy*?—just extended a hand and touched a finger to the magic button. With a gentle hum, the blackened glass rose ghostlike behind him, closing off his world from the sweaty Shangri-la the client was about to create in the back.

He waited.

No one waited like the driver. Other chauffeurs gathered in the casino parking garages for gossip, caffeine, text messaging, and—inevitably—smoking. In the strata of Las Vegas social groups, theirs was an archaeological history of shooting the breeze while their betters wiggled martinis at one another and hid behind their sunglasses at Texas Hold 'Em tables, preening like miniature gods. But the driver needed no cigarettes and even less camaraderie from those who understood the trade. Alone, his thoughts walked the steps of his imagination, and what he found at the path's end was always himself.

The door opened. Closed.

The driver felt the car's weight dip gently. He knew the vehicle intimately, like a captain with the first and only ship of his command, and judging by the minimal shift, he guessed the new passenger to be no more than a hundred and fifty pounds, give or take. And so the limousine welcomed aboard another actor, though the driver didn't care whether they knew their lines or not. All that mattered other than the sun rising tomorrow and his shoes staying shined was the client's fifty-one dollars an hour, plus tax.

Chapter 2

Later he let them out a block from where their wives were feeding slot machines.

When he opened the door for them, he caught his own reflection in the polarized glass. The cascade of colored lights here on Karen Avenue subtly transformed him. His skin was the kind of black that was neither so dark as to make his client uncomfortable nor so light that the man didn't look at him like he was a servant when he climbed out the car and said, "Nice tux."

"Thank you, sir." The driver had never worn a simple chauffeur's uniform.

The client hefted an uncertain smile to his face as another man followed him out, slightly rumpled. "I appreciate your circumspection this evening. By that I mean—"

"I know the meaning of the word, sir."

"Oh . . . yes, of course." The man tried to keep his smile in place. A hairline of sweat lingered on his upper lip. "Then I'm also sure you accept the good, old, devalued American dollar in lieu of a credit card." He palmed something from an inner suit pocket and offered his hand.

The driver, as he had done so many times before, shook.

"And if I should require your boundless prudence again in the future?"

Now it was the driver's turn to delve into his pocket. His tuxedo jacket wasn't custom-made but had at least been tailored so as not to give away its off-the-rack ancestry. From within it he retrieved a card.

ONE COOL GENTLEMAN LIMOUSINE SERVICE

The client accepted the card. "Very well, then."

With that, the two men struck off down the glaring Vegas sidewalk, veering apart from each other as they approached the Sahara.

The driver didn't even watch them go.

He closed the rear door without bothering to check on the aftermath, the spilled Courvoisier, the condoms in the tiny waste bin, the insistent scent. In the two years that he'd been the owner and sole operator of One Cool Gentleman, he'd shuttled senators, high-rollers, low-rollers on a weekend lucky streak, convention-goers, a handful of celebrities, mafiosi, honeymooners, and pricey prostitutes en route to or from the job. They could all be read, their lives examined and revealed by the flotsam they left behind. But they'd purchased from the driver more than just a ride; they also bought a few blessed miles of anonymity. And they remembered as much when they signed for the tip.

The driver slipped behind the wheel. The dashboard clock read 11:17 PM.

Feeding time in the city had begun, and the animals waited.

Chapter 3

At midnight the women started singing.

Somewhere in heaven, the driver knew, Whitney Houston was scratching at a sudden rash. The five bachelorettes had reached the chorus of "I Wanna Dance with Somebody," the only part of the song they managed without breaking into giggles and partially drunken words their mothers hadn't taught them. Because they'd insisted he didn't raise the privacy divider—the better to pester you with, my dear—he played out his prisoner's role of captive audience of one. At least they smelled nice.

He guided the car into a gentle turn.

The singing had, at least, trimmed off the conversation they'd been having about someone named Derek and the God-if-only-he-could-touch-me things *they* would say to him if they were that lucky bitch Laretta. And other tidbits: Jessica's new boyfriend, a promotion at work, the economy, open-toed pumps. They said *boobs* a lot.

The driver slowed, edging toward the curb.

"*. . . with somebody who loves me!*"

They broke into a cheer in which the driver detected a few ounces of sadness. He didn't intend to make note of the occasional strain in their voices, their unspoken sense that this marriage might change things between them. But his radar sometimes swept the local skies before he could turn it off. Thankfully it was time to shift into park and get out.

He held their door open. How many times had he performed

this particular action in the previous twenty-three months? How many times had he reached for a hand to help a lady plant her narrow heel safely on terra firma?

The first one smiled at him a little bashfully. She was probably the one he'd heard whispering about him being kinda cute. The next one wore a cocktail dress that was likely worth at least two payments on the limo. Two of them were white, two were black, and damned if the last wasn't Hispanic, a perfectly divided demographic right here on the sidewalk in front of the MGM Grand.

The tallest and least inebriated of them gave him a little wave. "Thank you so much."

"My pleasure, ma'am."

"Oh, you don't have to call her ma'am," another one said. "That kind of chivalrous nonsense goes straight to her bleach-blond head."

"And tequila goes straight to yours, Shondra," her friend returned.

Shondra pinched the corner of the driver's tie and gazed up at him. "I don't suppose you have time for a little nightcap? Sort of take the edge off . . ." She gave his tie a tug. "Hey, this isn't even a clip-on. I'm impressed."

Offering her a prefabricated smile, he carefully removed her hand before she could storm the Bastille of his bowtie. "I'm honored by the invite, but I'm on the clock."

"Sure, honey. Your loss."

Thankfully they'd paid in advance, because suddenly they drifted away, one of them removing her shoes as they went.

The driver checked himself in the glass. Women had this thing about touching a man's tie. He hadn't worn a ready-tied variety since that night a year ago when the sorority girl had reached for him with the quickness of a lioness and tried to untie it. When she realized the bow was pre-made and fastened around his collar by a strap, she'd laughed a mere foot from his face, while her embarrassed friends tried to lead her away.

Satisfied that all was well, he got back in the car and went to meet his one true love.

Chapter 4

Tully waged war with salami. As long as the driver had known him, Tully had craved little more than various incarnations of that particular cold cut. He called it a surrogate; ever since he gave up the sauce, Tully had screwed his cravings to wintergreen gum, salami on rye, and porn.

Munching the last of his sandwich, Tully dumped himself into the passenger's seat. He was fifty-six but could've passed for seventy. Faded tattoos that had lost their meaning covered both arms, hieroglyphs of a younger man's life. "Hey, maestro. You ever get the feeling that Jesus was like an Amway salesman?"

The driver checked his mirrors and pulled into the street. "Is it going to be one of those nights?"

"One of *what* nights?"

"You know what I mean."

"Listen, I told your pops I'd look after you, and now what's happening? *I'm* the one in need of lookin' after. You know how dedicated I am? I go to these meetings at midnight, goddamn *midnight,* because that's when the addicts in this town need help the most. Myself included."

"So?"

"So I'm dedicated, that's all I'm saying." He paused, exhaled. "You doin' all right?"

"Yeah, Tull. I'm chill."

"Now what the hell does that mean? Chill? That's something

a punk-ass kid would say. How old are you? Thirty yet?"

"Almost."

"Then do me a favor and say *cool,* capiche? We've been sayin' that since the fifties and it's worked out just fine. Can you do that for your old man's ex-partner?"

The driver permitted himself his first real smile of the day. "Whatever you want."

Tully swallowed the remains of his sandwich and wiped his mouth on his arm. "God, I'd lick the condensation off a goat's balls for a cigarette."

"Not in the car."

"So you always say."

"Impossible to get the smell out of the upholstery."

"Is all you care about this damn car? You know what you lack most in this second-rate life here on planet Earth?"

"What could that be?"

"Passion. You ain't passionate about shit."

"Sure, I am."

"Yeah, well then I'm Ray Charles because I sure the hell don't see it."

The driver said nothing more. He thought if he tested Tully's hypothesis too thoroughly, he'd do nothing but prove the man's point.

A silent minute passed.

Tully twisted in his seat. "You know I'm madly in love with you, right?"

"I'm afraid to answer that. What do you need?"

"Hey, give an old flatfoot the benefit of the doubt, will ya? I'm not askin' for any favors, for chrissakes. At least not any *additional* favors. I mean, these rides are enough. I'm already in your debt until the next life and all that shit. But I mean seriously. When I think about it, you're all I got. And *no,* I'm not about to start getting all touchy-feely and slap you on the back or anything and call you the son I never had. But I just wanted to say it. If we get hit by a bus tonight on the way home, for instance. Just so you know."

The driver had long been familiar with Tully's monologues and his routine expressions of brotherhood. Some of that simpatico stuff was only leftovers from the days Tully had spent on the beat with Malcolm, the driver's father. Some of it was straight from the AA playbook, as recovering alcoholics were encouraged to make amends and build bridges. But the rest of it, the core of it, was as true as the limo's engine, a motor with its own beating heart that took men where they needed to go.

"I hear you, Tull. We're cool."

"Good. Very damn good. As long as we ain't chill."

The driver laughed. "Perish the thought."

After he dropped Tully off at his apartment—though Tull insisted on calling it a *flat,* as if that could class it up a notch—he spent an hour at the car wash with his jacket off and his shirtsleeves rolled up, vacuuming out the telltales of the day's clients and realizing with no surprise at all that he'd already forgotten their faces.

He didn't mind. It was safer that way.

Chapter 5

Before picking up his next client the following day, he visited the pillar of salt his father had become. The Horizon Health Care parking lot was no place for the black Chrysler 300 with its seventy-inch stretch, its custom wet bar, and its fiber-optic lighting. The car and its upkeep were the driver's only overhead expenses. Everything about him was frugal save this Greek galley that sailed the seas of Las Vegas. In the trunk he kept two spare shirts and pants with creases like paring knives.

The nurse's assistant at the desk knew him by now. "Always good to see you, sir."

The tux, as always, took credit for the *sir.* The driver had often thought that if the gang-bangers wanted true respect from the world at large, they'd swap their red and blue rags and high-top shoes for a suit and the *sirs* it procured. "You doing okay, Laci?"

"Well, Hollywood hasn't called yet with any movie offers."

"But other than that?"

"Other than that I'm peachy. You?"

"I guess peachy works for me, too." He gave her a little nod. She was white and pretty and probably close to his age. Maybe if he ever found time to date . . .

He entered his father's room without knocking.

The former police sergeant occupied a wheelchair that faced the window. The limo's nose was just visible on the right, while on the left was a row of desert willows. It wasn't much of a view. The driver assumed his customary perch on the sill, positioning himself so that he blocked his father's field of vision. The man's eyes didn't shift. They stared at nothing.

"Tully says yo," the driver told him.

Nothing moved but his father's chest, rising and falling, rising and falling.

"Yeah, I'm still giving him rides two nights a week. You believe that? Man doesn't think he needs a car, so he sort of depends on me, you dig?" He slipped his hands into the smooth fabric of his pockets. "Still making payments on the beast, but I'm getting it cut down. Apartment's cheap, and I haven't run out and bought one of those fancy 3D TVs. I'm saving, right? Just like you used to say, laughing all the way to the bank."

None of this ever got any easier.

The driver crossed the room and poured himself a glass of water, then returned. "Hey, you want to hear a joke Tully told me the other night? It's a cop joke, so you've probably heard it before, but whatever. There's this officer who's decided to stake out a bar for DUI violations. When the bar closes up for the night, the cop sees this dude stumble out to his ride. He tries his keys on three or four cars before he finally finds the right one, then he sits behind the wheel for five minutes, messing around with his phone and his keys. While he's trying to get his car started, everybody else who was in the bar gets in their cars and drives off, so pretty soon he's the only one left. Eventually he cranks it up and starts to pull away, so the cop flashes him and pulls him over."

The driver watched his father. The man was a figure carved from wax. His hands protruded from the sleeves of his robe and lay motionless in his lap. The attendants hadn't shaved him in a day or two, and with biting clarity the driver remembered how those whiskers felt when rubbing against his cheeks. His father had loved football and his job and his son, with the order depending on the day.

The driver looked out the window for a moment, then sighed. "So the cop pulls this guy over. He gives him the Breathalyzer. But the results turn up a zero reading. The officer, he doesn't know what to think about this, so he asks the guy if he's had anything to drink. The dude smiles and says, 'Nope. Tonight I'm the designated decoy.' "

The driver waited. He actually waited for his father to respond.

"Jesus." He left the window and paced a few feet across the floor. His father was brain-dead and would grow old in that chair. Tully called it the Goddamn Throne of No Return.

"I've got to go, Pops." He squeezed his father's shoulder and left through a rear exit so as not to have to meet the intensity of Laci's smile.

CHAPTER 6

A mystery man had booked him for the entire evening.

The driver worked from five till midnight, six days out of seven. This was one of those rare nights when his phone's digital appointment book contained only a single client. At fifty-one dollars an hour, that tallied up to over half a car payment in a solitary stroke. The man's representative had paid in advance.

The driver waited within sight of the gondolas at the Venetian. A young Japanese couple kissed neared a parked Porsche. A faux cowboy in a sequined dinner jacket escorted a woman half his age on a stroll along the canals, the hotel's imitation Italian tower watching over them benignly. The lights made rainbows where once only cacti had grown.

When his client finally appeared, wearing a three-button navy suit and understated cufflinks, the driver was mildly surprised. The last time his services has been reserved by a travel agent who'd paid with a company credit card, the client had turned out to be a hip-hop artist of middling fame. His entourage had left a coin purse of Ecstasy in the car, along with a woman's earring and the smell of Dolce & Gabbana cologne. The driver had flushed the pills but saved the bling. No one had ever called about it.

But this was something different. No flamboyance here, no high-torque bodyguards with the tartar of menace between their teeth. The man had a single companion, a brunette in a tea-length dress and three-inch heels. The driver saw beautiful women nearly every night, so she made little impression on him. He didn't look at her but instead gave his client the full measure of eye contact as they approached.

"Good evening, sir."

The man was white, shorter than the driver by an inch, with hair ready for the boardroom. His cheeks and neck were smooth and bore no sign of the shadow that haunted most male faces this time of day. The driver was someone who shaved with deliberate care every workday at three-thirty in the afternoon, using a badger-hair brush and his father's shaving cup. So he respected the client's attention to detail.

The driver opened the door. Factory workers assembled widgets all day; the driver opened limo doors. "Ma'am."

"Thank you." The woman ducked and entered the car.

The client stopped, slipped out of his suit coat, and tossed it in after her. As he unfastened his cuffs, he appraised the driver. "My name's Austin Savlodar. We'll be headed to Soaring Court. You know the neighborhood?"

"Of course, sir." The street in question had room for only half a dozen houses, as each sprawled over at least eight thousand square feet. The cheapest probably went for two million dollars. "We'll be there in no time."

"Wrong."

"I'm sorry?"

Savlodar leaned an inch closer. He had a presence about him that was only magnified at point-blank range. "I'm not in any hurry. I want you to take the long way. The scenic route, as they say. Can you do that for me?"

"I understand, sir."

"Good. Then let's shove off, shall we?" His smile appeared suddenly, like the beam of a lighthouse or the grin of a mad prophet—the driver wasn't sure exactly which.

Chapter 7

Even with the divider up, the driver heard the occasional word.

Soundproofing had been an unnecessary expense, and so he'd opted against it, though more than once regret nibbled on him, urging him to pony up. Husbands cheated on their wives. Wives spoke like vipers about their husbands. Businessmen screwed their partners out of profits, and johns spoke dirty to their hired concubines. Most of the time the glass partition was enough. But sometimes people got loud. Thank God for the music.

But Savlodar hadn't bothered with the sound system, as impressive as it was. The satellites could've supplied him with whatever type of sonic camouflage he needed, but apparently his pangs were too demanding. The driver heard only one word—*spread*—and that was enough.

He accelerated easily from an intersection, continuing the tour.

Obviously this drive wasn't about getting from point A to point B, but about holding off B until Savlodar satisfied his desire, whatever that might entail. The limousine itself was purely a diversion.

I'm the designated decoy, the driver thought, the failed joke coming back to him.

He cared little either way. To each his own. So long as they didn't stain the seats.

The Chrysler eased onto Summerlin Parkway.

The driver worked the numbers in his head. Assets to one side, liabilities to the other. He was nobody's accountant—he had only two years of higher ed at Kaplan College—but regarding the sphere of his own finances, he was master and commander. By his shrewdest estimate, he could put away enough for a second car and one employee in twenty-six months. Optionally, he could hardwire that savings into investments and continue to go it alone while his portfolio grew. Granted, that risked working himself to the point of grinding exhaustion, but—

The woman uttered a single syllable of pain.

The driver bit his lower lip. The car's acoustics suppressed most of the sound, and the glass divider intercepted the rest . . . except when it didn't. He felt them moving around back there.

Another mile whispered under the tires. The sun torched the western horizon.

Savlodar's words were indistinguishable but his voice had that kiln quality to it, the tone of something cooked to hardness. A moment later, the woman let out a little moan that contained no pleasure at all. It was a noise infused with dread.

The driver clenched the wheel, then watched his fingers as they took turns relaxing. In two years he'd never had trouble, at least not any of the real kind. Some drunken club-hoppers had gotten into a scrum back there once, though they were chums again by the time the driver dropped them off. But this . . .

Damn. The last thing he needed was to lose a night's work explaining things to the police. If the woman suddenly grabbed her phone and dialed 911, Savlodar wouldn't be the only one taken downtown. So for his own well-being, the driver couldn't let things go that far.

Ignoring his most sovereign rule, he brushed the intercom button.

The thought of eavesdropping secreted a sour film along his

tongue. It wasn't that he was morally opposed to learning other people's business; he simply *didn't care* about their business. Good or evil, drunk or icily sober, what voodoo they practiced on their personal island had no effect on his. Tully had once told him that his lack of curiosity was unnatural. Perhaps so.

". . . you see this gun, bitch?"

Savlodar's hushed voice carried through the intercom and caused the driver to lift his foot off the gas. He held his breath, resumed pressure on the accelerator, and waited.

"I see it, Austin, please, put it away, I'll do whatever you want."

"But of course you will. Tell me, is it cold against your leg?"

"Jesus, Austin, *please.*"

"Hold still."

"Don't *do* this . . ."

The driver forced his lungs to resume their work. The guy had a weapon. Terrific. A felony assault was unwinding in back of the car.

"It's called a thirty-eight snubnose. Very compact. Wonderfully portable. How would you like it *inside of you*?"

The woman began to cry.

The driver concentrated on his teeth. He probed them with his tongue. No imperfections were to be found. He visited the dentist once every six months. No cavities, no fillings. He kept his teeth like he kept his fingernails and the Chrysler's interior, businesslike and clean.

He concentrated on that as Savlodar pushed the gun's barrel between the woman's legs.

Her response was muffled. The driver envisioned Savlodar's hand clamped over her mouth, his knuckles white with the force. With his other hand he violated her with a pistol.

"Little in and out for you, bitch? That turning you on?"

The sound she made was small but rhythmic and sharp with

distress. Their weight shifted, the movement transmitting through the chassis to the driver's seat. He kept both hands on the wheel—ten and two, like they taught in driver's ed—and a few feet behind him, his client who'd booked him for the evening raped a woman with a gun.

He turned off the intercom.

They said the monks in Bangladesh could meditate through monsoons. The driver imagined what that world was like, a place he'd never visited but one that had never seemed more appealing than it did now. He didn't know where it was located on the map. But if the Buddhists there could find the solace of silence in a raging storm, then he envied them that power as he drove the final few miles to his destination. There were a dozen reasons why he should be slipping the phone from his pocket and calling the police, and a dozen more why he should've pulled over and broken the bastard's leg with a tire iron. And he could produce only a single one for doing nothing at all.

It was none of his business.

Tully was wrong. He wasn't unnatural. He was simply discreet.

Minutes later, he stopped the car in the crushed-pebble driveway of a home with a roof of Spanish tiles and landscaping that fell away from the main property in gentle terraces of mint-green grass. When he stepped out of the car, he spent a moment with his cuffs, ensuring that they extended a quarter-inch from the black sleeves of his coat. It was the best form of meditation he could muster. The monks had their mandalas. The driver had his suit.

He went to the back door and touched its handle. It felt the same as it always did. He'd almost expected it to be different, somehow, considering what had transpired on the other side. Before the moment could grow more awkward than it already was, he opened the door.

Austin Savlodar popped out. “A smoother ride I’ve never had.”

The driver constructed a smile on his face in response to Savlodar’s. “Thank you, sir.”

“Darling?” He extended his hand into the car.

When the woman appeared, the driver stabbed his eyes at the topiary just beyond her shoulder. But his peripheral vision betrayed him. She held herself as if she were made of porcelain. Her face lacked expression. A single strand of hair hung in her face, but Savlodar nobly brushed it away.

The driver closed the door.

“I trust you’re up for another assignment?” Savlodar asked him.

“Of course, sir.”

“Very good. Some friends of mine are doing a bit of clubbing. They’re professional dancers, here to seek fame and fortune and all that rubbish. Do me a favor and meet them at the Tao. Take them wherever they want to go.”

“I understand.”

“After that, I’ll ring you if I need anything more. I found one of your cards next to the sherry. I hope you don’t mind.”

“That’s why it’s there.”

“Outstanding.” His hand on the woman’s back, Savlodar started to turn away, then stopped and looked at the driver with what seemed to be honest concern. “You feeling all right, friend? You’re starched a little stiff.”

The driver nodded. “I’m fine, thank you.”

“Here.” Savlodar handed him a folded bill without bothering to check the denomination. “Buy yourself a coffee or two along the way, perk yourself up. You may have a long night in front of you.”

“I appreciate it, sir.”

“De nada.” He escorted the woman toward the front of the

house, where a pair of bronze gazelles reared their hooves on either side of the door.

The driver stared after them longer than he intended.

Finally he jostled himself and returned to his seat. He ran a hand over his face. As he shifted into gear and pulled into the street, the money trapped between his fingers and the steering wheel, he cursed himself—not for driving away and leaving the woman on her own, but for activating the intercom in the first place. It was a mistake he wouldn't make again.

Chapter 8

Savlodar's friends stepped sideways from the Tao nightclub, laughing at their human chain, their arms slung around one another's shoulders. There were six of them, all young, the men with their shirt collars unbuttoned and the women with phones fastened to their hands. Lean and sculpted, they looked like athletes from ancient Rome.

"Dancers," the driver reminded himself as he watched them approach.

At least they were polite. As he held the door for them, each of them said thanks. One of the men winked at him.

Once they were sealed inside, he got behind the wheel and lowered the divider. He appreciated the sound of their excitement, their simple joy at being alive on a night like this, in a city like this; it helped him forget about recent events. At the first pause in their rapid-fire dialogue, he cleared his throat and said, "Where are we heading tonight, folks?"

The woman sitting closest to the front of the car—a blonde with eyes so blue she was surely wearing contacts—gave him a smile that conveyed her delight. "What do you recommend?"

The driver regularly engaged in these just-show-us-around conversations, so he was ready with a reply. "I'd recommend the city library. Or maybe a quiet museum."

She laughed. "Sounds thrilling, but I'm betting the library is closed."

"Ah, of course. You're right."

"Too bad, though. I'm sure it's a hoot. How about . . . um, something classy?"

"In this town?"

"Good point." She turned to the others. "Hey, anyone got anywhere particular you want to go?"

She received a variety of spirited responses, all of them facetious, so she simply gave the driver a shrug. "I'm afraid you're stuck with lunatics tonight. Our destiny is in your hands."

"Fair enough."

Before she could say anything more, he touched the switch and raised the partition between them. Though he might have been the leader of their safari, that didn't mean he had to join them in the hunt.

The ride to Tryst took only a minute, as it was a straight shot up the Strip. The driver always did his best to match the trendiness of his passengers with an appropriate club. He caught a green light at Buccaneer, with Treasure Island and its piratical croupiers on his left. His luck with the lights held at the Sands intersection, and he passed the Fashion Show Mall with only a single glance at its architectural flying saucer that beckoned shoppers from the farthest reaches of known space. He turned into the Wynn as he'd done so many times before, easing to a stop as close as he could get to the Tryst and its ostentatious indoor waterfall. While his passengers were inside, dancing themselves into a sweat, he'd wait somewhere down the street and probably again wonder why he hadn't brought along a magazine or portable DVD player. You'd think by now he would come prepared for protracted periods of thumb-twiddling. But he'd learned patience from his father. Back in the day, Malcolm and Tully could sit for hours on a stakeout. In fact, they'd been sitting on one the night Malcolm had been turned into a vegetable.

Scowling at himself for dredging it up again, the driver got out and opened the back door for the dancers.

One by one they bounded out, agile and invincible in the neons. The club beckoned them. The last of them to emerge was the one with the eyes. She was shorter than the driver by almost eight inches. It startled him when he glanced down to see her smiling at him.

"Ma'am?"

"Thank you for the ride, as short as it was."

"You're welcome."

"You'll be around?"

"Until either you're ready to leave or midnight, whichever comes first."

"Why? Your chariot here turn into a pumpkin at the stroke of twelve?"

For a moment he thought she was making fun of him, but then he realized there was no meanness in her eyes. "Something like that."

"Cool. Well, thanks again." She took a step, then looked back. "Hey."

"Yes?"

"What's your name?"

There had been only a handful of times during the prior two years when someone had caught him off guard. The attorney who'd paid a hooker a grand for a single blowjob. The businessman who'd called him a nigger. The woman who'd puked on his shoes. Those were his only surprises.

This one beat them all.

"You do have a name, don't you?"

He realized that several seconds had passed and he'd done nothing more than stand there like one of those wooden Indians his father had told him about, the ones supposedly outside the old cigar stores. He'd helped countless *Homo sapiens* from the

back of this car, and not one of them—not one—had eve
him that.

"Micah," he said, marveling at the sound of his own
"Micah Donovan."

She considered it. "Nice name."

And then she was gone, jogging to catch up with the oth

The driver—Micah Donovan—leaned against the smo
black steel until she vanished from sight.

CHAPTER 9

Three hours passed.

Though the night deepened, you couldn't tell by the Vegas skyline. Bright blues and reds chased each other like Chinese dragons across the hood of the parked limousine. When the lights blinked, the dragons changed positions, a never-ending yin and yang of a bored man passing the time.

Micah sat with his jacket off and the window down, stacking numbers on his phone. He'd learned a lot about spreadsheets since launching One Cool Gentleman almost two years ago, as well as a lot about math. It wasn't so bad, as long as you avoided that $x = y$ stuff they scared you with in junior high.

Would he be able to retire at fifty?

Assuming, of course, that he remained childless and didn't have to worry about diapers, prom dresses, and college tuition—the concepts were alien to him—could he rat-hole enough money to live comfortably so early in life? Barring a major medical problem that caused him to miss several weeks of work, could he conceivably—

The phone buzzed.

He'd swapped the obnoxious ring tone for a gentle vibration, and the phone shook in his hand, the spreadsheet on the screen replaced automatically by a number he didn't recognize.

He answered like he always did: "Driver."

"Evening, amigo. I trust you're still on the clock?"

Micah didn't immediately recognize the voice. A second

passed before it sank in. "I'm yours for another forty-five minutes, Mr. Savlodar."

"Excellent. Then I have one more favor to ask of you on this night of nights. One more mission, if you will."

Micah had been hoping the man wouldn't call for the rest of the evening. He had little desire to attend to the whims of a man Tully would've called a sick-o son of a bitch. But an obligation was, after all, an obligation. And a dollar was a dollar.

"Are you still there?"

"I'm here. What can I do for you?"

"I just called a cab to come pick up my most recent houseguest. I'm in the mood for another. Would you mind bringing her out this way?"

"Certainly, sir."

"Her name is Katelyn. She tells me that you dropped her off at a club. Could you be a chap and escort her to the house?"

"Not a problem."

"Damn, if you're not an efficient fellow. I like that. I'll have to keep you in mind. Last driver I had talked too much and smelled of cheap cigarettes. See you in a spell."

He terminated the call.

Micah thought no more of it. He got out of the car long enough to put his jacket back on, checked his cuffs and tie, and then captained the long Chrysler away from the curb. Fifty was not unreasonably early at all. If he were frugal, he could manage it. But then, what would he do with his time that first day of retirement? How would he fill up the suddenly vacuous forty-eight hours of his week?

"Better find yourself a hobby," he said to the dark eyes in the rearview mirror.

He tried to imagine himself fly-fishing.

By the time he returned to Tryst, he'd also considered woodworking, landscaping, and restoring vintage Plymouths.

He'd read somewhere that the punishing defensive lineman Rosey Grier had taken up needlepoint after his football days were finished. So there was always that. God knows what Tully would have to say about it.

He got out of the car to find the woman with the blue eyes waiting in front of the club.

"We meet again," she said, gliding toward him in a short dress that matched her eyes.

Micah slowed.

"Something wrong?" Her hair hung to her shoulders, slightly disheveled by the shifting energy of the club.

"Uh, no. Sorry. I just . . . didn't expect to see you here."

She smiled. "*You* dropped me off here, silly. Where else would I be?"

"That's . . . not what I mean." He sought salvation by turning and offering her an open door. "Please." He motioned her inside and realized that his hand wasn't steady.

Once she was in, he unbuttoned his jacket and assumed his position. The driver. That's what he was. That's *all* he was. He reminded himself of this as he got them moving toward Soaring Court, where Austin Savlodar waited.

Katelyn knocked on the raised divider.

Micah closed his eyes for a moment, even though he was driving. He opened them and waited.

She knocked again.

He had no choice but to lower the glass.

"Hey," she said.

"Do you need anything? Help yourself to the bar."

"Thanks, but I'm not a big drinker."

"There's water."

"Way ahead of you." She knocked back the bottle, then made a popping sound with her lips. "Guess what?"

Micah didn't look at her in the mirror. He would take the

swiftest route possible to Savlodar's house. He would drop her off and go promptly home.

"This is my first limo ride," she told him. "Actually my second, if you count a few hours ago. I'm trying to get a part in a new show that's opening in the fall. There's a big soiree on Friday where I'm supposed to meet the choreographer and basically grovel and throw myself at her feet."

"I'm sure you'll do fine."

"Only if I can manage not to have a nervous breakdown before then. Between the rehearsals and the nightlife, I'm borderline freaking out."

"It doesn't show."

"It doesn't? I hope not. Vegas is sort of the big time when you're in my line of work. This and New York. Yours too, huh?"

"I suppose so."

"You're not much for conversation, are you?"

"Most of the time my clients have . . . other things to do."

"Other clients? You're not Austin's personal chauffeur?"

"Freelance."

"Oh. Cool. Me too."

Micah hoped her phone would ring. Tully once told him that hell was other people's ringtones. Though that was likely true, Micah didn't care what hers sounded like so long as she occupied herself with something other than him. He wasn't trying to be rude—he couldn't recall the last time in his life he'd ever been intentionally impolite—but he simply wanted to raise the divider between his life and hers, both literally and figuratively. If he allowed himself to think about this beautiful girl alone in Savlodar's house . . .

"My name's Katelyn, by the way."

Micah tightened his grip on the wheel. Ten and two, baby, ten and two. "Pleased to meet you."

After a few moments of silence, she seemed to get the hint.

She settled back into her seat and used one of the car's fold-out mirrors to adjust her hair.

Micah just drove.

He'd never been uncomfortable with himself. Not once. But now the environment in the Chrysler's front seat compressed him, like a man too close to his own ocean floor. He rarely pushed the car beyond the legal limit, but he coaxed a few extra miles per hour from the 340-horsepower engine with its dual alternators and batteries.

The car—his livelihood on four wheels—delivered him twenty-two minutes later.

The elegant yard lights, arched like the necks of flamingos, fully illuminated the driveway. As he got out of the car, Micah fastened the top button of his coat and glanced around for no reason other than he was off his game and unable to focus. A fountain in the shape of a trident spewed three perfect curves of water. The night air smelled of the purple coneflowers planted in fluted troughs near the curb.

He went to the back and opened the door.

Katelyn stepped out, wonderment in her eyes. "Wow. This is one serious *casa.*"

Micah released her hand with haste. When he shut the door behind her, he avoided his reflection in the tinted glass.

"Will there be anything else?" he asked.

"Um . . ." She looked away from the sprawling manor. "I'm sorry, but I'm still new to all of this—am I supposed to tip you?"

"Not necessary, ma'am. Have a good evening." As he turned away, his cheeks burned. The most important thing now was driving home and letting sleep lay quiet claim to him. What went down here tonight was none of his concern. His life was a latitude line that ran parallel to others but never intersected them.

"Thank you!" she called as he closed his door.

He put the car in gear and drove away.

Chapter 10

The vacuum helped.

With his sleeves rolled up, he trolled the rear of the car for any specks that might catch the eye of tomorrow's clientele. The noise of the vacuum industriously doing its job was the sound he heard around 12:15 AM on most nights of the week. Once that was finished, he checked the two eight-inch TV screens, the MP3 player, and the contents of the wet bar. Half of the glasses would need washing—he kept two full sets in his apartment's kitchenette—but the crystal ramekin of caramel candies was still full and in no need of replenishing. He wondered if maybe he should go with the chocolates next time.

That task complete, he returned the vacuum's hose to its holder, wiped down the windows, and then surveyed the final product in the overhead lights of the car wash. Everything was as it should have been. There was only one problem.

She had asked his name.

It was as simple a thing as that. A trifle, really. She'd asked his name. So what? Yet he couldn't get around it.

He dropped behind the steering wheel and stared down the street at the layers of multicolored signs: CASH, CASINO, PAYDAY LOANS, XXX . . .

He told himself to let it go. Had Tully been sitting here beside him, the grizzled old charmer could've talked several paragraphs of sense into him: *What the hell you think you're gonna do? Politely punch the asshole in the mouth? Listen, O' son of my silent best friend, because I'm only gonna say this once. Nothing good can come of this.*

Undeniably it was true. If he accused Savlodar of anything or even upset the man, he'd put his business and his future in jeopardy.

When a rich dickhead is pissed off at you, Tully said, *you might as well put your thumb in the air and hitch a fast horse out of Dodge. At best, he'll beat your ass. At worst, he'll turn you into a pariah. You know what that means—pariah?*

"Yeah, Tull," Micah said. "I do."

He slammed the door and turned the key.

He couldn't afford to risk so much for so little. Then again, maybe it wasn't so little.

Pulling away from the car wash, he aimed the limousine toward Soaring Court.

Chapter 11

He turned into Savlodar's driveway without a plan, but eight seconds later he had one.

The bling.

Ever since the vixen with the hip-hop star had left her earring in the car, Micah had kept it in the glove box. He supposed he could've pawned it, but it wasn't his to sell. Now it would be his pretext, his designated decoy.

With the jewelry in hand, he left the car idling and headed up the walk.

He was aware of everything. The hard sound of his heels. The scent of the coneflowers in their immaculate beds. The musical splash of the fountain. And most of all his pulse, battering away in his wrists. He was not a confronter. Nor even an arguer. Yet here he was, homing in on the door and whatever waited beyond.

He stopped a few feet away. In his mind, Tully sighed and shook his balding head.

Micah lifted his hand toward the doorbell.

He didn't quite make it. What if he was wrong? What if Savlodar and Katelyn were innocently having drinks or watching an old Sidney Poitier movie or taking a swim in the pool that no doubt occupied a sizable portion of the back property? Who would be the tuxedo-wearing fool then?

"Just ask about the earring," he said softly. "Easy as that."

It sounded plausible. He would say, *I found this in the car and thought it might be yours,* to which she would respond, *Thanks, but it's not mine,* her blue dress in a color contest with her eyes, and then he would nod and offer a shaky smile, turn, and be on his way. It was as simple as it was believable.

He jabbed the doorbell just as she screamed.

The yawning insides of the house muted her cry so that it barely reached him, but its message was clear.

Startled, Micah took a step in retreat. He looked around, but he was alone. The neighborhood rested quietly in the night. His phone was ensconced in its holder on the dashboard, so if he was going to call the cops then he'd need to rush back to the curb—

No time for that. He was in this by himself and nothing Tully said at this point mattered. He ran a hand across his forehead and found it slick with sweat. If anything happened to her, who would be to blame?

Before he could change his mind, he drove his foot into the door.

His kick was well placed, landing just below the heavy latch. He was six-one and weighed one-eighty-five, and for the first time in his life he broke open a door. It swung wide on polished brass hinges to reveal a foyer with a parquet floor and a staircase curving up to the second level.

Carried by a momentum he couldn't explain, he stepped inside, crossed the foyer, and looked up, anticipating activity upstairs.

His intuition failed him. The danger came from his right.

"God*damn* you!"

He turned to see what appeared to be a study, a room stuffed with books and antique maps. Austin Savlodar, shirtless, was already on the move, running for his jacket that hung on the knob. In the light of the green-shaded banker's lamp, his bare skin was nearly albino white.

On the desk behind him, Katelyn held her dress to herself

with her hair in her face and one shoe missing. Crying, she slid awkwardly to the floor.

Micah processed it all in a single moment. Savlodar's jacket held his gun—*Very compact,* he'd said as he was raping the woman with it, *Very portable*—and he could shoot Micah dead for breaking into his house and probably get away with it. The idea of having a gun pointed at him was too incredible to comprehend. That was not his world nor anything resembling it. But the force that had borne him across the threshold didn't relent; it hurled him into the study.

He collided with Savlodar just as the man tore the revolver free of his coat. A few feet away, Katelyn, breathing hard, located her shoe. Micah lost sight of her as he grabbed the man's wrist in both hands and drove him down.

Savlodar hit the floor, his back absorbing the brunt of the impact. He barked in pain. Micah landed mostly on top of him, his body infused with a fear and frenzy he'd never known. He jerked Savlodar's arm, but the gun remained trapped between them. His face inches from Savlodar's, he saw the man's eyes narrow and his muscles harden to the point where the veins stood out like wires in his jaw. He turned into an animal, and Micah didn't have the instincts to match his transformation. Savlodar twisted suddenly and pulled the trigger.

Micah's panic saved him.

In his desperation, he shook Savlodar's arm as hard as he could, his fingernails trenching into the flesh of the man's wrist. At the moment Savlodar fired, Micah wrenched his arm sideways, altering the bullet's course as it left the barrel.

It bored into the meaty part of Savlodar's leg.

Micah went rigid as the sound of the shot filled the room, but it wasn't until Savlodar started screaming that he realized he hadn't been hit. He gasped loudly, amazed that he'd been missed. In one brutal whipping motion, he tugged Savlodar's arm in such a way that the man lost his grip on the weapon. The gun tumbled beyond sight as Micah rolled off and saw the blood and the crazed mask that was the man's face.

"I'll fucking kill you!"

Micah peddled backward on his hands, away from Savlodar's fury. He bumped into Katelyn and latched fast to her arm.

Savlodar tore his jacket from the knob and wrapped it violently around his leg.

Together Micah and Katelyn found their feet. He was thankful as hell for her, because he didn't think he could've stood up without assistance. His body trembled even more than hers.

Savlodar, breathing hard through his teeth, lashed the jacket sleeves into a tourniquet.

Micah couldn't look away from him. Not even as he took that first staggered step toward the door. Not even as Katelyn squeezed painfully on his hand.

"Run!" Savlodar yelled at them. *"Run, you motherfuckers!"*

Micah stumbled, almost fell, and then got moving, Katelyn behind him. Nothing made sense, not the saliva in his mouth, not the heartbeat drumming behind his eyes. In a manner of seconds his carefully arranged life had—

"You stop and you die!"

Micah veered into the foyer, not sure if he was pulling Katelyn along or if she was driving him forward. All that mattered was getting out, getting safe, getting away.

"You stop and you fucking die!"

They ran through the open front door and toward the street. Lights burned in nearby windows. Silhouettes watched them from the sanctuaries of million-dollar homes.

Micah didn't care. Right now he saw only the driver's door—he yanked it open—and the momentary refuge inside. He started to tell Katelyn to get in, but she was already scrambling across the seat.

He threw himself in after her and thanked God he'd left the engine running.

Chapter 12

They drove for miles in the dark.

But nothing was ever dark in this city, not really. Every third neon promised sanctuary in one form or another, though Micah believed none of them. He slowed at intersections, turned, and accelerated again without thought for where he was taking them or what they might find when they arrived. One block melted into another, the bedazzled buildings without form.

At some point his breathing returned more or less to normal. He wasn't aware that it was happening. But driving slowly through the confluence of Western and Highland Drive with Cheetah's topless wonderland on his left—its sign sporting a series of red lips making promises the club would never keep—he realized that his chest was no longer heaving, his stomach no longer bunched between his ribs.

He looked over at her, his latest and most improbable passenger.

Katelyn leaned against the passenger door, knees close together, arms hugging herself in a tight embrace. She stared silently out the window.

Micah summoned his voice from wherever it was hiding. "Are you cold?"

She nodded without looking over.

Though the night was warm, Micah keyed the heater. He didn't know what else to say.

The light turned green.

Where was he supposed to go now? What was he supposed to do? He kept his foot on the brake and tried to align his thoughts, but reason eluded him, like a sparrow leaping away from an outstretched hand.

"Katelyn?"

"Just drive."

Her words came out in little more than a whisper, but they connected with him in a way that nothing else could. Without knowing it, she'd given him the one command he could obey without doubt.

He flexed his fingers on the wheel, touched his foot to the gas, and drove.

Chapter 13

"You can turn the heat down now."

This was the first she'd spoken in half an hour. Micah did as she asked.

He wasn't even sure where they were. Somewhere around Los Prados, by the looks of things. The limo still had a quarter-tank of gas, which was good, since he hadn't thought to check the gauge until now.

"We're in trouble, aren't we?"

He glanced over at her. Still she gazed from the window, as if she might find a form of solace in the sky that couldn't be found here on the mundane ground.

"I guess so, yeah."

"He has my purse."

Micah had no response to this, and Katelyn said nothing more.

In small increments, logic returned to him. He knew what to do. He was a creature of order, but only now did he finally reclaim that part of himself that had fled when he'd thrashed on the floor with a man who'd tried to kill him. Unsure of where to go next, he defaulted to the only sure thing remaining.

Tully's building had no parking garage, so Micah parallel parked the Chrysler, taking up two spaces and hoping the cops didn't choose tonight to get picky about such things. Of course, as it was well past one AM, it was no longer tonight but tomorrow.

"Where are we?" she asked.

"A friend's."

At last she turned to him. He could barely see her eyes in the dark. "Are you sure?"

He didn't understand the question. Was he sure about what? That this was the right apartment? Then he figured it out. She was asking whether or not he trusted this person.

"It'll be okay."

"I don't think I believe you."

He couldn't blame her. Nor did he try to convince her otherwise. He may have been skilled at chauffeur–client banter, but finding any reassuring words in this disaster was beyond him. "It's the best I've got."

That seemed to be enough. She opened her door and met him on his side of the car. He started to make his way to the building's narrow staircase, but she snagged his sleeve and stopped him.

"Thank you," she said. "For getting me out of there."

He wasn't sure how to reply. This was not his element, not his venue, not his life. He wanted to say something macho in return, but he settled for something simple and real. "You're welcome."

Together they made their way silently up the stairs.

Chapter 14

Tully wiped his forehead with a beer bottle full of iced tea. "You. Have got. To be *shitting* me."

Micah sat on one end of a couch from the Reagan era, Katelyn on the other. He looked around the room as he sorted his thoughts, his eyes passing over the motel-style art, the ceramic ashtray, the stack of curling *American COP* magazines. Framed newsprint showed a pair of uniformed officers looking heroic and magnificently young.

Eventually he settled his gaze on Tully. "It happened too fast. I was in there only for maybe a minute."

"Yeah? Well evidently a minute's more than enough time to help a prick shoot himself in the leg." For a moment Tully looked like he might laugh, then he settled for tapping the bottle's neck against his forehead. "If this wasn't *you* sitting here telling me this, I wouldn't believe it for a second. But you've never been the most imaginative kid, pardon me for saying so."

"Tully, I need to know what to do next."

"Wait a sec. This rich would-be rapist, he got a name?"

Katelyn said it first. "Austin Savlodar."

Tully glared at her as if he were wondering who'd given her permission to speak. Maybe it was her dress or her youth or her looks, but he seemed affronted by how she clashed with his environment. Then it seemed to occur to him what she'd said. "Savlodar?" he asked.

Micah confirmed it with a nod.

"As in Richard Savlodar's boy? *That* Savlodar?" Tully grinned without mirth and rolled his eyes at the ceiling. "Oh, man, you might as well have picked a fight with the son of Jack the goddamn Ripper. This guy will cut out one of your kidneys and make you watch while he shoves it in a blender. Jesus Christ, you screwed yourself past the point of rescue with this one. I mean, *holy shit* this is bad."

"Who's Richard Savlodar?" Micah asked.

"Been in lock-up at Ely for half a dozen years for racketeering. They couldn't ever prove a mob connection because there wasn't one. Old Rick the Dick was plenty good at intimidating the hell out of people without the need for backup from Guido and Luigi. Even when your pop and I were on the beat back in the Jurassic age, Dick Savlodar was already a menace to the manor-born. One of his goons, some Asian guy, almost killed a poor bastard from Carson City by crushing his feet in a vise. In a *vise,* for God's sake."

"What about Austin, the son?"

"Who knows? Never met the man. And I don't exactly have my ear to the tracks when it comes to policework anymore, so as far as I know he's straight. But if I were you, I wouldn't be expecting a Christmas card and an apology anytime soon." Tully drained his tea and stared at the bottle, shaking his head. "Do you two have any idea, any *inkling* of the size of the shitstorm you're in?"

Micah glanced at Katelyn. "We're beginning to get the picture."

Tully grabbed the seat of his chair and walked it bow-legged toward the couch, dragging the chair legs across the floor until he was only two feet away. "Micah Donovan, you are my godson in spirit, the next-of-kin of the bravest man I ever knew, the child I never had and all that prissy shit, and I promise you that I'd go out in the street in this instant and get hit by a Peterbilt for you. But in the last hour, you have screwed yourself in a way that is beyond my ability to comprehend. Do you realize what you've lost?"

"I haven't lost anything."

"Not yet you haven't, but if you think this guy is gonna let bygones be bygones then I'm about to hit you in the teeth with this bottle. Why, *why* did you have to ring his doorbell?" He shot a fast look at Katelyn. "No offense, doll, but my boy here doesn't know you from Patty the Pole-Dancer." Then he snapped back to Micah. "So please tell me so those of us in the cheap seats can figure it out, *what the holy hell?*"

Micah sat still and considered it. He listened to Tully's diatribe because he always let the man have his say. Tully was his only real friend, and more often than not he spoke the truth, even when everyone around him was planting seeds of lies. But Micah had been down this path already, and as for *why* he did it, that was something that Tully—for all of his gutter-ball wisdom—would never understand.

When he finally spoke, he let it happen slowly, as he wasn't entirely sure what he needed to say. "The fact of the matter is that it happened. Savlodar tried to . . . have his way with her. I broke in. We fought. He got shot. We took off. Now, I came here because I need to know if I should go to the cops—"

"Are you joking me? I wore the badge, so believe me when I tell you that your panty-waist rich boy has *already* called Las Vegas's finest and he's *already* told them the story, which happened just like you said, except for the part about him trying to stick his joystick in the girl here."

"Her name is Katelyn."

"I don't give a shit. And you shouldn't either. Don't you hear what I'm saying? This guy has got you in a corner and you don't even know it. You told me you busted his door in. How many neighbors heard the shot and then saw you running your

black and white asses out the front door like two-thirds of an Oreo? Huh? The cops won't be after him. They're after *you.*" He pointed at Katelyn. "And you too, by the way."

Micah felt his heart again. It had settled in the limo only to rediscover its gallop. Everything was moving away from him so quickly, like ribbons in the wind . . .

"And don't even get me started about your word against his. No, sir, in that department, you don't have a chance. This guy's got enough dough to hire a *team* of lawyers, a whole *attorney assembly line.* He'll throw so much money at this thing that people will be tripping over themselves to run you down, turn you in, rat you out, and lock you up. He won't even need to send his leg-breakers after you. He'll drop the law on you like Zeus with a goddamn thunderbolt."

Tully stood up abruptly. "I need a beer but I'll settle for another tea. It ain't exactly hair of the dog, but it's swell with lemon. You two want anything?"

Micah shook his head. Katelyn didn't move at all.

"I'll be back. Try not to shoot anybody in the leg while I'm gone."

Micah let him go, glad for the respite. He fixed his eyes on the lampshade, where a stain in the shape of Puerto Rico made him wish he could close his eyes and suddenly be there, somewhere on the shore, away from these choices he'd made. If matters played out like Tully predicted, Micah's business was in serious peril. And thus his life. Even if he avoided jail, which he hoped was still possible, Savlodar would make it difficult for him to attract any new clients. And then what would he have left?

Suddenly Katelyn slid next to him. "Look at me."

Micah did. Her gaze was steady.

"This is not over," she said. "I don't want to give up."

"But—"

"He's right. Everything he's said is true. I don't have any family. Nobody high and mighty owes me any favors. So if that . . . that *sack of shit* sends police or hitmen or whoever after me, there's nothing I can do to stop him. And frankly that scares me to death. So I need something, Micah. Some kind of . . . some kind of plan. Please. Lie to me and tell me you've got something."

"I never lie."

"Why doesn't that surprise me?"

"Would it do any good if I did?"

"Maybe. I'm easy that way. When a man in a tuxedo tells me something, I tend to give him the benefit of the doubt."

"Okay, fine. I have a plan."

She nodded once, thought about it, then nodded again. "Good. That's very good. For a moment there I was starting to get worried." She gave him a smile, but there was more sadness in it than Micah cared to see.

Tully reappeared, a fresh bottle in hand. For the last twenty-odd years, Tully had brewed sun tea in his windowsill and disguised the finished product as beer. He said it made him feel better about being sober if he could still look at the labels. "You two are blowing my mind here, you know that?" He resumed his seat in front of the couch. "Look, neither of you should call anybody, got it? So if that's on your mind, I'm officially disappointing you. Doll, your girlfriends will just have to assume that you went ahead and spent the night with the guy. No texting, no waking up daddy back home."

She stiffened. "There is no daddy and I lost my phone, but I get the point, thanks."

"Great. A quick study, I like that. I figure our best option is to lay low for the rest of the night, see what tomorrow brings in way of police activity. I'll give it till mid-morning, then I'll call a buddy of mine at the precinct and nibble around for intel. If

Savlodar's gonna get the authorities involved, he won't waste time. By then we'll know what we're up against, and hopefully you can show your faces without getting arrested. You down with that?"

Micah was thankful for the guidance. It was the first thing that sounded rational.

"Terrific." Tully waved his bottle in a negating gesture. "And don't even think about going home until then to powder your noses or grab some clean undies. If that scumbag has opted not to call nine-one-one, then odds are strong that he'll take a page from his old man's playbook and send the Four Horsemen to your doors. You don't want to be there when they arrive, trust me."

"So where do we go?" Micah asked.

"You know, I've got a thought on that, and it involves getting that long black hearse of yours out of town for a few hours. It's not exactly the most inconspicuous ride on the Strip."

"Agreed."

"You ever meet my skinny sister?"

"Excuse me?"

He grinned, showing his smoker's teeth. "I got two sisters, one fat, one skinny as a twist of sticks. The skinny one's never been able to find a man, but the fat one with dinosaur thighs managed to snag a wealthy stockbroker and now lives in a lake house in Tahoe. Go figure."

Micah tried to predict where this was going but came up empty.

"Anyway, her name's Rhonda, the skinny one. Lives in a trailer in the middle of the goddamn desert out on I-15. Keeps lizards for pets and watches truTV all day. I'll call her and tell her you're en route. I'll have to look up her exact address, but just get on the road northbound and I'll let you know the details along the way."

Micah looked at Katelyn. "Are you okay with this?"

"I'm not okay with any of it."

"You can sleep while I drive."

That seemed to resonate with her in a way that Micah hadn't expected. She gave him a tight smile. "Sold."

"Smart choice," Tully said. "Now you two vamoose the hell out of here. I got your cell number on the trusty old speed-dial. I'll call you later when I have something to report. But don't get anxious. This might take a while."

"I'll need to let my clients know. I'm booked for the evening."

"Do what you need to do. Pass 'em off to some other service. God knows we got enough limos in this pretentious-ass town of ours. But do that while you're on the road. Now scram, the both of you. You're overdressed for my flat and it's starting to depress the piss out of me."

They stood and made for the door. Micah signaled his thanks but Tully waved it off with his bottle. "Just get on the highway, you handsome punk. Put some miles between you and the end of the world."

Micah thought it was the best advice he'd heard all night.

Once they were outside and heading for the car, Katelyn said, "Forget it."

"Forget what?"

"Sleeping while you drive. I've never been less tired in my life."

Chapter 15

The desert at this hour looked like outer space.

Miles earlier, they'd finally escaped the city's manic gravity, and the nebula of neons was replaced by honest stars. When Micah tipped his head to the left and looked up, the vastness beyond the window eased some of the pressure between his ribs. In a galaxy like this, where the stars were nearly without number, surely there was a chance that all of this would end in a way that left him healthy and whole.

"If you don't talk to me," Katelyn said after a while, "I'm going to grab the wheel and drive us into the ditch."

Her voice pulled him from his reverie, grounded him. "I don't know what to say."

"Anything."

"How about you start and I'll chime in when it sounds good?"

"Okay. Do you own this limousine?"

"The bank owns most of it, but yeah, it's mine."

"No boss? No supervisor?"

"Well, Tully gets pretty bossy sometimes."

"How long have you known him?"

"All my life."

"He was a policeman?"

"With my dad."

"And you're dad is . . . gone?"

Micah drummed his thumb on the wheel. "More or less."

"Wife? Girlfriend? Boyfriend?"

"None of the above."

"Too busy?"

"And rotten at socializing. I don't do the club thing."

"So you're a hermit?"

"I play basketball with some guys on Sundays. Other drivers."

"Are you good? On the court, I mean."

"I get by."

"What about music?" she asked.

"What about it?"

"I noticed we don't have the radio on."

"We can, if you want. Go ahead."

She accepted his invitation, and the dashboard lit up with the cool blue outlines of the stereo's digital readout. She flashed through a few stations.

"It's satellite," he told her, "so pick your poison. They've got it all."

"What do you prefer?"

"You choose."

"No, really. Who do you listen to?"

"I don't know. Older stuff, mostly. Stuff I got from my dad."

"Such as?"

He didn't want to look like he was totally out of sync with the top forty, but there was no avoiding it. "Some Luther, Marvin, that kind of thing. Nothing you've probably heard."

"Hey, give me some credit. I know Luther Vandross. And just last year I did a routine to a Marvin Gaye medley, thank you very much."

"A routine?"

"Dance. That's what I do. Contemporary is my favorite, but I can also manage some hip-hop and ballroom if the situation calls."

"No ballet?"

"Sorry, not my line."

"Tap?"

"Not so much."

"What about square?"

She looked at him, her hand still on the stereo. "Pardon?"

"Square dancing. You know, 'swing yer partner round and round and do-si-do.' "

She laughed. "Now *that* would be a little out of my comfort zone."

Micah smiled to himself. Her laughter was mission accomplished.

They pulled over at a last-chance convenience store that seemed to exist in its own dimension, so far was it removed from civilization. As Micah slotted his debit card into the gas pump, paranoia curled around his feet like a low-lying mist: in the movies they tracked you like this, when you got sloppy and paid with plastic, leaving an electronic trail.

He scowled at himself and went in to buy some food. Unsure of what she might like, he grabbed a variety of nutritionally dubious products along with a six-pack of water.

The man behind the counter gave him the onceover, noting his attire. "Hot date?"

"Not exactly." He paid with the same card that was probably lighting up computer monitors in Savlodar's study, the LVPD, and the National Security Agency.

Apparently the paranoia was here to stay.

"Give my regards to Broadway," the clerk said as Micah left the store.

Katelyn paced at the back of the car. Her arms were crossed in the cooling night air, her eyes on the same sky that Micah had been observing minutes before.

He set the bag on the trunk lid and then did something he'd never done before. He took his suit coat off with the intention of giving it away.

"Here," he said. "You look like you're freezing."

Her face changed; worry was replaced by appreciation. "It's not so bad, but thanks." She accepted his offer and slid into the coat. The tips of her fingers barely reached the end of the sleeves. "I guess I got lucky."

"What do you mean?"

"You're a nice guy. I could've been rescued by an axe murderer."

He removed the fuel nozzle from the car—the nineteen-gallon tank had reached capacity while he was inside buying Zingers—and returned it to the pump. "Why would I want to murder any axes?"

It was a weird attempt at humor. After what they'd experienced a few hours ago, were either of them in the mental mood for wordplay?

But miracles happened. She rolled her eyes and smiled, if only faintly. "I'll attribute that one to lack of sleep."

"I'm not sure they get any better after a full night's rest."

She started to respond, then noticed something and furrowed her brow. "What is that?"

He looked at himself. "What's what?"

She stepped toward him and lifted his arm toward the bug-crazy light above the pumps.

On his sleeve, near the cuff, was a Rorschach print of blood.

The sight of it sobered them. Without another word, they returned to the car. Micah gestured toward the bag on the seat between them, and Katelyn silently helped herself.

Before putting the car into gear, Micah rolled up his sleeve so he wouldn't be reminded of whose blood he wore on his arm and how it had come to be there.

Chapter 16

From twelve thousand miles overhead, satellites showed them the way.

Using the address that Tully had provided shortly after they left Vegas, Micah programmed the dash-mounted navigation system. It directed them to a two-lane blacktop intersecting with I-15 somewhere in the barrens of the northeastern Mojave. Two minutes later the asphalt surrendered to dirt. Occasional lights stood like lone soldiers in the darkness, the only evidence of human habitation.

"In eight hundred yards, turn right."

"That voice startles me every time," Katelyn said.

"Never leave home without it." Micah slowed as they neared a side road marked by a reflector glowing orange in the headlights.

"I need to call and report my credit cards missing," she said.

"That's probably a good idea."

"He's got my driver's license, my insurance card . . ."

"We'll take care of it."

"Will we? I'm holding you to that."

Micah turned onto a long driveway. A mobile home on cinder blocks waited at the far end.

"And I know your friend said I shouldn't, but I really need to get in touch with Dezi and let her know I'm okay. Last she knew I was being all daring and running off to have drinks with a millionaire. She's probably sent me forty-seven text messages by now."

"You can use my phone. I guess you may have to leave out a few details."

"No kidding. I don't want to lie to her, but I also don't want her calling the police because I didn't return her messages."

Micah stopped the car near a collection of metal yard art. The yard itself was grassless, with a single Joshua tree standing sentinel over a family of cast-iron jackrabbits.

He shut off the engine. It ticked like a bomb.

"This whole thing is so weird," Katelyn said.

"And then some."

"I thought he was cute. I'd only known him for three days, but I thought he was cute and harmless." She snorted. "I guess I'm not a poster child for female intuition."

"It's not your fault."

"Tell that to your friend. He seems to believe I'm going to cause you to lose your company. I don't think he likes me."

Micah thought about it for a moment, then shrugged. "It was never much of a company, anyway."

She turned toward him, though he could see only half her face in the gloom. "I know you don't mean that. You really seem to have your act together, and then—boom—you kick in one door on my behalf, and now you could lose everything."

Micah knew this was possibly true, and it worried the hell out of him, but it didn't do any good to let her hoard the guilt. "Nobody's lost anything yet, okay? Except for your purse. I'm counting on the sunrise to clear everything up so we can both go home."

"Your glass is half full, huh?"

"Until somebody knocks it over, yeah."

"So why did you do it, anyway? Why did you come back after dropping me off?"

Micah was surprised she hadn't already wondered about it. The truth was that he wondered about it himself. And because he didn't have an answer for either one of them, he did something he never did: lied. "I found an earring in the car. I thought it was yours. When I got to the front door, I heard you inside. You sounded—"

"Scared shitless and mad as hell?"

"Pretty much."

She stared at the Joshua tree. Its leaves were like green bayonets. "I won't tell you *thank you* again, because I believe in saying it only once. But I'm very glad you found that earring even though it isn't mine."

Micah let it go at that. The truth was too complex to sort out under these lonesome Nevada stars at this hour of the morning.

The door at the summit of three concrete stairs swung open. A woman stepped out. In the porch light, all Micah could see was a pink T-shirt and a pair of knobby, middle-aged legs.

"Just like Tully described her," he observed.

"I just hope she's nicer than her brother."

They got out and stopped when they saw the gun.

Chapter 17

"I ain't *never* seen no Rolls Royce parked outside my front door."

Micah didn't see the point in correcting her. After all, she was holding a rifle.

"There was a time," she continued, "when a colored man and a white girl getting out of a car like that meant trouble. And from what my brother says, that's just what you two are bringing to my doorstep."

Micah glanced at Katelyn. They stood in front of the car near a rusting silhouette of Kokopelli. Katelyn apparently read the message in his eyes—he had no idea what to say to this woman—and took a step toward the porch. "Ma'am, my name is Katelyn. A few hours ago a man tried to rape me. Micah saved me. And now we need a place to stay."

Maybe it was the clarity of her words or what she was wearing—a knee-length blue dress, heels, and a tuxedo jacket too big for her—but something about her must have affected the woman with the gun, because she lowered the barrel toward the ground.

"Name's Rhonda Tullmacher. And if that degenerate son of a bitch comes looking for you here, sweetie, he's getting a bullet from a thirty-ought-six where the sun don't shine. Come on in, coffee's brewing."

Somehow comforted by her confidence, Micah followed the women into the house.

He expected birds. Though he had little experience with folks who lived alone in the desert, for some reason he envisioned them surrounded by an oddball animal collection, with living rooms that smelled of droppings and air-freshener that fought a losing war. He'd always lived in the city. But Rhonda's home seemed animal-free. Instead, it flourished with jungle intensity. With the exception of the gas range in the tiny kitchen, every flat surface supported plant life. Dozens of pots of every imaginable shape stood on shelves, the top of the television, end tables, and cabinets. Plants spilled from these containers, vibrant and healthy ministers of life in the middle of an otherwise dry and dead world. Where there weren't windows to provide direct light to this unexpected ecosystem, Rhonda had placed lamps with warm blue bulbs. The ceiling fan was immobilized by years' worth of ivy that had been coaxed to climb the wall.

"Talk about your green thumbs," Katelyn said.

"Yeah, it's gotten a little out of hand," Rhonda admitted. "I can't sew, sing, or cook worth a damn, but I do all right with anything in dirt."

"It's incredible."

"It ain't bad. If only men had chlorophyll in their veins, maybe I wouldn't be an eternal spinster. Take a seat there on the divan. I'll get the coffee."

The cushions nearly devoured them. A peace lily tickled Micah's neck from behind, and as he shifted, he saw the little sign sticking up from its pot: GARDENERS DO IT BENT OVER.

"So Ernie tells me you're a limo driver," Rhonda said as she stood the rifle in the corner and gathered the mugs.

Micah raised an eyebrow. "Who?"

"My dumb brother. You probably know him as Tully. That's what everybody on the force always called him, and now everybody in AA. I'm sure as hell he doesn't say, 'Hello, my name is Ernest and I'm an alcoholic.' "

"I guess I never realized he had another name."

"He's never liked it. Our sister Ruby used to call him Ernesto the Pest-o. Lucky for me that nothing rhymes with Rhonda." She brought them matching cups and then claimed the only other chair in the room, a rocker within easy reach of the remote control. "I hope you take it black."

"We're not really picky at this point," Katelyn assured her.

Rhonda looked from Katelyn to Micah and back again. Though her hair hung listlessly around her face and her clothing was unremarkable, her eyes gleamed with what Micah suspected was rootsy wisdom. It must have run in the family. Tully had his own variety, an intelligence belying his appearance. "Well," she said after a while, "I think Ernie gave me enough of the sordid details that I don't need to know any more. But if you two are afraid that guy'll send the cops or his henchmen after you, you're welcome to crash out here as long as you like. There's no way they'll ever find you. Of course, I might put you to work with a trowel if you're not careful."

Micah didn't yet risk the coffee; the steam warned him of a scalded tongue. "Tully said he's going to make some calls in the morning. Hopefully we'll be able to head back around noon. We don't want to inconvenience you."

"Sounds to me like you might need to get yourself a lawyer."

"Maybe."

"Or a shovel."

"I'm sorry?"

"To bury the body when you kill that creep."

Micah shook his head. "It won't come to that."

"Okay, maybe you'll need the pruning shears instead. Plants need to be cut back every so often, for their own good and yours. Sometimes you just need to do a little pruning."

Katelyn slipped out of her shoes and folded her legs under

herself. "I think he could stand for a particular bit of pruning."

"Give him the old snip-snip, huh?"

"We'd be doing the world a favor."

"You're probably right. Though most men have more or less evolved past the Cro-Magnon state, you've still got your throwbacks. He's probably been forcing himself on women for years and using his money to get away with it."

Micah chanced a sip. It wasn't as hot as he expected. The warmth moved down his throat.

"I don't have an extra bedroom, but I can certainly provide blankets and pillows for the divan and floor, if that's good enough."

"That would be fine," Katelyn said, "though I'd be surprised if we got much sleep."

"Only to be expected. That's why the coffee's decaf. Last thing you two need is a pound of caffeine in your veins." She put her mug aside and stood up. "I'll see about those blankets. And you're welcome to the shower in the morning, but I can't offer much in the way of a change of clothes."

"I have some in the car," Micah said, though it occurred to him that his cache didn't include any socks or underwear. He kept the spare pants and shirt in case a client spilled champagne on him. He wasn't prepared for gunshot wounds and slumber parties in the plant-rampant houses of strangers. He looked at Katelyn. "Maybe we can stop somewhere and get you something."

"I've got a better idea. When we get the call that the coast is clear, we can just go home to our own clothes. We're keeping the glass half full, remember?"

"You bet."

"Sounds like my kind of philosophy," Rhonda said as she made her way down the narrow hall. "One crapload of quilts and covers, coming up!"

After a few moments of silence, Katelyn said, "What are you thinking?"

Micah took a well-timed drink to buy a bit of time and then told his second lie of the day. "I'm just thinking about that shower. Looking forward to it."

"Me, too. And I really need to get some other shoes. Nothing puts a damsel in more distress than being forced to run away while wearing heels."

He smiled, and she did too, though in his head he kept hearing what she'd said when they arrived here: *Micah saved me.*

He didn't know if that were true, but he liked the way it made him feel.

Chapter 18

Just after sunrise, Nirat drew the blade across the wood as if shearing flesh from bone.

For seven years, Alex Niratpattanasai had worked for Richard and Austin Savlodar. When the elder had gone to prison, Nirat's life had simplified. Now he was asked to be cruel only to the imperfections in wood, which he sanded and planed until smooth.

"Behold," he said to the length of fine mahogany, "you are made pleasing where once you were splintered and raw."

The new railing of the rear deck didn't reply. Too bad. Nirat wanted a bit more mysticism in his life. They said it used to be everywhere over in the motherland.

"Alex? You back there?"

Nirat chose not to respond. Though he was no Buddhist like his father—he was, in fact, nothing religious in particular—he knew the value of patience and the comfort of an empty mind. When Austin called for him like that, it was usually because he had an errand more fitting for a butler or delivery boy.

"Yo, Alex? Where the hell are—oh, there you are." On a pair of aluminum crutches, Savlodar the Younger swung his way to where Nirat was bent over what would soon be the central component of the new deck surrounding the pool. "We need to talk. Right now."

Finally Nirat looked up. Austin's tie was loose at his throat. The servant girl, Carmilla, had said he'd fought off a burglar.

Nirat let it go at that.

"Follow me." Austin hobbled to the pool house.

Nirat reluctantly set aside his rabbet plane and followed his employer into the spacious poolside suite. He enjoyed his work recently, which hadn't always been the case, but now his employer's son was going to ruin all of that. Nirat, like a soothsayer from his family's native Thailand, saw it play out before it had even begun.

"Shut the door."

Nirat complied and then stood with his hands crossed in front of him.

"You heard what happened?"

"Yes."

"The hospital took it upon themselves to call the fucking cops. I spent an hour getting cornholed for having a gun."

"Do you not have a permit?"

"Of course I have a goddamn permit. I told them it was an accident. I told them I was playing Dirty Harry in front of the mirror and the thing went off. Into my leg. Total bullshit but eventually they bought it. Considering my family name, they're not exactly overly concerned for my well-being."

Nirat believed it best to say nothing. He thought about his woodworking, how the dark grain would shimmer in the evening light.

"Look, what happened was . . ." Austin stopped in front of a framed black-and-white photograph that hung on the wall near the shower. One of Nirat's favorites, it depicted two sailors in a dinghy, alone in a vast expanse. Nirat often stood before it and wondered who the sailors were, where they were bound, and how the photographer had captured them in such a moment full of possibility. "Never mind. This is not the kind of shit I can deal with right now." Austin clawed a business card from his breast pocket and held out his hand.

Nirat didn't want the thing, whatever it might say. But he owed this man's father his life. Prisoner to the inevitable, he accepted the card and read it.

"Find out where he lives," Austin said. "Don't touch him if he's there, but someone he cares about, that's what I want. Do you understand? I want you to hurt that person, whoever it is—wife, daughter, his minister, it doesn't matter. Hurt them, Alex, like you would've done had Richard asked you to. Hurt them like the old days."

"These are not the old days."

"No shit, Sherlock. Just humor me."

"Are you certain of this course of action?"

Austin darkened. His right hand trembled—with a mangled cry he slammed the crutch against the boat on its empty sea, shattering the glass. The picture dropped from the wall, the corner of the frame striking the floor. The wood cracked, split open, and the thing fell on its face amid the shards. *"Like the fucking old days, Alex."*

Nirat took a step back, half expecting the crutch to swing in his direction. Of course the weapon would never find its target; Nirat had not survived the crucible of his former life by being too slow to avoid so crude an attack. But he was not about to put his reflexes unnecessarily to the test.

"You do this thing," Austin said, "and then it's over."

Is it? Nirat wondered.

"Now go."

"So be it." With a slight *wai,* hands together, head bowed, Nirat left him to his anger. With a certain wistfulness he passed his unfinished work at the deck and went instead in pursuit of other, less noble but sometimes equally fulfilling labors.

CHAPTER 19

At eight-thirty in the morning, Micah put on a clean shirt and added the tie because that was part of the deal. When you wore tuxedo pants and shirt, you were obliged to don the tie or risk feeling incomplete.

This was not a day he could stand to be incomplete.

He spent twenty minutes checking the car, the early sun warming his face. On any other day he would've been asleep, having turned in about an hour after midnight. Very soon his bedside alarm would buzz, and it would likely keep buzzing until he finally made it home and silenced it.

The trailer door swung open to reveal Katelyn wearing yesterday's clothes. Apparently she'd borrowed Rhonda's brush, but otherwise she was repeating her blue dress and oversized tux jacket. If Micah took a moment to admit it to himself—and he did—then he supposed she didn't look too bad in the outfit.

As she joined him at the car, she said, "My kingdom for a toothbrush."

"I settled for mouthwash."

"Me, too. But still."

"I hear you. We'll stop along the way."

"Has he called yet?"

"Nope. We've got a three-hour ride back home. I'm sure he'll check in when he's got something."

Rhonda emerged with a cardboard box, duct tape holding it shut. She tromped down the steps and placed the box on the

Chrysler's hood. "It ain't much of a care package, but it's the best I could do under the circumstances."

"You've already done enough," Katelyn said.

"Hogwash. Sleeping on that bumpy divan surely didn't do you no favors, and don't get me started about the floor."

Micah hefted the box. "It wasn't so bad."

"Did either of you sleep at all?"

Micah left that one for Katelyn to answer, busying himself by transferring the box to the front seat.

"We were *fine,*" Katelyn said. "You're a wonderful spur-of-the-moment host."

"And you're a good liar, sweetie, and I appreciate it. Here, let me give you a hug for the road."

The women embraced, and then Rhonda offered Micah her hand. "Why do I get the feeling I'm never going to see you again?"

He shook her hand. "Never can tell."

"Uh-huh. I guess we'll see."

"Thanks again." Micah got in and started the car. He watched Katelyn say a few last things, then she joined him and slammed her door.

Micah carefully turned the long car around.

Rhonda waved.

Katelyn returned the gesture as Micah got them moving along the driveway and then onto the dirt road that would eventually link them to I-15.

After they joined the interstate, they rode in silence for a while, watching the sun's alchemy change the desert rocks to gold.

"Why don't you check the box?" Micah suggested, just for something to say.

"Right. Sorry, I was fazed out."

"I don't blame you." He rubbed his chin, where the landscape wasn't quite as smooth as it was a few hours ago.

"Pining for a razor?" she asked, guessing his thoughts.

"More than you know."

"Hey, we won't even mention my legs."

"I was just thinking of something my dad used to say."

"What's that?"

"There are two things a man should be able to do well. Throw a football. And shave."

Katelyn narrowed her eyes as she considered it. "Hmmm. Not bad advice, I guess. I'm sure I throw like the girl that I am, and I always cut this place behind my ankle. Your dad sounds like an interesting gent."

"He was." Micah stared at the road without seeing it. His dad hadn't been his dad in years. The man who laughed with all of his heart was no more, having left behind only his exterior. And his son.

"First item up for bids," Katelyn said, delving into the box, "is a plastic baggie full of chocolate-covered raisins. Followed by two bottles of root beer, one bruised apple, some paper towels, and what appears to be a small geranium."

"She gave us a plant?"

"That is a fact. Think it would look good on the dashboard?"

"Not if we have to stop suddenly."

"Good point. He can live here on the seat then." She placed the plant between them. "You ever have a geranium in your car before?"

"It's a first."

"Thought so. Let's see, we have one more thing in here, wrapped in a towel."

Micah glanced down at the little plant. The significance of Rhonda's gift was slow to reach him, but when it did, he realized how much it meant. She'd taken that which represented her more than anything else and given it to them, a kind of talisman against their troubles. There was more than a little bit of mojo in that plant.

"Uh, Micah?"

"What is it?"

She lifted it from the box. "A gun."

Chapter 20

The limo idled in the breakdown lane. Micah and Katelyn had moved to the back, where he felt safe enough to examine the weapon.

In a past life it had been a shotgun. Some industrious soul had, for whatever reason, sawed away most of the wooden stock, leaving only the curved handle. Turning to a hacksaw, this would-be gunsmith had truncated the weapon's two barrels so that the whole thing was now only about twenty-one inches long. At the press of a thumb latch, the gun would fold in half, permitting the operator to slide two shells into the pipelike barrels.

Rhonda had also supplied a box of ammunition.

"I vote we throw it out the window," Katelyn said.

"Probably not a bad idea."

"Why would she think we'd need this?"

"That's just how she's built, I guess."

"I think I've already had enough shooting to last me a while, thanks."

"Me, too. And this thing probably isn't even legal."

"So if the cops really *are* after us, then they can also nail us for an unlawful firearm. This just keeps getting better."

Though he wanted nothing to do with the weapon, Micah decided against tossing it onto the side of the road. He imagined a hitchhiker finding it and using it to commit a double homicide. Leaving it lying around in the open, however, probably wasn't the best idea.

He touched a latch under one of the leather seats, causing it to lift upward like a toilet lid. In the space beneath was a bottle of glass-cleaner and two neatly folded rags. He returned the gun to its towel swaddling and stowed it and the shells under the seat.

"Is that safe?" Katelyn asked.

"For now."

"For now? What about for later?"

"We'll worry about later when it gets here."

She was about to reply when Micah's phone buzzed from its holder on the dash.

He reached over the front seat and was relieved to see Tully's name flashing on the little screen. Katelyn looked on, so close that Micah could smell the shampoo she'd found in Rhonda's shower.

"Driver."

"*Buenos dias* and all that shit."

"What's the good word?" He hoped there *was* a good word.

"You two okay?"

"We could use a change of clothes but otherwise we're cool."

"Not chill, huh? Honestly cool this time."

"Tully, come on."

"Okay, damn, you sound strung out. Sorry. Let me set your mind at ease by saying that Savlodar didn't call my friends in blue."

"You're sure?"

"I talked to them myself, so yeah, I'm sure. I've got a friend, been on the force damn near thirty years. I was as subtle as I could be, but I definitely had to mention the scumbag by name. I left you out of it, though."

"So Savlodar didn't say anything?"

"Are you not listening to me? The prick didn't call. He *did,* however, haul his ass to the ER, and *they* made the call. But don't sweat it. They sent a couple of uniforms to interview him, but he told 'em the injury was self-inflicted."

"It *was* self-inflicted."

"True enough. So it was easy to prove. But I got the impression that nobody downtown would shed any tears if the guy had hit himself in the head instead of the leg."

Micah realized that he'd barely been breathing. He took a moment to settle back in the seat and let his lungs resume their work.

Katelyn's eyes had never left him. "The coast is clear?"

Instead of answering, Micah said into the phone, "What about the apartment?"

"Just got back from there," Tully said. "I took a cab and did a ride-by—twice—but I didn't see anything out of the ordinary. No dark sedans sitting at the curb, no gunmen in the grassy knoll. Looks like Savlodar decided not to press things, considering he could get accused of attempted rape if he makes a mountain out of this particular molehill. Now do you feel better or do I have to come out there and pat you on the bottom?"

Micah gave her the thumbs-up.

Katelyn, visibly relieved, sank down beside him on the long, J-shaped seat.

"We'll be back in a couple of hours," Micah said. "And thanks."

"Who says there's never an ex-cop around when you need one?" He hung up.

Micah lowered his phone and looked at Katelyn.

"Let's go home," she said.

"You want to drive?"

"Seriously?"

"If you want."

"I appreciate it, but I think my limo-driving skills are probably on par with those of my football-throwing and leg-shaving."

He laughed, partly because of her and partly because he was simply glad it was over.

Chapter 21

Nirat stood in a stranger's living room, thinking about broken glass.

The apartment belonging to Micah Donovan, owner of One Cool Gentleman Limousine Service, might have performed double duty as a clinic. The kitchen floor looked to have been recently waxed. The countertop was free of crumbs. The windowsills were dusted and the panes clear.

From the bedroom came an insistent locust. The alarm clock throbbed with a steady *skree-skree-skree.*

Nirat wanted to return to the pool house and clean up the glass. His favorite photo still lay on its own bones, waiting to be resurrected. Thinking of the jagged pieces reminded him of the last time he'd done a job for Richard Savlodar, thirteen days before the man was arrested and held without bail. There had been a gambling addict from Kansas City. For every ten grand of his debt, Nirat had inserted a sliver of glass beneath a fingernail. Bamboo splinters weren't so readily available. And they were dreadfully cliché.

In a room used as an office, Nirat discovered extensive records: medical, financial, personal. He relaxed. The anal retentives of the world were so much easier to trace. The only out-of-the-ordinary item in the entire apartment was a large container in the kitchen; curiously, it was filled with dollar bills. Nirat had no explanation for it.

He'd parked two blocks away and walked to the apartment,

expecting to find a wife or live-in lover, some co-ed who'd gotten knocked up and now spent her time watching the soaps while her man ferried the rich about town. Instead, he'd entered a realm of order and tranquility. There wasn't much verve in the place—no knickknacks, no autographed baseballs, no girlie magazines in the john—but what it lacked in artifacts it made up for in access. Nirat easily navigated the man's life, plumbing the paperwork of his existence.

Hurt them like the old days.

Nirat's first task was locating the right person. His second would be finding some glass.

Chapter 22

The two hours it took them to reach the city limits were not silent, as Micah had feared, but filled with the kind of conversation he hadn't encountered in . . . had it been so long?

"Okay, I've got one for you," Katelyn said. She sat sideways in her seat so that she could face him, her shoulder harness barely holding her in. "Imagine that you're on a desert island—"

"Hold on a second."

"What?"

"Is it *desert* island or *deserted* island? I've heard it both ways."

"Heck if I know. Whichever you like. Tomato, tomahto, you know. We'll say deserted, so it's not like a wasteland or anything."

"Got it. So I'm on this island."

"Right. You can bring only three things with you *and*"—she waved him off before he could say anything—"you can't say your car or your suit or your shaving cream."

Micah balked in the face of such stipulations. He wore a variation of the same outfit 312 days of the year. He shaved at least fifty days more often than that. If Katelyn disallowed the obvious choices—

"Clock's ticking. We need your answer, sir." She hummed the tune from *Jeopardy*.

"Okay, uh . . . a toothbrush . . . some deodorant . . ."

"Boring!"

"But that's what I'd choose."

"*Boring*. You have one chance to redeem yourself in the eyes of the gods."

"Uh . . ." He rattled his hands on the wheel.

"Three, two . . ."

"How about—"

"One . . ."

"A bottle!" he yelled.

Katelyn frowned. "Come again?"

"A bottle."

"Say *what*?"

"A bottle. Like a soda bottle or beer bottle."

"Yeah, okay, but why?"

"Why do you think? So I can send a message. Put it in the bottle, throw it out to sea. Wait for someone to find it so they know I'm out there, hanging on."

She thought about it for a while, and then apparently decided that his answer was acceptable. "Okay, you're off the hook."

"What about you?"

"Don't change the subject."

"Since when did I become the subject?"

"You're more interesting than I am," she said.

"Hardly."

"I'm just a dancer who refuses to get a real job. There are thousands of us out there. We're like starving artists but we tend to be a bit more physically fit. Otherwise I might as well be a poet at open-mic night at a college bar."

"They call that paying your—"

"Paying your dues, yeah, I know. I've spent three years living from one audition to the next. I've been in a few decent productions and a lot of mediocre ones, and I even tried out for one of those dancing shows on TV. Trust me, dues are being paid."

"What about that party you mentioned? On Friday, right?"

"Yep. It's invite-only. Lots of bigshot dancers there. My goal is to trap a certain choreographer in the bathroom and force her to offer me an audition."

"Sounds a little extreme."

"Maybe so. But you can drive a limo forever, while I've got a pretty narrow window before the bod gets too old to throw itself across a stage."

"I think you're still a long ways away from that point."

"Thanks, but you know what I mean. Sometimes extremism doesn't feel so extreme."

Micah found that a little too esoteric to explore, so he steered things back to earth. He realized he was having actual discourse with an actual human being, and he didn't want to interrupt their rhythm. It sure beat jawing with the other drivers about engine sizes and subwoofers. "How long have you lived here?" he asked.

"Long enough to know I'm not in Kansas anymore. Or in my case, Indiana. I share a place with another dancer. And yes, before you ask, having roommates sometimes sucks. You know what I mean?"

"I live alone."

"Lucky duck."

Micah wasn't so ready to lay claim to that title. "I guess you could say it has its pros and cons."

Katelyn offered nothing in reply. Micah resisted the urge to look at her in an effort to guess her thoughts. Who was he to start being Mister Empathy? He lived his life with wheels beneath him, he kept his own counsel, and his best friend was either this car or a pot-bellied misanthrope who drank tea with beer labels.

When they finally left the barrens behind and entered the city proper, with civilization rushing up from the sand, Katelyn said, "You know, sometimes I want that bottle in real life."

"I'm not sure I know what you mean."

"You said you would want a bottle if you were on that

deserted island. I have days like that. Too many of them, actually. Sometimes I just want someone to find my message floating in front of them because I can't reach them on my own."

Micah heard the change in her voice and recognized it as his own. He lived his life as an arrow between two points of separation. He fired himself from his daily routine toward the goal of security when he was older. But there were times when he felt marooned.

His phone hummed.

His eyes went automatically to where the instrument stood in its holder on the dash. The caller ID showed the name of the nursing home where his father lived. If you could call that living.

Suddenly, he was afraid to answer. The home rarely called. This time it might be the one that he'd been dreading and at least a little bit hoping for, ever since he realized that Malcolm was never coming back.

Katelyn saw the name. She looked at him. "Micah?"

"They look after my dad."

"Oh. I thought he was . . ."

"It's okay. Mostly he is." Shrugging off his cowardice, he grabbed the phone. "Driver."

"Mr. Donovan? This is Laci. Laci Gueterez. I'm a nurse's assistant here at—"

"Has something happened?" He stared at the street in front of him without seeing it.

"Your father is fine. I'm sorry, I didn't mean to scare you."

Micah gathered a stabilizing breath. "That's all right. What can I do for you?"

"There was a man here. I thought he was visiting Mrs. Pocheski in room twenty-two, but I guess he was in there with your father."

Micah tried to guess where this was going but couldn't. Other than Tully, nobody stopped by room 23 except for Micah himself. Sure, there was the annual Christmas visit by some of his old colleagues from the department, but each year there were fewer of them, and they looked increasingly uncomfortable with the brief time they spent there.

"He left a card here at the desk," Laci said.

"A business card?"

"Yes."

"Who was he?"

"I don't know. The card has, uh . . . it's *your* card, Mr. Donovan."

Micah thought he'd misheard her. "I'm sorry?"

"The man tore your card in half and dropped it on the desk as he left."

"He what?"

Katelyn stared at him so forcefully that Micah felt the pressure of her eyes. He shot her a glance to convey his rapidly mounting certainty that Tully was wrong. Austin Savlodar had not gone quietly into the night.

"My father's okay?" he asked her, hating the tightness he heard in his voice. "You're sure? You checked on him?"

"I just came back from there. He's fine. His condition is unchanged. Mr. Donovan, is there something I can—"

Micah ended the call and dropped the phone on the seat.

"It's him, isn't it?" Katelyn asked.

"Yeah."

She looked upward and blinked several times, warding off the tears. After a few seconds, eyes turning toward the window, she said, "Don't worry about dropping me off. We should go check on your father."

"It's none of your—"

"Don't you dare say that. This *is* my business. You hear me? The whole damn thing is my business. We go together. End of discussion."

It was the kind of statement that refused rebuttal. Micah wanted to argue, but he was also secretly relieved. Not only would it save time not having to cut across town to her apartment, but if they were still in danger, he didn't want her to leave his side.

CHAPTER 23

He usually said hello to the invalids parked in their chairs near the building's main entrance, but now he hurried through without acknowledging them. Katelyn quick-stepped behind him.

The lobby smelled like it always did. An automated unit in the corner periodically emitted a fragrant burst, a whisper of spring here in the winter of the bedridden.

Micah turned left, his long strides forcing Katelyn nearly into a jog.

"Aren't we supposed to sign in or something?" she asked.

"They know me here."

The door numbers came and went. With each, his anger rose and fell, like the moon pulling a dangerous tide. How had Savlodar learned of this place? Nothing on Micah's business card connected him to the Malcolm Donovan who was a resident here, which implied a certain amount of research on Savlodar's part. Tully had miscalculated. The man wanted revenge, whether he deserved it or not.

He stopped at 23. The door was open, held in place by a hinged doorstop, its rubber cap wedged against the tiles.

"Pops?"

Though Laci had assured him that all was well, he wouldn't be satisfied until he confirmed it. He entered the room, hating the quiet, wishing yet again that he'd arrive to find his dad watching noisy daytime TV.

Malcolm sat in his chair. The attendants moved him several times throughout the day, and apparently they'd already finished the morning transfer from bed to windowside seat. Micah saw him in profile, a fifty-something black man as serene as a bronze bust.

"Yo, Pops, it's me."

Micah swung around in front of the chair, eyes searching his father's body for any sign of Savlodar's visit. They'd dressed him in a brown-checked robe and matching slippers. He was still in need of a shave.

"Is he okay?"

For a brief moment, Micah couldn't make sense of the voice behind the question. Every time he came here, unless he happened to bring Tully, he'd come alone. Never once had he invited a friend, so he experienced a mental lag before remembering her.

He knelt before his father. "He's not okay. There was an accident during a stakeout." Funny, but he'd never told this story before. And he promptly decided that he wasn't going to tell it now. "It's not important."

"Looks pretty important to me."

"He's fine, that's all that matters. I don't see any indication that . . . that anyone did anything to him." Without thinking about it, he adjusted his father's foot on the chair's steel stirrup.

"We should call somebody," she said softly.

"Who'd you have in mind?"

"The police, I guess."

"And tell them what? That someone left a torn-up business card on the front desk?"

Katelyn said nothing.

Micah straightened the folds of his father's robe. As he did so, he felt something in the breast pocket. Instantly his radar came alive again.

Katelyn sensed the change in him. "What? What's the matter?"

From his father's pocket he withdrew a driver's license. He stared at the photo.

Katelyn snatched it from his hand. "What? This is *mine.*"

Micah stood up. "It's a message."

"Oh, shit." She turned away from him, hand over her face. "Oh shit, this is bad."

Micah didn't know what to say.

"What are we supposed to do?" The rasp in her voice presaged tears, and by the time Micah got in front of her, they flowed down her face. She bunched her fists in front of her, gripping the plastic license. *"Tell me what we're supposed to do."*

"Easy, easy." He hesitated, doubting himself, then said to hell with it and put his arms around her. "We're still on our feet, right? That ol' glass is still half full."

She pressed herself against his chest.

Micah looked over the top of her head at his father, who stared into a black hole.

"Come on, now. If there's one thing my old man can't stand, it's watching a woman cry."

She withdrew just enough to gaze up at him through shimmering eyes. "I'm sorry about your dad."

For a second Micah thought he might join her in her tears. His eyes stung momentarily; he blamed it on her damned sincerity. "Thank you." He lowered his arms, and she stepped away.

"We're going to be fine," he told her, wondering if it were true.

She sniffed and dashed a hand under her nose. "I think I stained your shirt."

"I've got extras."

"I bet you do."

"I need to talk to Tully. I can take you to a friend's place."

"Appreciate the sentiment, big guy, but no way."

"It's safer."

She shook her head, eyes still rimmed with moisture. "No way. No how."

"Katelyn, please—"

"Three things. Are you listening? Three things. I'm only going to list them once, and then we need to get out of here." She took a step toward him and held up her fingers. "One, he's after both of us. Two, I don't have anywhere safe to go. So three, we're doing this together."

Micah thought of at least a dozen instant counter-arguments, but before he mustered one, Laci appeared in the doorway. "Is everything all right?"

Micah surprised himself by how easy the false smile appeared. Since when did he become so adept at artifice? "It's all good. But you didn't happen to talk to that man who was here earlier, did you?"

"He didn't say anything. He just dropped your card on the desk."

"What did he look like? Caucasian, light hair?"

"Uh, actually he was wearing sunglasses, so I couldn't really tell much. But I'm sure his hair was black. Is there some kind of trouble? Because I promise you we normally greet everyone who comes in and ask them to register . . ."

"It's cool. No harm done."

She plainly didn't believe him, but nodded, backed away, and left them alone.

Micah returned his attention to Katelyn, who'd never looked away from him. "Partners in crime, huh?" he asked.

"Looks that way to me."

Chapter 24

The Virgin Atlantic jet parted ways with the earth, leaving behind a blurry nebula of superheated air. Micah watched it lift heroically higher as he drove toward the parking garage at McCarran International. He wondered about its destination and what the weather was like there. Not for the first time, he reminded himself that he'd never seen the ocean.

Katelyn handed his phone back. "Dezi thinks I'm crazy."

"But she believed you?"

"Doesn't say much for her perceptive skills, huh? Usually I'm a rotten liar."

"Sounded like she was asking a lot of questions."

"Mainly about him. She thinks I slept with him. That I'm having a great time as a millionaire's floozy. That I'm living it up and barking at the moon. Yeah, right."

"She didn't ask when you'd be back?"

"Oh, she knows I'll be around before the party with the choreographer on Friday. When is that—two days from now? I've lost track. And she reminded me that the rent's due. You have a charger for this? Your battery's on its last leg."

"Glove compartment."

Darkness dropped over them as they pulled into the vast garage. Tully had suggested the airport after Micah realized that he had to hide the car. He couldn't risk being such a conspicuous target. The plan from here involved taking a cab to a hotel until he decided to brave any possible curbside watchers and return to his apartment. Without the limo, he'd be forced to retrieve his father's Cutlass, a car he normally used only one day a week. It was like driving a time machine, and on certain days he feared where it might take him.

"What was that word again?" Katelyn asked.

"Regrouping. Tully uses it a lot. Whenever he's having a bad day, he says he needs to get home and regroup, collect his thoughts or something like that. Get things in order. So regrouping. That's what we're doing."

"Where at, exactly?"

"I hear Australia's nice this time of year."

"If only."

"I guess our second option is a hotel." He stopped the car in a dark corner near the back, consuming two parking places and figuring they were going to charge him double. That was fine. This wasn't a day for quibbling.

They got out and went in search of a ride. Micah brought along the box that Rhonda had given them, including the geranium but minus the shotgun, which he left in its lair beneath the seat for fear of being caught with an illegal weapon. Katelyn carried the phone charger and her newly discovered license.

"I'm going to ask you a question you may not want to answer," she said as they wove through the cars toward the terminal.

"Go ahead."

"Whoever was in your father's room, he left without doing anything. Anything bad, I mean. But what do you think would've happened if your father wasn't . . . you know. Would he have hurt him?"

Micah had already considered it. Had Savlodar's man expected to find Malcolm merely infirm? Most residents of the home were at least semi-responsive if not completely alert. Malcolm and one old-timer in the east wing were the only two who were fully catatonic, as far as Micah knew. He guessed that the intruder had been surprised by Malcolm's condition and thus left him unharmed. What did that say about the man?

"Never mind," she said. "You don't have to answer that."

"No, it's just . . . I don't know. He wants to get back at us without drawing too much attention to himself. Like Tully said, the cops don't think too highly of him. So he's not going to, you know, kill anybody or anything along those lines."

"You sure about that?"

"As sure as I am about anything today."

At the terminal, a parade of taxis waited to receive newly arrived travelers. Micah went to the first in the queue and gave a simple nod, the only sign required to set the transaction in motion. In moments they were moving.

"Where we goin' today, folks?"

"Australia," Katelyn said.

"Huh?"

Micah wished it were possible. "There's a hotel at South Decatur and Meadows, the Regent Suites. You know it?"

"West of that shopping mall?"

"That's the one."

The cab lurched away.

"Do you think he's been to your house?" Katelyn asked.

"Do you think he's been to yours?"

"If he was there, Dezi never knew it. Then again, the place usually looks like it's been ransacked, so that's not saying much." She was silent for a moment, then shook her head. "This whole thing sucks."

There was really nothing Micah could add to that. For the first time since he'd launched his business two years ago, he'd been forced to call clients and make other arrangements for them. He was rarely sick, and when he *was* sick he drove anyway, never passing a ride off to another service. But now he'd lost at least a little control, and the only way to get it back was to wait for the storm to move on, its rain and lightning finally spent.

"What I need more than anything," Katelyn said, "is a change of clothes."

"Right. Sorry, I didn't even think about that. I dress like this nearly every day, so I didn't, you know . . ."

"Don't worry about it. I'll live."

"No, we can fix you up."

"We're not really in a position to go on any shopping sprees."

"I'll take care of it." He leaned forward. "Driver?" Immediately he realized what he'd said. The irony of it pushed a smile to his face, if only for a moment.

"Yeah, what's up?"

"Forget the hotel. Just drop us at Meadows Mall. We'll walk the rest of the way."

"You're the boss."

After he leaned back, Katelyn said quietly, "I don't have any money. He has my debit card."

"Have you ever done any shoplifting?"

She looked at him to see if he was serious, then smirked. "Sure. I'll distract them while you stuff a clean bra and panties down your pants."

"Nah, I never steal underwear."

"Hey, at this point I'm not choosey. I'd settle for a maternity blouse and a pair of NASCAR boxer shorts."

"We'll see if we can do a little bit better than that." He wanted to keep going, just chase that line of lightheartedness as far as he was able, but the thought of a trespasser in his father's room subdued him. He sat with the box in his lap, anger stirring beneath his fear.

Chapter 25

Nirat framed the sea.

He settled the new pane of glass into the frame that rested facedown on his work table. In order to keep the photo from touching the lite, he added plastic spacers around the edge. That done, he used an air gun to blow out any tiny bits of debris.

Then he picked up the photo, which was mounted to an acid-free backing.

The dinghy either rode the waves or was about to be capsized by them. The photographer had captured the moment in an ambiguous amber of time. You couldn't tell if the two sailors were masters of their vessel or prisoners to it. Neither was it evident if they were man and woman, father and son, young or old. Their coats and hoods concealed them and gave them a gravity they wouldn't have had on sunny days.

The door swung open behind him.

"You found someone?"

Nirat settled the photo into its frame. "Actually I've never had an easier time of it. The man is fastidious. His files indicated only one living relative, along with a current address."

Austin Savlodar crutched his way to the table. "If it was so easy, then why do I get the feeling that I'm not going to like how this ends? Did you find this relative or not?"

"I did. He is a former police officer in the latter half of middle age. He is also completely without brain function."

"Explain."

"The newspaper clippings detailed an injury he received years ago while on duty. He was shot in the side of the head. He survived, but in body only. He's been living in a round-the-clock care facility near the Palm Valley golf course ever since."

"Damn. Tough break. So what did you do?"

"Do?"

"You paid this zombie a visit, right?"

"I think it would have done little good to cut him with the glass shard I'd brought along, as he has no capacity to feel pain."

"Drop the smartass routine, Alex. I'm not in the mood."

Nirat finally looked up from his work. "You're right. I apologize. I simply wanted to convey the uselessness of using the man as either leverage or bait."

"I understand that. But we have jobs to do. Yours is now to find these two, not anybody's father or mother or fat aunt from the suburbs. Since that's apparently a dead end, we'll take what's behind door number two. You understand?"

Nirat needed no explanation for Austin's insistence on vengeance. Richard had been the same way—in spades, as they said. Though Richard had never personally murdered anyone—at least as far as Nirat knew—he left behind a wake of cowed lovers, intimidated business partners, and bleeding enemies. On Richard's behalf, Nirat had once tapped out a man's front teeth with a ball-peen hammer. Until this morning, he'd assumed those days were over.

"They're hiding," Austin said. "Flush them out. Fucking cripple somebody."

He left Nirat alone with his half-framed picture and his memories of bolder men.

Chapter 26

When Micah returned to their room from the hotel cleaners, he was glad to hear the water still thrumming the shower walls. Katelyn deserved whatever comfort the steam could provide.

Having dropped off one set of shirt and pants for dry-cleaning, he felt a bit more in command of his surroundings. That particular activity was part of his routine, a component of the ritual that conveyed him from one day to the next. Thinking became easier.

The answers, though, eluded him. Despite his sudden clarity, he didn't see how to resolve this without someone getting hurt. On the street it was a common problem. You pissed a guy off and then spent the next week waiting for paybacks, a razor in the face or bullets sprayed across your house from a black-market machine pistol. That had never been Micah's life; his father had made sure of it. But he knew the rules.

The water shut off.

She'd protested the use of his credit card, but ultimately he convinced her that it was the only way. *When you're a world-famous dancer one day,* he'd said, *you can send me a check.* His eyes settled on the white cross-trainers, still nested within the tissue of the shoebox. Katelyn had wasted no time trying on a second pair or waffling over any other part of her impromptu ensemble. *This is a record for me,* she'd told him. *Usually the act of shoe-shopping requires at least half a day and the opinions of three or four nitpicky girlfriends.*

The hotel-provided hair dryer came to life behind the door.

Micah supposed he was fortunate. Maybe it was the luck of Vegas rubbing off on him, but he could've gotten stuck with a woman less inclined to hold things together. Katelyn had succumbed to only a few renegade tears. Everything else was grit.

He drained the last bottle of water and stared at the plastic cap in his hand, wishing a plan would appear within it, however tiny it might have been. At this point, even something small would suffice.

Eventually the dryer stopped. A few minutes later, the bathroom door opened, too soon for that plan to materialize in his palm.

"I saved you a towel."

He looked up from the bottle's lid, a cheap crystal ball that had failed him. Katelyn was barefoot, wearing jeans and a simple cotton top that were less than an hour old.

"The shower door leaks a bit," she said, "so pardon the water on the floor."

"I'll check it out in a minute." He'd bought shaving supplies and deodorant, and the thought of cleaning up had its appeal, but he couldn't relax quite yet. Not until they decided what to do next, where to go, how to bring this to an end.

Katelyn sat on the ottoman in front of his chair. Her nearness made it impossible for him to look anywhere else. "Don't think you're hogging all the gloomy thoughts to yourself. We've got enough to share."

He leaned forward, forearms on his knees, the empty bottle turning in his hands.

"We can still go to the police," she suggested.

"You know it won't do any good."

"Why not? We'll tell them the truth. Everything. From the start. The truth shall set you free and all that baloney, right?"

"And what will Savlodar's lawyers have to say about that? I

broke down the man's door. There's no evidence at all that he tried to hurt you. The neighbors saw us running out in the middle of the night like a couple of hoods. And we can't prove he had anything to do with whoever was in my father's room. At best, we could have him investigated for assault or something for what he tried to do to you. And that's not much. But his legal posse can inflict a lot more damage on us than we could on him."

"So that's it? We give up? We spend the rest of our lives scared that he's going to send someone to run us over or throw a brick through our window or do a drive-by when we're sitting on the porch?"

"Not the rest of the our lives. But at least the rest of the day."

"While we regroup."

"Something like that." With nothing else to offer, he spun the bottle slowly and hoped that time could cool the fires he'd inadvertently ignited. Savlodar would consider himself lucky for not getting accused of attempted rape, and by and by he'd busy himself with more important things than a rookie dancer and an anonymous chauffeur. It wasn't as if Micah had shot the man. He'd never even gotten his finger on the trigger. Surely Savlodar had adversaries more worthy of his time.

"I want to add one more thing to your list."

Micah looked up from the bottle. "List?"

"The one you learned from your father. This morning you said he told you that a man should be able to do two things really well."

"Throw a football and shave."

"Right. But I think he was missing something."

Micah was glad for the diversion, as temporary as it was. "Lay it on me."

"Well, the waltz, of course." She gave him a look that said, *Duh, what else?*

He offered her a smile and a dismissive wave of the bottle. "Maybe in my next life."

"What if we don't get a next life?"

"Then I'll miss out."

"I'm serious about it."

"I think we have other things to worry about. Besides, I don't dance."

"For one thing, I'm making the offer mainly for selfish reasons. I need something to take my mind off of everything, and dancing is the only thing I know. Secondly, just because you *don't* dance doesn't mean you *can't.*"

"How about after this is over? We can celebrate by me tripping over myself on the dance floor."

But her eyes abided no deserters to her cause. "One move at a time, that's all it takes. A single move per day. That's what I ask. It's not a big deal, so shut up and live with it. I *need* you to live with it. First lesson's tonight." She grabbed her shoes and socks and returned to the bathroom without looking at him again.

He didn't have to see her face. He knew that her eyes were not always so brave.

Chapter 27

I'm giving you one last piece of advice, Tully had said, *then I'm hanging the hell up.*

Micah had braced himself for whatever it might be.

Have some goddamn pizza delivered. Feed that girl and put some meat on her bones.

Two hours later, the pizza box lay open on the desk like a great book, over half of its pages missing. Micah's hunger had overrun him, and Katelyn wasn't far behind. Other than the food, nothing could separate them from their worry. No matter which channel they found on the room's oversized TV, the programs failed to hold their attention. They failed, even, to seem real at all. It was like staring through a telescope at pictures of sharp objects when you lived in a world made of knives.

"You might as well get up and get it over with," she said after a while, muting the television.

Micah carefully folded his paper napkin. "Meaning what?"

She got to her feet. "We're meeting Tully in the morning at your place, yes?"

"If it's safe, yeah."

"And that's not till the *morning,* yes?"

Micah sighed. What he wanted was to put a fresh pillow over his face and hope he fell asleep. He'd spent only a few hours on the floor at Rhonda's, and his body craved something more substantial.

"If I have to watch one more stupid reality show," Katelyn

told him, "I'm not going to be able to pretend like I'm paying attention anymore. That stuff is idiotic even on a normal day. I can't call Dezi and I can't hide in the bathroom all night. So either get on your feet or get your ass to a liquor store so we can drink ourselves stupid. It's up to you."

Micah held up his hands in surrender. "Okay, I hear you. It's cool." He stood up, already feeling foolish.

"You act like you've never danced before."

"Every now and then, you know, when some of the other drivers would drag me out."

"You mean club dancing."

"Yeah, I guess."

"That's not what this is. At all."

"I get it. I've seen it on TV."

"Good. Then don't act like its alien or something." She narrowed her eyes at him. "What's wrong?"

"It's not exactly my thing."

"Feeling out of your element?"

"Way."

"Then you know precisely how *I* feel. I've been out of my element since last night. I need to focus on something other than my imminent anxiety attack. This is the only chance I've got. Now straighten your back."

For her sake, Micah complied. But his apprehension must have shown in his face, because she planted her hands on her hips and glared at him. "This isn't a vasectomy, for God's sake."

"Sorry. I know. It's just . . ."

"Wow, you really *are* out of your element. I thought I was kidding. But this is the first time I've seen you uncertain of yourself. You can kick in a guy's door, get in a death-match on the floor for a gun, and handle a car like a test pilot—but the thought of learning to dance in a perfectly private place where no one else can see you, *that* makes you uncomfortable?"

He gave her a shrug. "Hey, what can I say? I'm a closet wimp."

"Now *that* I don't believe at all." She stepped toward him. "Arms out."

Micah supposed there was no escape. Men had probably gotten out of Alcatraz with less trouble. He did as she instructed.

"Now this is where we'll begin." She put her right hand in his left and moved closer to him. "Put your other hand behind me."

Micah had seen the dance performed, so he knew the general look. Still, it was one thing to catch a few minutes of it on cable and another to stand at ground zero while it happened.

"A little higher, near the shoulder blade. There, that's better. Try straightening your back a bit. Slumpy shoulders do not a dancer make."

Micah concentrated on it. If he was here, he might as well try and not embarrass himself.

"Now, listen up. The waltz is all about rising and falling, but not with your shoulders. Okay? The shoulders need to remain level and parallel to the floor. And when we move, our steps will tend to be long. Or at least they're supposed to *look* long."

"Rise and fall, shoulders steady, long steps."

"Ah, an honor student. I like it. The only other thing you need to worry about for now is how you place and lift your foot. When you take that first step, try and put the weight on your heel, then move to the ball of your foot, and then rise up on your toes for the next step."

"Got it." He resolved at that moment to be good at this. His father hadn't cared what his son chose as a career, as long as he didn't do it half-ass. With Malcolm, you were in all the way or you went home. "Ready when you are, coach."

"Okay. The first step. It's an easy one because it's straight ahead. Now, this is kind of weird for me because I'm going to be leading for now even though I'm moving in the woman's position, but this is what we do first."

When she moved, Micah was ready. He stepped forward with his left foot.

"And then go here." She glided to the right.

Micah mirrored her and put his right foot down the way she described it, then brought his left beside it.

"Hey, not bad!"

"You know what they say about beginners."

"No, sir. You're confusing luck with the natural dancer blood in your veins. Okay, now the next thing you do is take a step backward with your right—"

The phone on the side table gave two short rings.

"Front desk," Micah said. "My cleaning must be finished."

"You're trying to tell me you're saved by the bell?"

He grinned, broke contact, and went to answer the call of clean clothes.

"We're not done, you know."

Micah hummed as if he didn't hear her.

Chapter 28

In the darkness, Nirat waited.

Micah Donovan lived in the Camden Cove apartment complex on West Rochelle. For a bachelor, the digs could have been a constellation that mapped the way for any number of lovers of either gender and diverse inclinations: resort-style pool, balconies, covered parking, fireplaces to while away the hours in another's arms. But Nirat had been inside and seen the stark utility of Donovan's environment. His CD collection consisted of only eight albums. The pictures on the walls were apartment-neutral landscapes in grayscale, and if there were bikini bombshells prowling the pool during the afternoon, there was no evidence that Donovan had ever invited any of them up.

Sitting in one of Austin Savlodar's cars across the street, Nirat wondered how such a man had gotten himself involved in a shooting. It seemed too messy a thing. At first Nirat had assumed that Donovan and the girl had tried to set Austin up or blackmail him or perhaps outright steal from him. Sharks did, after all, attract sharks. Now, however, having studied the man and seen his meticulous and civically responsible records, he'd discarded that theory in favor of another: Donovan had interrupted Austin in the act of molesting yet another unfortunate damsel, and matters had promptly gone down the shitter.

It didn't matter. Nirat would spend the night and at least part of tomorrow morning in surveillance, simply because Donovan appeared to have no exterior weaknesses to exploit. He was a man with only a single familial bond, and Nirat saw little point in torturing a mindless lump of human clay.

So he waited and watched. In the briefcase on the seat beside him was a Taser and a pair of bolt-cutters with tempered steel blades.

Chapter 29

Micah awoke in a strange bed.

For several minutes he lay there, trying to remember the last time this had happened. Had it been over a year since his questionable decision to sleep at Janelle's house? Their short-term stab at romance had expired only a few days later, and he'd dated no one since. Tully called him a eunuch.

Micah sat up.

Gloom still shrouded most of the hotel room, though the dull light from around the edges of the drapes cast a camouflage pattern of gray on the walls. In the darkness, his recently cleaned tuxedo jacket hanging from the clothes bar looked almost human, as if a silent guardian had kept vigil over their sleep.

He looked at the other bed.

Katelyn's face was the only visible part of her. The blankets were drawn against her chin. Though Micah could see little of her features, he hoped her dreams were untroubled. He had a sudden impulse to wake her up and tell her that she'd become his friend in roughly thirty-two hours. There were people he'd known for years who hadn't yet earned that distinction.

He blinked the notion away. If all went well, everything would settle down today, they'd return to their pre-Savlodar lives, and odds were strong that he'd never see her again. He suspected she'd text him every so often and ask if he'd found any more lost earrings, but that too would fade after she landed a steady gig in New York or L.A.

The shower beckoned him.

After he was through, his body infused with warmth, he stood before the mirror in his towel and wiped a circle in the fog. His day-old beard softened by the hot water, he applied a minimal amount of shaving gel to his face. This wasn't the perfect solution. The perfect solution involved a non-comedogenic shaving oil, followed by a cream applied with a brush. The badger-hair bristles were drawn upward, against the grain, ensuring that the hairs weren't flush on the skin. But without the amulets of his usual ceremony, he made do with stunt doubles purchased at a convenience store. The blades of these things were notoriously barbaric.

He survived unscathed.

The suit came next. Maybe he should've picked up something more practical at the mall, but traipsing around in cargo pants and Southpole shoes on a weekday would have only reminded him how badly his life had jumped the tracks. He thought again of the monks with their prayer beads and mandalas to center them.

He left the bathroom to find Katelyn cursing the coffee maker.

"Just brew already, dammit. What am I doing wrong here?"

"Here, let me. I don't want the hotel to charge us for property destruction."

"It's early. I destroy when it's early."

"I'll keep that in mind."

"Are you finished in the restroom?"

"Go for it."

"I won't be long. Then we can get out of here and get this over with. I'm tired of having my life offline. Time to reboot. You look great, by the way."

Micah glanced up from the coffee maker, but by then she was already through the door, closing it behind her.

Shaking his head, he finessed the machine into compliance.

After that, things sped up. Tully called to say he was on his way in a cab. Micah and Katelyn ate muffins from the continental breakfast downstairs, and by ten AM the three of them were bound first for Micah's place and—assuming they didn't find it in shambles, with death threats scrawled on the fridge—they'd give Katelyn a ride home. At last.

". . . but look at me," Tully was saying in the back of the taxi. "I'm a slouch in twenty-year-old slacks and a Shriners windbreaker. I ain't ever *been* in the Shriners. You two, though, the young and the restless, you got prospects."

"You're retired, right?" Katelyn asked him.

"Would I have time to chaperone you kids if I wasn't?"

"Okay, then. If you're retired, does that automatically mean that you don't have prospects?"

"Oh, sure, I got prospects out the ass. The AARP sends me shit all the time to remind me about my prospects. Then there's always arthritis, liver shooting craps, maybe goddamn Alzheimer's if I'm lucky."

She turned to Micah. "Is he always like this?"

"It grows on you."

"I'll take your word for it."

"Doll," Tully said, "if I was thirty years younger, I'd have the black stallion here thrown out of this cab so you and I could get hitched by Elvis over at the Shalimar."

"A sideburned man in a sequined suit is definitely in my future wedding plans."

"See there? I got all kinds of prospects." He laughed and gave her just enough elbow that she couldn't help but join him.

Micah was glad to see the two of them getting along. Tully had been his father's partner until the accident. He'd turned in his badge the next day. Things had gone wrong that night. And the wrongness had haunted Micah ever since.

A few minutes later, the taxi delivered them.

"Wait here," Tully ordered the cabbie. "When we're done inside, I'm gonna need a ride back home."

"It's your nickel, friend."

"I can give you a lift," Micah told him.

"In your old man's car? No way I'm getting into that thing. Might as well climb into a goddamn casket."

Micah understood. Though his father hadn't died in the Cutlass, too much of his ghost remained.

They got out and left the idling cab at the curb.

"Let me go first," Tully said, shouldering his way ahead. It was only then that Micah noticed that Tully's right hand was riding in his jacket pocket. The kids on the street would've said that Tully was strapped.

"You sure that's necessary?" Micah asked him.

"Staying alive is necessary. Everything else is optional."

As they ascended the steps, Micah took the rear, keeping Katelyn in front of him where he could see her. If someone were waiting inside and this turned south, he wanted her to be within reach. Strange, this compulsion to protect her, but there it was.

Tully stopped at the door, tested the knob.

"Still locked?" Micah asked.

"Doesn't mean much. Shitty lock like this, an amateur with picks bought online could be through it in less than forty seconds. Gimmie the key."

Micah took the keychain from his pocket. It held only three keys: the limo, his apartment, and his father's car, which currently rested under a polypropylene cover beneath the parking awning. "It's the middle one."

"Thanks for the tip. I guess I won't try the ones with the Oldsmobile and Chrysler logos."

Katelyn said, "Remind me again why you like this smart-aleck?"

"Doll, if it's all the same to you, I prefer the term smart-*ass.*" He swung open the door but kept his body safely out of the line of fire.

After a moment, Micah said, "Well?"

Tully put his head around the corner, hand still in his pocket. "Any assholes in here?"

The only reply was silence.

Tully stepped across the threshold, looking more alert than Micah had seen him in years. Even the way he moved was different, as if his instincts hadn't died but were only dormant. He wondered how much of the old Tully was the same way, lying in wait. Back in the day, he'd been less steel wool and more gunmetal.

"God, this must be what it's like living in a dentist's office. You need some dirty dishes in the sink, my son. Maybe a *Penthouse* calendar and a dartboard."

They followed him inside. Micah placed the box with the geranium on the kitchen table.

Tully checked the rooms and returned, visibly relaxed. "The one thing I know for sure is that the place definitely *ain't* ransacked."

"I like it," Katelyn said, fingers of both hands thrust into her back pockets. "Plenty of room to stretch. Cool fireplace, too."

The last woman who'd stood on his living-room floor had been Janelle, and now Micah couldn't even remember her last name. "I guess I'm not a big fan of *stuff.*"

"Hey, it works for me."

Tully wasn't impressed. "Guy even puts the lid down on his own john, if you can believe it, after all the years I've spent trying to teach him to behave like a proper Neanderthal. Anyway, it looks like that fag Savlodar's decided to cut his losses. Now, that doesn't mean he might not have you both mugged in a week or so, or send some crack-heads to slash your tires, but that's the nature of the beast. It's ugly out there, so you both best be on the lookout for the next couple of months. Buy some pepper spray or something, and don't go out alone after dark."

"That's it?" Katelyn asked. "It's over?"

"Like I said, maybe it's over and maybe it ain't. He's either dropping the issue so as not to get on the police shit list like his daddy, or he's waiting a few days before sending some punks to break your arm or something."

"Looks like I'll be investing in that pepper spray."

"Smart girl." To Micah he said, "Stick around this broad for a while and maybe her brains will rub off on you. God knows you're in the market."

Micah absorbed the insult with a knowing smile. Tully, for all of his Ebenezer remarks, would have gone to his grave if Micah asked him. There was no one else out there like that, at least not in this life. Maybe there was in the next.

"Since there's nobody hiding behind the couch," Tully said, "I'm hittin' the road."

"You sure you don't want that ride?"

"Sooner drink lighter fluid and piss on a wildfire." He ambled out the door and down the stairs.

"Thank you!" Katelyn called.

He grunted something unintelligible from the base of the steps.

Micah closed the door, but before he turned away, he twisted the deadbolt home. Already caution was shifting his gears, making tiny changes in his routine.

"So now what?" Katelyn asked. "We're off to buy brass knuckles and bulletproof vests?"

"I'll run you home in a few minutes. I need to get some things together first, see if I can salvage a few of today's clients. You don't mind waiting?"

"Not as long as I can sit on your sofa and drink all your beer."

"And smoke all my cigarettes?"

"Only if they're menthols."

He smiled. "Make yourself at home."

Back in his bedroom, he opened his laptop and used its USB cord to connect his phone. If he didn't keep everything synced—phone numbers, calendar, pick-up times—then there was a chance he'd fail to provide his passengers with what the marketing gurus called a seamless experience. While the computer did its thing, he removed his shoes and found a glossier replacement pair.

"Uh, Micah?"

"What's up?" he yelled from the closet.

"You're not moonlighting as a male stripper, are you?"

The question was so off-planet that Micah couldn't guess her meaning. A stripper? Holding one shoe in his hand, he walked to the kitchen. "Say *what*?"

Katelyn pointed at the large terra-cotta flowerpot near the stove. Sixteen inches tall, the pot contained no plant, but was filled to the brim and beyond with one-dollar bills.

"Have girls been sticking these down your Speedos?"

Micah felt the grin tugging at his mouth but resisted it. "I didn't want to tell you. But yeah, I have to make ends meet. I work for Chippendales on the weekends."

She studied him intently, searching his face. "No, if you *did,* then you'd know how to dance, which you've already admitted isn't the case."

"Maybe I was lying to you about not being able to dance."

"Maybe you're lying to me *now.*"

He gave in to the grin. "I had you for a second there."

"Okay, sure, but only a *split* second. Now really, what's this all about?"

Micah crossed his arms and leaned on the wall, his lone shoe held against his chest. His good humor seeped through his pores, sweated away by the truth. Though telling her about the collection of dollars should not have been an intimate act, it had that sheen to it simply because he kept so much of himself behind the battlements of his heart. On any other day with any other woman, he might have changed the subject. He was, after all, a subject-changer from way back. But this wasn't any other day, and Katelyn was certainly no other woman.

She cocked her head to one side. "So . . ."

"I charge fifty-one dollars an hour for the limousine service. Gas is free for all in-city destinations."

"Okay."

"When I first considered buying the car and starting the business, my rate was going to be fifty an hour. But then I decided to make it an extra dollar and see how long it takes me to reach five thousand and fourteen."

Katelyn let him have his few moments of silence before prompting him. "And then what? You splurge on a hot tub?"

"No, actually, I . . ." This wasn't something she needed to hear, but for a reason he couldn't define, he wanted to tell her. "I'm going to use it to pay off the last of Tully's legal debt."

Obviously this wasn't what she expected. She matched his pose without realizing it, crossing her arms.

"He's been having to make payments to a lawyer for a long time now," Micah explained. "I just want to help him get it over with."

She chewed on her lip for a moment. "I'm afraid to ask, and you don't have to tell me because it's none of my beeswax, but why did Tully need a lawyer?"

Micah sighed. "For shooting my dad."

CHAPTER 30

Nirat followed the cab.

Sitting across the street when the three of them arrived at Donovan's, he'd sorted through the variables carefully. Here at last was the couple who'd ruined Austin's evening and caused him to discharge a .38 into his thigh. Nirat was mildly amused by that and bore these two no ill will. But he owed Austin's father his life and would do as he was instructed.

The older man intrigued him.

At first Nirat assumed he was the young woman's father, but their posture toward each other convinced him otherwise. The way he entered the apartment, going low through the doorway, hinted at experience. He came out a few minutes later, having apparently satisfied himself that the couple wasn't about to be ambushed. He wore faded polyester pants, and his hair was little more than a half-circle of wild gray connecting his ears. But looking at him, Nirat thought he'd found his man.

When the taxi pulled away, he eased into the street behind it.

There was no use trying his luck at the apartment, not when both of them were in there. Nirat was not about to take on two at once; he hadn't come so far by making poor calculations. His next option, then, was to try yet again to locate one of Donovan's friends or relatives, but Donovan seemed to be without either. Hopefully this man in the cab could provide those answers. All Nirat needed was a name.

The apartment building matched its tenant, a nondescript affair that had seen better afternoons. Nirat's family had moved to the States in '81, his father a failed Thai businessman and his mother the American paralegal bent on saving him. He suspected that this building hadn't been so morose back then. The Cold War kept everyone angry.

He got out of the car, the briefcase bumping against his leg. He didn't want to fall too far behind his quarry, so he hurried to open the trunk and grab his gardening hat, a soiled trucker's cap bearing the legend A COUNTRY BOY CAN SURVIVE. Coupled with his wide-lens mirrored sunglasses, the hat rendered him effectively incognito. Because of his tinted complexion, he could easily be mistaken for a Latino, so long as he didn't remove the shades.

Pulling on a pair of driving gloves, he took the steps two at a time.

He arrived on the second floor in time to hear a door shut. As he advanced along the hall, he remembered the day that Richard had called him "my fearless half-breed hunter." At the time the remark had mildly annoyed him, but later he realized that annoyance was a sign of truth. He was just that, a half-Thai, half-*farang* commando who also happened to be handy with a carpenter's square. Richard kept him around for both reasons.

He stopped, cleared his throat, removed the Taser from his case.

Damn Taser. A silly weapon, really. A pair of prongs on a flying wire—any warrior of the old code would've refused to use such a thing. There was little honor in it and even less guts. You either had the balls to hit a man in the mouth or you didn't.

"Alas," Nirat said, and knocked on the door.

"Who the hell is it?" The door jerked open. Up close, the man had a bartender's jowls and rampant eyebrows.

Nirat showed him the Taser, pointing it at his navel.

The man looked at the weapon, then—scowling—stared straight into the reflective lenses. "You gotta be shittin' me."

"Back up, please."

"I'm gettin' robbed by a guy with an electric dildo."

Apparently the man shared Nirat's opinion of the device, but that changed nothing. "Back up. Now."

He did as he was told.

Nirat entered and closed the door gently.

"Take whatever the hell you want. Let me hear how much the fence gives you for my eight-track player. I'd like to know."

"Remove your hands from your pockets, please."

The man hadn't yet taken off his windbreaker, and he stood there with a hand in each of its two oversized pockets. A few seconds passed without him moving. He was past his sell-by date and his apartment reeked of unwashed laundry, but Nirat suspected he still had some red marrow left in his bones.

"You will do this now, and you will do it cautiously, or this electric dildo will put you on the floor in a very ignominious way."

Slowly the man lifted his hands. In the left was a phone. In the right was a revolver.

Interesting. Red marrow, indeed.

"Put them both on the floor."

"Suck my cock."

Nirat paused. Had it been so long since he'd gotten his hands dirty that he'd forgotten how to deal with a little bit of spine? Nirat's respect for the man was inversely proportional to his waning patience. "After I shoot you in the stomach with this, I'll have the option to cut your throat open while you're convulsing. It's up to you."

The man's eyes were mere slits. Color flushed his cheeks. "Pussy." He bent over and placed the phone and gun on the uncarpeted floor.

"Now sit down."

The man raised his voice. "You gonna rob me or bore me to death?"

"Down."

The man removed a pillow from an armchair, sat, and put his hands atop the pillow in his lap, wisely keeping them in full view. Then, after a moment of consideration, he held up his middle finger.

Nirat ignored it. He walked to the Formica-topped table and glanced down at the stack of unopened bills. "Ernest Tull . . . Tullmaysher?"

"It's pronounced Tull*mocker,* if you wanna know."

"You're an associate of Micah Donovan?"

At this, Tullmacher shifted in his seat. "Ah, I see. Right. I get it now. This ain't a robbery."

"No."

"Well that changes things. Let me save you some time, pal. Micah didn't shoot anybody. He heard some broad in trouble in the house, and he did the right thing."

"Actually, I believe you."

"Actually, ask me if I fuckin' care."

Nirat moved closer. Beyond fifteen feet, the Taser might as well have been a can opener. "Is his father his only living relative?"

"Not counting me, yeah. So what?"

Nirat raised an eyebrow. "You're related?"

"What, you don't think in this day and age that a honky burnout can be kith and kin to a brother in a classy car? Welcome to the modern world, shit-for-brains."

Enough.

Nirat used his free hand to throw the latches on the briefcase. He took out the orange-handled bolt-cutters. They were sixteen inches long, with a hardened alloy head. Their teeth could slice through a bolt nearly half an inch thick. "I've been sent as a matter of recompense. An eye for an eye. You know how it is."

For the first time, Tullmacher appeared to lose a bit of his Kevlar. "I reckon I do."

"Once we're finished here, balance is restored. We'll be even-stevens, as we used to say when we were kids. Unless, of course, Donovan elects to elevate the matter, in which case I'll be forced to respond in kind."

"Shouldn't be a problem. Micah . . . he's too smart for that." He blinked several times. "So, uh, what happens now?"

"Now? I thought for starters we'd cut one of your Achilles tendons."

"Sounds a little extreme, but there's one thing you should know."

"I'm listening."

"I stopped being afraid of puddles of shit like you a long time ago." He vaulted from the chair.

Nirat lost a second in surprise, but that second was enough for Tullmacher to lift the pillow from his lap and hold it in front of him. With a mangled scream, he lunged at Nirat with his makeshift shield.

Nirat fired.

The barbs impaled the fabric. The voltage discharged into the thick cotton batting without effect.

Tullmacher crashed into him.

Even as Nirat was falling, he wanted to laugh madly at his own folly. The red marrow had gotten the best of him. He would be killed by a troll who'd used a pillow for defense.

He landed hard on his back. The impact with the floor was a flat stone between his shoulder blades, the pain pulsing outward in concentric circles, rippling down his arms and lower back. Tullmacher's face, suddenly only inches away, bunched in rage, a spider's thread of saliva dropping from his lip.

Nirat kneed him between the legs.

The effect wasn't as dramatic as he'd hoped, but it gave him the space he needed to roll clear and get to his feet.

Tullmacher, far from paralyzed by the blow, pushed himself up and went for the gun.

Nirat sat up and swung the bolt-cutters, catching the back of the man's leg. Tullmacher collapsed, hissing through his teeth. Nirat, his breath scraping up and down his throat, lunged for him and swung the tool that had become his bludgeon.

He hit Tullmacher in the center of the back, driving him to the floor. Tullmacher barked out an animal noise. Though his backbone might have very well been cracked, he frantically groped for the gun until his fingers finally clenched it.

In that instant, Nirat panicked. He stood up. Caught in the cannibal frenzy of his own pulse, he gripped the steel club in both hands and brought it down like a man with a hammer on a carnival bell.

The steel head buried itself two inches deep in the man's skull.

The sound was blunt and wet. Blood gurgled from the trench.

Nirat yanked the bolt-cutters free.

Tullmacher's legs jittered. One arm bounced up and down, as if belatedly electrified by the Taser. His blood drained rapidly through the hole Nirat had carved in him, he gasped, and then his limbs relaxed and lay still.

Nirat tried to swallow the mass in his throat but couldn't. Staring down at the body, he breathed in short, painful gulps, the hyperventilation wicking away his eyesight like a guttering candle. The bolt-cutters, slickened with gore, trembled in his hand.

CHAPTER 31

Leaning against the kitchen wall and clutching a black cap-toe shoe, Micah said, "Tully and my father were like an old married couple. Half the time they just sat around and argued. But they knew it was them against the world, and you couldn't get to one without going through the other. They'd been partners for seven years."

Standing on the other side of a flower pot full of one-dollar bills, Katelyn could not have been a more attentive audience. Her eyes never left him.

"They were on a stakeout that night. It wasn't even really anyone important they were looking for, just some punk they suspected might know something about a liquor-store robbery. They were going to follow him, see where he went. He didn't even have a record. No big deal."

A bass beat from the next apartment softly vibrated the wall. It made Micah realize how lonely his words sounded in space. Maybe he should've put on some music so this didn't feel so much like the tragedy it was. Though he'd finally moved beyond the grief, he still had his days.

"I don't know what went wrong. Nobody does. But Tully and Pops heard shots from inside the building, so they radioed it in and then did their thing. It's like on TV, you know, plainclothes cops with their pistols out, running up the steps, watching each other's back. It was only like the second or third time either of them had needed to draw their guns. All of this was in the reports, the paperwork. And there was a lot of it. I've got copies."

Part of him wanted Katelyn to say something. Part of him wanted to draw her in with this story so that maybe after he dropped her off in a few minutes, they wouldn't fall out of touch. But she only watched him, her gaze curious and intent. He remembered thinking that she probably wore contact lenses, though she'd given no indication this was true.

"They went inside. There are diagrams about how it went down, stuff the review committees drew up based upon bullet trajectories and Tully's account. It took them almost a year to close the case. But the bad guys inside, they panicked. It was dark. The techs ended up finding a total of forty-three shell casings from five different semi-autos. My father"—he gathered himself and confronted the beast one more time—"my father was hit two inches above the right ear."

Katelyn looked down at her hands.

"They ruled it an accident. The lab proved definitively that the bullet came from Tully's gun. It was dark. Things happened. But one of the investigators from the D.A.'s office wouldn't let it go. He got wind of Tully's on-again, off-again romance with the bottle, and he pushed it, said maybe it was criminal negligence. Tully had a good lawyer and ended up in the clear, but it put him in debt without a job, and then his drinking kept him there."

When Katelyn lifted her head, her eyes were rimmed with unfallen tears. "And he's had to live with that amount of guilt all this time. I can't imagine."

"Yeah. Anyway . . ." Now that it was out, Micah felt adrift, as if the story alone had tethered him and now he had nothing left to keep him afloat. "That's why things are the way they are."

"You never blamed him?"

"At first. Maybe I even hated him."

"So what happened?"

"I grew up, I guess. One day I just realized that I loved him a lot more than I disliked him. But he's still a pain in the neck more often than not." He followed this with a distant smile. "That's part of his charm."

She thought about it for a while before responding. "Thanks for sharing. I know that sounds goofy, but really. It means a lot."

Micah considered adding details of his father's condition, his police pension, and Tully's struggle to recover, but he decided to save those for another time—assuming there *was* another time. He bent down and laced up his shoe, shrugging off the bad mojo. "I think I need a change of scenery. Let me give you that ride home."

The first step was removing the cover from the car. Revealing Malcolm Donovan's 1983 Cutlass/Hurst was always a breathing exercise: hold your breath, let the car do a number on your heart, resume breathing. The paint still gleamed like black pearls despite the years that had passed since it rolled from the showroom floor. Malcolm had loved it for what it provided as standard features, primarily the rear spoiler, red accent stripes, dual exhaust, and the 307 four-barrel V-8 under the hood.

Micah didn't share his father's fascination. Though he appreciated the car's vintage quality, his relationship with the vehicle was quietly antagonistic. It was freighted with too much of the past. But like a true co-dependent, Micah couldn't bring himself to buy an ad in the paper and get rid of it.

"I'm not much of a car person," Katelyn admitted, "but this looks pretty sweet."

"So they tell me." He put the cover in the trunk, unlocked Katelyn's door, and held it open for her.

"You don't have to do that," she told him. "I'm not a limo passenger anymore."

"Habit. Sorry."

"Don't be sorry. It's nice."

Micah had no sooner settled into the driver's seat than Katelyn said, "Now *that* is something I've never seen before."

The car's strangest feature was its gearshift. Three separate sticks sprouted from the middle console.

"Looks like the thrusters on an airplane," she said.

"Yeah, it's weird. It works almost like a normal automatic transmission, except the middle shifter is for second gear and the one on the right is only for first."

"And why is that?"

"Not sure. Street racing, maybe."

"A guy thing, huh?"

"Not this guy."

"You're telling me you never burn a little rubber in this baby?"

He twisted the key. "Not my style."

She studied him for a moment. "I'll buy that."

He got them moving, but they made it only a block before his cell buzzed. He fished it from his inner pocket and saw Tully's name on the screen. "Driver."

Nothing.

"Tull? Can you hear me?"

Then, from what sounded like far away: *"You gonna rob me or bore me to death?"*

Micah took his foot off the gas.

Katelyn saw his reaction. "Oh, shit, don't tell me it's bad news."

Micah pulled to the curb and concentrated on whatever was happening on the other end of the phone.

"You're an associate of Micah Donovan?"

He barely heard Tully's response: *"I get it now. This ain't a robbery."*

"No."

Micah sorted through the possibilities and settled on the most likely scenario. Tully had speed-dialed him. He was facing off with Savlodar or—more likely—the man Savlodar had sent to the nursing home, the one who'd dropped the torn card on Laci's desk.

Katelyn reached across the trio of gearshifts and touched his arm. "Tell me what's happening."

"I don't know. I'm not sure."

"Then guess."

"Is his father his only living relative?"

"Not counting me, yeah. So what?"

The phone clamped against his ear, Micah hit the gas. The Cutlass surged into the street.

"Micah, please."

"He's there, somebody's there with Tully, somebody looking for us, for *me.*"

"Oh, God."

Micah glanced both ways at an intersection and flew through it. He wanted to pour himself into the phone, to crawl through the line and stop whatever was happening. The needle clocked higher on the speedometer. He drove with one hand wrenched to the top of the wheel and his head banking left to right. And all the while the distant words continued.

"Unless, of course, Donovan elects to elevate the matter, in which case I'll be forced to respond in kind."

"Keep him talking," Micah whispered. "Just use your head for once, you old fool, and keep him there a few minutes more." He knew the streets as well as anyone. He'd been driving them professionally for two years. And as his father's engine deepened its growl and brought them up to fifty-four on a residential street, he did the calculations and came up at three. Three minutes and he'd be there, two and a half if he got lucky at the corners.

"What's he saying?" Katelyn asked.

"I thought for starters we'd cut one of your Achilles tendons."

"Jesus." He didn't have two and a half. He thrust the phone at her. "Take it."

She'd barely touched it before he snapped his hand to the wheel and bent himself to the task of turning the car into a comet. They hurtled through a red light and left behind a wake of blaring horns.

Katelyn braced herself on the dash as he tapped the brake and cornered hard, the tires blurting against the asphalt. He put his foot down, slapped the gears, and the car roared back to speed.

Katelyn took her free hand from the dash and covered the ear that wasn't jammed against the phone.

Micah shot her a quick glance. "What do you hear?"

She squinted, as if this might somehow clarify the far-off sounds.

"Katelyn, what do you—"

"No!" she screamed. "Tully, no!"

"Katelyn!" Micah, helpless, could only drive.

"Tully!"

Micah wanted to tear the phone from her. *"What's happening?"*

She bent over and rocked up and down in her seat.

"Katelyn, talk to me."

"I don't know, he's gone, they're both gone, I can't hear anything, Micah, *I don't know what to do.*"

He ripped the thing from her hands and listened.

The only sound was that of a phone left on in an empty room.

He broke the connection and drove the last minute as fast as he could without imperiling them. If they collided with anyone, they'd never reach Tully's place in time, the dump he called a flat. The final hundred yards felt like a mile.

The Cutlass jumped the curb and slammed to a halt. Micah threw the thing into park even as their doors were flying open. He ran for the building, and Katelyn chased after him.

He didn't wait for her, taking the stairs three at a time.

"Tull!" He hurtled down the hallway. Threw himself against the door.

The first thing he saw was the gun. It drew his eyes, capturing his attention and momentarily making him wonder when Tully had bought it. After the accident, he'd left his .45 lying on his precinct desk.

From there he tracked to the nearby cell phone, Tully's battered relic that never seemed to keep a charge. A few inches away he saw the hand, and then the arm to which it was attached and the body and the blood.

Katelyn ran in behind him. If she made any kind of sound at all, Micah was beyond the ability to realize it.

Tully lay facedown, his windbreaker riding high on his back. He looked like he might have given in at last to the drink that called him and—seduced by it—fallen in a stupor to the floor. But that wasn't right. That wasn't how it happened. Someone had made a cave in the back of his head.

Micah took a step, then another, then dropped to his knees. He opened his mouth but had no air. The room became outer space, a vacuum that emptied his lungs even as it flooded his eyes with tears.

A single pellet of blood, like a red raindrop, released itself from Tully's splintered skull.

With a painful compression of his lungs, Micah lowered his fists to his sides, lifted his face toward the sky beyond the ceiling, and howled.

CHAPTER 32

Nirat dropped the burning matchbook like a flaming butterfly. The siphoned gas ignited the pile on the desert sand.

He'd spent the last two hours distancing himself from civilization, driving into the wilderness realm of scorpions and empty skies. Each mile had been an opportunity to consider what he'd done, to curse himself for his reflexive actions, to curse Tullmacher for his fatal bravery, to curse Austin for starting it all. Because the younger Savlodar couldn't keep himself from groping random women, a man was dead and Nirat had gone from building decks to burning an evidence pile.

He stepped back. The clothes he'd worn at Tullmacher's became a pillar of fire.

He added the man's wallet to the blaze, following it with the bundle of paperwork he'd seized as a diversion. Along with the radio and cigar box full of cheap jewelry, it would appear as if Tullmacher had interrupted a robbery. Or so he hoped.

Would it be enough? He hadn't followed the man home with the intention of murdering him. Consequently he wasn't prepared to eradicate all of the thousand tiny particles that television police were always using as forensic Rosetta Stones to prove a man guilty. Only twice had Richard ever instructed him to dispose of someone, and those someones were fringe-dwellers in debt to their gonads, unmissed after they were gone. Ernest Tullmacher, though—hell, Nirat knew nothing about him. He might have had choir lofts of adoring friends and been brother-in-law to the director of the FBI.

Things could get bad. Then again, things had been bad before.

He waited to be sick. Surely the raw memory of the act would squeeze a bit of humanity from his stomach, like someone twisting soured water from a rag. But Richard, damn him, hadn't selected him for his qualms. He'd selected him, actually, because Nirat could kill a man with a pair of bolt-cutters and have the wherewithal to get away with it.

That reminded him: he needed to dispose of the cutters and the Taser. When that was done, he'd return to the house and finish framing the picture of the dinghy on the sea. Oh, at some point he would have to update Austin on the situation, but for now he believed it was best if his employer remained ignorant. That way, Austin would seem far more authentic if questioned by the police. Nirat supposed such a questioning was inevitable, as Donovan and the girl would probably confess the entire story, in which case a pair of grim-eyed detectives would want to ask Austin why he lied about shooting himself in the leg while cleaning his gun.

Yes, things could go bad. Tullmacher had stupidly attacked him, and now Nirat was back where Richard Savlodar had placed him years ago, in the middle of a snake's nest, eating the heads of other serpents in order to survive. But nothing would be determined in the next hour. Nirat had time to contemplate and even to find something to eat. So he turned and headed for the car that was parked a mile away on a two-lane road. During his hike he could let these things play out in his mind and try to guess the order in which they would ultimately occur.

Behind him, the fire ground the evidence to ash, the flakes carried away in the whisper of the desert breeze.

Chapter 33

"Coffee?" A hand extended a dented mug. "Tastes like motor oil, but at least it's hot."

Micah shook his head. Or did he? Everything felt disconnected. The tiles on the floor of this police interview room seemed to blur whenever he moved.

Someone sat down beside him—not across from him like they did in movie interrogations, but like one guy sitting beside another on a bus. He wondered why they were being so friendly. They must have felt they owed it to his dad.

"I've spent the last hour and a half talking to your friend," the officer said. "Now I'd like to hear your side."

By *friend* he meant Katelyn. Micah wondered how she was holding up. Probably better than he was.

"Mr. Donovan? I know this is hard. But I need your help here."

"I don't think I"—he left the coffee on the table but pawed the water to his lips—"I don't think I have any more help to offer."

"You might surprise yourself."

"I already told somebody what I saw in the flat. I talked to a sergeant or somebody. He wrote it down."

"I appreciate that, I do. I think we've got a pretty good idea of the state of things when you arrived at the apartment. But I need to know about a man named Austin Savlodar. Your friend told us about him and an altercation that might or might not have happened at his house. I'm Ling, by the way." He held out a hand.

Micah shook it but had no strength. Tully would've called him a limp dick for having a handshake like that. Micah wished he could hear those words now, but Tully's good-natured insults were finished.

"So what happened that night at Mr. Savlodar's residence?"

Micah thought again about the blood around Tully's head. There had been so much.

"Mr. Donovan, I really don't want to keep you here any longer than I have to. The sooner you tell me about the alleged incident with Mr. Savlodar, the sooner I can determine who did this thing today. So throw me a line, man. Please."

Micah sat up and leaned back. His eyes ached. "Savlodar hired me."

"Hired you?"

"I'm a driver. A limousine. That's what I do."

"I understand. That was in the sergeant's notes. We can sort of fast-forward through that. I know how long you've been driving, I know your address, and I know of your relationship to the deceased. Our captain used to call him Ernie T. What I *don't* know is how you ended up back at the Savlodar residence after dropping the young woman off. Why did you return?"

Even in his numb state, Micah sensed trouble. Was Ling asking him something he couldn't reasonably answer? "What do you mean?"

"I mean you turned around. Isn't that right? You escorted a woman you'd never met to Mr. Savlodar's house, and maybe half an hour later, you went back. Why?"

Did they call it perjury when you lied to the cops? Or was that term used only in the courtroom? Either way, Micah stood on the precipice. He could attempt to explain his true reason for going back for her, which didn't make sense even to himself, or he could risk traveling the very serious road of lying to a police detective in the middle of a murder investigation.

"Mr. Donovan?"

"The bling," he said, hoping he wouldn't regret it later.

"The what?"

"The first place I went after dropping her off was the car wash. I found an earring in the car. It looked expensive. I thought she'd want it back."

"An earring."

"Yes."

"And you drove back to deliver it."

"Yes."

"Was it?"

"I'm sorry?"

"The earring. Was it hers?"

"Oh. I don't know. I never got the chance to ask."

"Do you still have it?"

"It's in the car."

Ling apparently decided that he wasn't going to let Micah's coffee go to waste, hot oil taste notwithstanding. He hoisted the mug and took two sips. "Then what?"

Micah remembered Tully's last birthday. As a joke, Micah had bought him a personal ad in the paper, and Tully spent a week fielding calls from women who were evidently okay with a Single White Male, A Little Husky, Who Enjoys Homemade Tea and Cuddling. Tully didn't stop swearing for days, but in between the epithets was laughter. He was delighted that Micah had done something so out of character, though he also promised revenge.

"What happened when you got there?" Ling asked.

Micah shifted in his chair. The seat was metal, and one of the legs was missing its rubber cap. "I left the car and walked to the front door."

"This was your third visit there, right?"

"Yeah, I guess."

"You guess?"

"I mean yes, it was. Sorry. First I dropped him off, then I came back with his . . . date. The third time was for the earring."

"So you're at the door, bling in hand. Then what?"

"I was about to knock and I heard something."

"Something?"

"Some*one*. I heard a woman scream."

Ling waited.

"I could tell she was in trouble. There was a sound in her voice, you know?" Now that he'd returned to the safety of the truth, the story came easily. "I knew it wasn't a fight, not a shouting match. It wasn't that kind of scream."

"I hear you."

"I think I might have even looked around, like I was waiting to see if there was anyone else nearby who was going to help. But it was dark. The street was empty."

"Did the screaming stop?"

"Only after I kicked the door open."

"Not an easy thing to do. I know from experience."

Micah shrugged. He hoped they weren't giving Katelyn the third degree. She'd been through enough. "When I got inside, I saw them in a room just to the right of the foyer or entryway or whatever you want to call it. She was upset. Her dress was . . . he'd tried to pull it off, and she'd been trying to get away."

"It was obvious?"

Micah nodded.

"Did you have a gun with you?"

Micah didn't even bother scoffing. He didn't have the strength. "The gun was his. I saw what was happening, and I didn't know what else to do, so I told her to follow me out of there. He drew the gun. He was mad. *Enraged,* I guess is a better term."

"Did he fire any shots?"

"One. And by then we were fighting for it. The gun, I mean. We were on the floor, and I kept thinking that I was going to be killed, just like that, just out of the blue on a normal day. When the gun went off, I seriously thought I was dead. It took a few seconds to figure out I wasn't hit."

"The shot hit him instead."

Micah knew it wasn't a question so he didn't bother answering it. "When I got up, the two of us ran out, just trying to get out of there before . . . you know, before it got any worse."

Ling communed with his coffee. Micah let him ruminate in silence. He'd told the truth, for the most part, and assuming Katelyn had done the same, Ling would hopefully release them and do whatever was necessary to bring this to its end. In the meantime, Micah would bury his father's partner. Could he do that? Did he have the strength?

"So you believe Austin Savlodar killed your friend to make a point?" Ling asked. "He did it out of . . . vengeance?"

"Or he sent someone to do it for him."

"The robbery angle, then, is bullshit? We believe some things might have been missing from his house."

"It wasn't about that. It was my fault."

"The hell it was. Don't let yourself think that."

Micah said nothing.

"Come on. I won't take up any more of your time. We can talk again tomorrow. Ernie T. was a good cop. So was your dad."

He led him through the room and busy offices beyond. "We'll have Savlodar down here within the hour. That's a promise."

Micah didn't reply. He just wanted out of here.

"You sure you don't want that coffee? Maybe one for the road?"

The walls here needed paint. The walls needed paint and the chairs were too loud when their legs scraped against the floor. The lights were the worst. Fluorescents without any soul.

"Mr. Donovan?"

He moved his head. He'd already forgotten the officer's name. "No, thanks."

"Just thought I'd offer. And don't forget your jacket."

He accepted the black tuxedo coat, only vaguely recognizing it as his own. His was used when greeting honeymooning couples and the occasional foreign dignitary. His was not involved with body bags.

"Here, let me get the door." The cop hurried over and held open the door to the hall or lobby or somewhere; Micah wasn't sure where it led. "You certain you're going to be okay? Don't take this the wrong way, but you don't look fit to drive home in the dark."

Dark? Had they been here that long?

"Goodnight, officer."

"Take it easy, man. I'll contact you as soon as I know anything."

Micah got himself moving. He looked at the floor. The pattern in the tile reminded him of oil on water. He decided to concentrate on that. The floor looked safe.

He ended up counting his steps. His shoes still gleamed, which was nice . . . he remembered reading somewhere that shoes made the man. Maybe this wasn't true—it could've been the tie or the shave—but thinking about it kept the rest of it away, the stuff that kept yelling at him from across the tarmac of his mind, its luggage full of grief.

Just count the steps. Count the damn steps. He made it as far as eleven before—

"Micah."

The police had spent several hours referring to him exclusively as *Mr. Donovan,* which reminded him of his father. Malcolm was the mister in the house.

"Micah, I'm so sorry."

He looked up. Katelyn rushed across the room.

Micah barely managed to open his arms before she was against him. He enclosed her and realized several seconds later that his head was resting against hers, the scent of her hair pushing back against the public smell of the police lobby.

They held on. She was saying things and crying again, her body shaking against his chest. He knew she was unaware that, if she stepped back, he'd fall over for want of support.

After a while she looked up at him. "Can we leave?"

He nodded.

Katelyn wiped her eyes. They walked side by side through the glass door and into the night beyond. Micah wondered where they were going. They didn't have a car, as they'd ridden here in the back of separate police cruisers.

Katelyn got them a cab. She helped Micah into the back and followed him in.

The ride made little sense.

The cop had been wrong. This wasn't dark. Nothing in this city ever was. The lights competed for his attention, and he looked from one neon promise to the other as if he'd never seen them before. Suddenly, they all seemed so interesting. He could get an advance on his paycheck or rent fetish Blu-Rays or GO ALL IN at the craps tables. He'd driven these streets for what felt like forever, but only now was he taking the time to consider a manicure, a Chicago-style pizza, or a marriage in fifteen minutes.

At some point they got out of the cab. And here at Tully's curb was the black carriage itself, the ghost of fathers past, the

1983 Cutlass with its red laser stripe and absurd gearstick configuration.

"Keys."

He kept his eyes averted as he handed them over.

"Get in." She ushered him to the passenger's side and shut the door behind him.

Katelyn got behind the wheel and groped for the seat adjuster until she found it. That done, she slotted the key and fired the engine, which responded as it always did, as if wondering where its original owner had gone and when he'd be back to kick some bad-guy ass.

"I learned to drive in an old VW Bug with a stick shift," she said as she pulled into the street. "You should've seen it. Talk about grinding some gears. It made my teeth hurt. I had to get dental work after every trip."

Dental work. Micah let that be his buoy as he floated across the shallow waters of his thoughts. The sharks didn't live in the shallows. He needed to make another appointment at the dentist's. He got a teeth-cleaning every six months. That was the secret to good hygiene. Make every routine a religion.

"I started dancing when I was sixteen," she said. "Had some good instructors. I haven't been able to get anything steady since then, but another show always seems to want a dancer just when my bills are starting to stack up. I've always been crappy at promoting myself. I haven't had any eight-by-ten headshots taken in months, and my Facebook info is *way* out of date."

Micah lowered his head. The lights were too much. He stared at his fingers, which he'd scrubbed clean at the Vegas Metro Northwest Area Command station after . . . after checking Tully for a pulse.

"So where should we go?" Katelyn asked.

He swallowed, wishing he'd accepted that coffee. "Just drive."

"Copy that." With both hands high on the wheel, she carried them deeper into the night.

Chapter 34

Micah came back to himself.

He wasn't sure why it happened. One moment he was lying on his back and the next moment he was sitting up, realizing that Katelyn had rented them a room in the same hotel they'd left this morning. The only light was that which spilled from the open bathroom door and the red numbers on the bedside clock that informed him it was nearing midnight.

He sat up and thought about Tully. They'd killed him because Micah had turned the car around to help a woman he didn't know.

He looked around and saw her in the other bed, her arm over her eyes. She didn't deserve any of this. She was going to meet a choreographer tomorrow night—her big break waiting to happen, now derailed.

A glass of water waited nearby. He took his time with it.

The police knew everything. They'd grilled Katelyn first. Apparently Micah's story had meshed with hers, because the detectives seemed satisfied they weren't being bluffed. Micah had lied only once. He saw no harm in the falsehood about the earring, as it gave him the incentive to return to Savlodar's house without having to explain the real reason.

So you believe Austin Savlodar killed your friend to make a point?

He told them yes.

The robbery angle, then, is bullshit?

Same answer. Tully hadn't been killed for walking in on a

burglar. He and Katelyn had heard the two men on the phone only seconds before he died.

Ernie T. was a good cop. So was your dad.

Apparently some of the officers from back then, when all of that unfolded, were still working this precinct. Their sympathy was undisguised.

We'll have Savlodar down here within the hour. That's a promise.

Micah didn't want their promises. He only wanted it to be over.

He finished the water and rubbed his face. The anger was down there, if he looked deeply enough, but he had no desire to summon it. Now that he had his senses back, as dulled as they might have been, he wanted to concentrate on getting past the hurt. Tully was all he'd had left. Like conjoined twins, they were bound together by their love for a man in a wheelchair and by the events that had put him there. Now that Tully was gone, all Micah had was a flower pot full of pointless dollar bills.

Needles stung the edges of his eyes. He blinked to fend off any exploratory tears.

Setting the empty glass aside, he stood up, needing escape. To sit here in silence would be to fall apart, and that wasn't a road he wished to travel. At least not yet.

"Katelyn?" He thought she might be asleep. "Kate?"

She uncovered her eyes. "You okay?"

"No." Before he could reconsider, he went to her and held out his hand. "One a day, right?"

"One *what* a day?"

"The waltz. I learn one move a day. Wasn't that our arrangement?"

She sat up. "You're serious?"

Micah just waited.

"Are either of us really in the mood?"

"It's the only thing I have right now."

"We could go home," she suggested. "I just thought that you wouldn't want—"

"It would be even worse there, alone. You were right."

She looked at his hand, still extended. "Are you sure?"

"Please. Just give me something else to think about."

After a moment's hesitation, she took his hand. He helped her up.

"You called me Kate."

He didn't know what to say to that.

"It's nice. Kate sounds like a tougher person. I could stand being tougher for a while." She didn't bother faking a smile, just pointed toward the window. "We should move over there. There's more room."

He had no desire to dance. But he understood that his life had chosen the best possible moment to fracture, because he wasn't fighting those fractures by himself. Ever since his father had left him, he'd made it a point to depend upon no one but the man he saw in the limo's window when he bent to straighten his tie. Yet now he leaned on another human being—one hand in hers, the other lightly on her back—and wanted to keep telling her thank you until she asked him to please shut up.

Her eyes were red but dry. "Ready for your next lesson?"

"Just tell me what to do."

"First we'll go over what you already know. We'll need some music for this eventually, but in the meantime this'll do. Here we go."

Micah stepped as she'd taught him. It wasn't so hard.

"Good. Now, the waltz is performed to music written in three-four time. It doesn't matter whether or not you know what that means, as long as you can count to six. On the one count, you step with your left, on the two count, you move sort of diagonally with your right, and on three you bring your left beside your right, like we learned before. On four you step back with the right and reverse everything. That's it. Now, let's try it. Ready . . . *one,* two, three, *four,* five, six . . ."

Micah found a small miracle in the movements. They demanded enough of his attention and dexterity that he had none to spare. Though greedy hands reached out from the dark places of himself, shaking with emotion, he eluded them with a box step that was far from expert but good enough for now.

"You're doing really well," Katelyn told him.

"You have no idea."

Chapter 35

When his phone shook him to life, Micah looked first at the clock—7:39 AM—then at the room's other bed. With obvious effort, Katelyn opened her eyes. "Were you expecting a wake-up call?"

He shook his head.

Somehow sleep had found him, a lurker in the alley of night, though he couldn't remember surrendering to it. Katelyn had called a truce at two-thirty in the morning. The student had proven more relentless than the teacher had anticipated. *You learn this too fast,* she'd warned, *and you'll forget it all by morning.*

He didn't think that was true.

"Want me to answer that?" she asked.

"Sorry. It's early. I'm slow."

"I won't hold it against you, considering." She covered her face with the blanket.

Micah picked up the phone and opened it. "Driver."

"Mr. Donovan? Detective Ling. We spoke last night."

"Yeah. Hey."

"I apologize for the early hour, but I thought you'd want to know that we interviewed Mr. Savlodar."

Micah sat up. "I'm listening."

"Normally you wouldn't rate a courtesy call, but your father had a lot of friends on the force, myself included."

"Thank you."

"Anyway, like I said, we talked to Mr. Savlodar, and I'm here to tell you that his alibi is fully verifiable. He spent the entire afternoon with colleagues at a business meeting and the other half of the day entertaining those same cronies at the blackjack tables at the Mirage."

Micah was disappointed but not surprised. He'd never thought that Savlodar was the man who'd visited his father and confronted Tully. He noticed his choice of words—*confronted* was as far as he could get; *murdered* brought too much leverage against him.

"He confessed that he'd omitted a few details about shooting himself," Ling continued. "Claims you entered his home illegally, which you admit is basically the truth. The point where your stories diverge is that you allege he was about to force himself on his date, and he says it never went that far."

"Why didn't he mention any of that when he gave his original statement at the hospital?"

"Said it wasn't worth it. Just wanted to forget about it. He seemed more embarrassed at the time than anything. Still does, actually."

"So . . . that's it?"

"Richard Savlodar was well connected, knew a lot of people from the streets. Assuming his son has access to the same contacts, then I'm afraid we may be facing quite a challenge in locating any possible agent he might have sent to do his dirty work."

"By *agent* you mean hitman."

"The only thing I mean at this point, Mr. Donovan, is that the case is wide open. The lab is still crunching the data from Ernie T.'s apartment, and I'll be speaking personally to the nurse who reportedly saw the man in your father's room. That's as much as I can say without putting my own neck on the line, but trust me when I tell you that we're moving on this as fast as we can."

"I understand."

"Good. Then I need you to do me a favor."

Micah couldn't begin to guess.

"Talk to Ms. Presley and convince her to file her complaint in a formal report so we can get this guy charged with something that'll stick."

Micah tried to make sense of that. He didn't know anyone by that name. Detective Ling had lost him.

"If Austin Savlodar really did assault Ms. Presley," Ling said, "then our hands are somewhat tied unless she helps us out. We can still go after him, but without her on our side, we can only get so far. Her cooperation would make things a hell of a lot easier. Last night she told me she'd think about it. I want you to do what you can to convince her of the wisdom of that."

And then Micah realized, until that moment, he hadn't known Katelyn's last name.

"We need to put some heat on this guy, Mr. Donovan. We get him hot enough, melt him down, there's no telling what might spill out. You savvy that?"

"Yeah, I hear you. I'll talk to her."

"Call me back at this number for any reason, night or day, and we'll see about nailing the bastard who did this."

"Okay."

"Later." He hung up.

Katelyn said, "Talk to her about what?"

Micah turned the phone over in his hands. "Your name is *Presley*?"

"Yes, but I'm not related, so no, I can't get you free tickets to Graceland."

"I guess there are probably a lot of different Presleys in the world."

"Millions. You didn't answer my question."

"Ling wants you to go on record about what Savlodar tried

to do to you."

"I *am* on record."

"He wants you to give him an official statement so they can press charges."

"And what good will that do at this point?"

"Savlodar had an alibi for . . . for what happened at Tully's."

"Surprise, surprise."

"The guy Savlodar sent after us killed Tully, but we have no idea who he is. Unless they find his fingerprints or some other kind of evidence at the scene, they'll never know who did it. By putting a little pressure on Savlodar—"

"By putting pressure on him," she said, standing up and heading for the bathroom, "I will piss him off beyond the point of no return, and then he'll send that mysterious someone after *me*. Sounds like a wonderful idea. I'll be in here singing about how wonderful it is." She closed the door.

Micah was sorry immediately. He didn't want her upset. But worse than that, when she was gone, he was alone, and solitude focused his anger, the rage that refused to cool.

Savlodar was going to get away with it.

Assuming Tully's murderer had left behind no damning prints or fibers or the like, the only lead Ling had was Laci's description of the man—silver sunglasses and dark hair. Richard Savlodar probably knew a Rolodex worth of hard-eyed men, and if his son had made use of these resources, his hired hand could've been from anywhere, local or global, Vegas, Atlantic City, Havana, or the storied streets of Palermo, Sicily. Any bookie in town would've placed odds that he was already on a plane.

Micah noticed his hands. He gripped the phone so tightly that the tips of his fingers ached.

He told them to let go, but his muscles led a little revolt and just kept on clutching. Someone had beaten Tully to death—*beaten him*—when the man had spent the recent years of his life only trying to make amends, to right the awful wrong he'd accidentally done. In the end, he'd fought for his life, but not because he was afraid to die. As he'd once said to Micah, *If hell is guilt, then heaven must be self-forgiveness.* Tully had lived every day in hell, so no monster under the bed was going to rattle him, no matter how dire. He'd died without fear.

When Micah felt the phone's plastic casing start to give, he forced his hands to release it.

Katelyn opened the door. She stood there brushing her teeth.

Beaten him.

"So what now?" she asked around the toothbrush.

"This isn't right."

She grunted an affirmation.

"Tully . . . he didn't even *do* anything. He wasn't involved."

She watched him, working the brush.

Micah bent over and gripped his knees. It was either that or give voice to the firebrand of rage that felt as if it were burning a hole through him.

"Micah?"

It only got worse the longer he remained here. It only seemed more unfair. Tully was going to be cut open in autopsy—they did that to murder victims—because Micah had turned the limousine around. Maybe all of it was his fault. And maybe Tully was right when he said that about guilt.

He lifted his throbbing head. "I'm going to the airport."

"Hold on." She disappeared, spit, rinsed, returned. "First of all, *we're* going to the airport. Second, why?"

"The car's parked there."

"So? We already have a car. Why do we need to go to the limo?"

Micah stared at her.

Katelyn held his gaze. She tapped the toothbrush against her chin.

And then she knew.

Chapter 36

"You see this ass?"

Nirat said nothing, only stood with his hands cupped carefully in front of him.

Austin jabbed a finger at his own crack, and Nirat was thankful that the man hadn't dropped his trousers to make his point. "The cops spent three hours with their hands up my colon *because you killed a total fucking stranger.*"

They were miles from the house, standing in an empty office owned by a subsidiary of Richard's real-estate firm. The vacant property on Eastern Avenue near Henderson was the only place Austin felt safe to vent his wrath. It was his first encounter with the possibility of electronic eavesdropping, and he was coping less than graciously. His father, by contrast, had rarely raised his voice.

"For the love of God, Alex, please. Tell me. What the fuck?"

Nirat had spent the evening running through this very conversation. Though he was fairly confident he'd left behind no crumbs for the investigators to follow through the trees, he also knew that he could remain a cipher only if he disappeared. The police would systematically scroll through the list of Richard's employees and associates. Perhaps they'd even pay the old man a personal visit at Ely. Sooner or later, the name of Alexander Niratpattanasai would blip to life on their radar, and he needed to be in a far time zone when that happened.

"Matters got out of hand," he said for lack of anything more original.

Austin's eyebrows leapt high on his forehead. He seemed trapped between a laugh and a scream. "You don't fucking say." He turned, using the crutch as a pivot, as if he could no longer bear looking Nirat in the eye. "They know what happened between the girl and me. They scared the bitch into coming clean. Which means they're none too happy with me for fibbing to them, to say the least."

"I have a plan."

Austin spun around, the rubber tip of his crutch squeaking against the floor. "Do you have any idea what you've done? What kind of position you've put me in? I don't have a criminal record. I am not my father's son. Does this mean I'm the reincarnation of Gandhi and I'm here to rescue humanity from itself? Hardly. I cultivate my indiscretions just like everybody else. But now? Now I may just be arrested for *conspiracy to commit murder.*"

"I said I have a—"

"I don't want to hear your goddamn plan! I want you out of here. Don't take this the wrong way, old friend, but I never want to see you again. The only reason I don't turn you in myself is because of my father."

"You turn me in, you go down with me."

"Predictable of you to say so, but there's nothing concrete that ties me to what happened yesterday. Think about it."

Nirat had already done just that. And it was true. If Austin decided to betray him . . .

"This is our last meeting as professionals and as friends. They might already be watching the house, so you can't go back and collect anything." He withdrew an envelope and handed it over. "Consider this your severance pay."

Nirat watched his own hand reach for the envelope. His body

felt detached. Was this his fate, abrupt and without ceremony? He'd led a simple life and did what was asked of him, and now, because Ernest Tullmacher had chosen the wrong moment to try for the Medal of Honor, he was excommunicated.

Austin said nothing more. He left, leg swinging, the shoulders of his expensive suit bunched around his neck.

Nirat looked at the envelope but didn't open it. Having dual citizenship, he could relocate to Thailand and never in this lifetime be found. There was probably enough cash in here to make things easy. As for Austin, he would bully and bribe his way through the ordeal. At worst he would face a minor charge for pawing the Presley girl, but little would come of it, as she hadn't been hurt. More than likely, his attorneys would be able to turn the legal spear so that its tip was pointed at the girl instead.

And where would Nirat be? Hunting for work in Bangkok.

He struck the sharp corner of the envelope against his palm. The sailors in their painted boat came back to him. He pictured them in his mind, hoping to glean a bit of mariner's intuition from them, but whatever they'd come to tell him was lost on the darkening waves.

Chapter 37

Sitting in the airport parking garage, Micah raised the seat and pulled out the gun. The previous owner had sanded the handle so that the edges where the saw had done its business were now smooth against the skin. Within a thumb's reach was an oiled lever that would cause the barrels to drop, revealing the dual tunnels where the shells were placed. As a younger man, he'd learned to fire his father's .45 at the police range. He hadn't touched a gun since then.

"I don't like this part," Katelyn said.

Micah traced a finger around the cusp of the two barrels.

"You can't kill anybody. I'm not going to let you. Besides, you're not that kind of person."

"You know me so well?"

"Don't I?" She positioned herself in such a way that he was forced to look at her. "Hey, I'm not going to pretend I know what you're feeling. Yeah, sure, I saw Tully dead there, with blood all over the floor, but he wasn't my friend. He and I didn't have what you guys had. But I *do* know that what you're thinking about is just reflex. You're mad and sad and somebody should pay for what happened."

"I'll take you home first."

"Yeah, whatever. You know I'm not going anywhere, so save us both some time and stop saying it."

"Why? Why do you have to be involved anymore?"

"*Why?* Do you really have to ask that?" Her voice dropped. "I like you, Micah. Despite all the . . . all the *shit* we've been through in the last two days, I think I might actually enjoy hanging out with you on a normal day. Maybe we can play Scrabble instead of run for our lives. Might be refreshing."

Micah let that pass through him, examining it. Clinical technicians were going to cut up Tully's body on the medical examiner's table and no one would be punished for putting him there, yet here was this woman with eyes like the desert sky telling him she thought he was okay. And maybe more than okay. "I've never played Scrabble," he said.

"Yeah, well, stick around long enough and I'll show you the other six wonders of the ancient world, including but not limited to going to the movies and eating dinner. That's what normal people do. Can you hear what I'm saying? I want a chance to be normal people with you."

"What about Laci?"

"Who?"

"The nurse's assistant. She saw Tully's murderer."

"So?"

"Don't you think that puts her in danger?"

"I haven't thought about it."

"I want to talk to her."

"To make sure she's all right or to try and track this guy down?"

He couldn't lie. "Both."

"Fine. For the sake of argument, what happens if you find something? And don't take the cheap way out and tell me that you'll play it by ear. At the present time I don't have time for half answers."

"I suppose I'll go whatever direction she points me and see what happens next."

"Whatever direction? You say that like it's going to be easy. This guy could be *anywhere* by now, Micah. He doesn't even need to leave town. There are, like, a gazillion places to hide in this city."

"Then I'll burn the city to the ground."

She leaned back. Looked at him.

He felt himself losing her. She'd become his friend, though now she slipped away. But then, not for the first time and probably not the last, she surprised him. She leaned forward again and put her hands on his. "You saved my ass. So now I'm going to save yours." She slowly slid the gun from his grasp.

He watched as she returned it to its hiding place below the seat. "I have a compromise for you, monsieur driver."

How could he not be intrigued by this person? Perhaps if he took a moment and considered his luck, he'd find better things to do than chase a murderer.

"I'll go with you," she said. "I'll go with you, and we'll talk to this nurse. If we find out anything useful, we'll tell the police or just go hunt the guy down and blow his head off, whichever comes first."

He couldn't tell if she was being serious about that last part, but he wouldn't have wanted to be the man who tested her resolve.

"But first . . . *first* you're making me a promise."

He almost said, *Anything,* but then decided he might not be able to live up to it. "Go ahead."

"At some point today we're going *somewhere* so I can get a change of clothes."

He allowed her to bait him into a smile. A smile, despite everything. "Are you going to make me shake on it?"

"Like this." She held out her little finger.

"A pinky shake?"

"It's the only way it really counts."

"Says who?"

"Says *me.*"

"Good enough." He hooked his finger in hers and sealed their pact.

CHAPTER 38

They drove the Cutlass to a place it had never been. Micah had never brought the car to the nursing home, for fear of something he couldn't explain. This was his dad's ride, and the man who'd waxed and loved this car was trapped in there, a prisoner in the cell of his body.

"What about your clients?" Katelyn asked as they headed up the walk. "Are you going to work tonight?"

"Are you?"

"If you count the twenty hours I put in each week at the coffee shop, the answer is no. It's my part-time life that squeaks me by when the rent comes due, but it's nothing that I can't miss. Not for something important. Not for this."

"We need to call Detective Ling about pressing charges."

"I told you I'm thinking about it."

He held the glass door open for her. "Why do I get the feeling that you're going to keep putting this off?"

"Maybe because I don't like the idea of becoming lunchmeat for the guy's lawyers."

There was no point in arguing. Micah knew her well enough by now.

Wheelchaired men and women of various ages stared at the TV or at the floor or at nothing at all. Unlike the residents of a senior-care facility, these were refugees from earlier life, people kicked prematurely to the curb by accident or disease—quadriplegics, victims of paralysis and nervous-system disorders, and others who'd been transformed beyond the care-providing abilities of their families.

Though Micah often took the time to say a word here or there as he passed, this was his second consecutive visit where he hurried by without noticing them. Yet he noticed them, anyway, if only on his periphery, and he promised himself he'd make up for his haste when all of this was over.

He stopped at the desk, which was, as always, decorated with flowers and fresh plants. Seeing the plants reminded him of Rhonda. Had anyone called her about Tully? Did she even know her brother was dead?

"Why, Mr. Donovan. It's always nice to see you."

It wasn't Laci, but an elegant black woman with red hoop earrings. Her name was . . .

"Hello, Gladys." She'd always been unfailingly kind to him, but sometimes her mothering morphed into pity, and that did neither Micah nor his father any good. "Is Laci on duty today?"

"That girl? She'd work herself silly if we let her. She's around here somewhere. Shall I page her?"

"Please. We'll be . . ." He gestured down the hall.

"I know where you'll be. You're a good son, Micah Donovan."

They found Malcolm in his Los Angeles Rams jersey, the one he claimed to have gotten from Eric Dickerson himself. No one had ever doubted him.

Though Micah entered the room without hesitation, he noticed that Katelyn paused briefly at the door. He knew the feeling. It was like passing through an airlock onto a space station. The atmosphere was different here.

"How you doing, Pops? You remember Katelyn?"

Malcolm didn't move. Micah had stopped imagining little motions from his father, encouraging twitches that weren't really there. Still, he never stopped looking for them, because . . . you never knew.

Katelyn had the look of someone whose helplessness waged war with her sadness, resulting in frustration. Micah recognized the emotion because he'd been there, squatting in the trenches and knowing that reinforcements weren't on the way. She went to the window and, as she passed Micah, she squeezed his arm.

He silently thanked her. Maybe there was such a thing as reinforcements, after all.

"Got some bad news, Pops." He sat on the bed, elbows on his knees. How to begin? "Yesterday, your old pal Tully got into some . . . into some trouble." He didn't want to be sitting here saying this, or even thinking about it, because it was all too raw. The solution would be to curl up on the bathroom floor and let his body accept the river of his sorrow. But there was no time for that. "Tully, you know, he's stupid sometimes. He gave it all up for me."

"For *us,*" Katelyn said.

"For us. Katelyn and I needed him, and he came through. Just like he always has." His throat burned, and he got up quickly and rammed a glass under the tap in the room's tiny sink. He didn't stop drinking until it was empty.

"Mr. Donovan?"

He managed to return the glass to its place beside the sink without dropping it.

Laci stood in the doorway. "Gladys said you were looking for me."

"Hey, come on in. This is Katelyn."

Laci smiled professionally and gave a little wave. "Hi."

Katelyn nodded.

"I thought maybe the police might've stopped by," Micah said.

"Yes. They told me they were investigating the man who left your card. I'm sorry if I did anything wrong."

"No, you're fine. You just happen to be the only person who can identify him."

"But I don't think I can."

"That's what you told the police?"

"I was working at the computer. You know how you can sort of see someone coming without really paying attention? That's how it was. When I finally looked up, I saw him only for a second before he dropped the card on the desk and left. Is he wanted for something?"

"Looks that way."

"The police wouldn't tell me. They said he was a person of interest. That's their phrase, not mine." Her eyes swung between Katelyn and Micah. "Is everything really okay? Because it doesn't feel that way."

"Nothing else about him you can remember?"

"There was something written on his hat, but I didn't get the chance to read it."

"You didn't happen to notice what car he was driving?"

"After I saw the torn-up card, I looked up while he was walking out. He parked right out front, next to one of the handicap spots. His car might have been silver or gray, but I'm not sure. He wasn't here to . . . to hurt anyone, was he?"

"Maybe." Micah wanted something more, that one clue that Detective Ling had missed, the arrow that would point him to this man. "Tell me about the hat."

"I couldn't tell what it said. He turned away. I just know there were words there. I'm sorry I can't remember anything else . . ."

"What kind of hat?"

"What do you mean?"

"Was it a cowboy hat? A lot of guys wear those around town."

"No, nothing like that. It was a baseball cap."

"Was the brim flat like it just came from the store or was it bent?"

"Uh, bent, I think. Does that matter?"

Micah wasn't sure if it did or not, but if he was playing the fashion stereotypes, then a bent brim ruled out street soldiers, hip-hop fans, gangsta wannabes, and a good portion of males under the age of twenty-five. "Would you mind telling me if the police asked you anything else?"

She shrugged. "Other than my name and things, they wanted to know what time the man was here, how long I think he stayed, if anyone else saw him . . ."

"*Did* anyone?"

"No. I'm really sorry we just let him walk in like that. I totally apologize. It's just that most of our visitors are family members and we always—"

"No sweat. If your supervisor gives you any hassle about it, send him my way."

That seemed to make a difference. Laci relaxed and took a step into the hall. "Well, uh, if you need me, you know where I'll be."

"Sure thing."

After she was gone, Micah looked at Katelyn. "What do you think?"

"Honestly?"

"Always."

"For one thing, I think that we don't have much more information than when we got here. And for another, I think that she's sweet on you."

"She's *what*?"

"Oh, come on, don't play the I'm-just-a-dumb-male-who-can't-see-the-obvious routine because I know that's not true, not with you. It's no big deal, so there's no need to stand there with that look on your face."

Micah closed his eyes. It was easier to align his compass in the dark. When he was fairly certain that he still had his footing, he opened them to find her staring at him.

"Tell me what we're going to do next," she said.

"We need to find him."

"You convinced me of that already. Where do we go from here?"

"There's only one place left."

She looked away. "Yeah. I guess there is."

Performing an encore at Savlodar's house was not something Micah wanted to say aloud, so he was thankful for Katelyn's telepathy. "We can stop at your apartment along the way, pick up that change of clothes."

"Yeah, that'll go over really well. I have no idea what I'm supposed to say to Dezirae. I was always the sensible roommate. And now look at me."

"We could skip it. Swing by the mall."

"I've done enough damage to your credit card already."

"No big deal. I recently came into a flower pot full of cash."

For some reason, those words cracked the dam. Katelyn was silent for a while. Then she pursed her lips tightly and shook her head as the tears welled in her eyes. *"I'm so sorry for what's happened."*

Micah reached for her—"Hey, come here"—and gathered her into his arms.

She cried against him. Micah held her, fighting his own battles, while a foot away his father watched them without seeing them at all.

Chapter 39

Before leaving this place forever, Nirat had one final order to ignore.

He owned little in the way of material things, and other than his expensive digital camera, he supposed there was nothing in his drawers or closet that he'd miss. So it wasn't for any of this ephemera that he risked returning to Austin's house on Soaring Court, but rather for the picture. The damn photo of the boat.

Austin would never miss it. Nor would he grasp its metaphor if it were explained to him. Nirat planned to remain at the house only long enough to retrieve it. First he'd call a cab, so that by the time he had the photo free of its frame and rolled up, his ride would be waiting. Then he'd have himself dropped at the bus station on South Main, but only as a diversion. If by some deductive miracle the police settled on him as a suspect, they might—with the assistance of yet another act of God—figure out that he'd taken a taxi from the Savlodar residence. There was the dim chance that they would locate the proper cabbie and question him. So to prepare for the wildly improbable event that he was both identified and tracked to the bus station, Nirat would instead head to the airport and leave them thinking he was on a Greyhound bound for Omaha.

Austin had told him not to come here again, and Nirat decided that this was the first time he'd ever knowingly disobeyed either the father or the son.

He pulled the silver Lexus into its customary spot and left

the keys on the seat. The afternoon was bright, the sun warming his face as he made his way around the kidney-shaped pool. So much for finishing the new deck.

The poolhouse interior felt more akin to a sauna, as no one had bothered with the AC. The weekend orgies that Austin so loved to host like an Armani-clad Bacchus would likely be suspended while he waited for the heat to die down, as the popular saying went. Nirat realized that he'd never used that phrase before, not in his entire clandestine career. Until Tullmacher had surprised him, Nirat's handiwork had never elicited attention. Hence Richard's love for him.

He found the picture where he'd left it, resting on the table in its new cherrywood frame. He quickly undid his previous work, liberating the print and carefully rolling it. Then he secured it with a rubber band at either end, wondering if the airline would find it odd that a man was traveling halfway around the world with a single cardboard mailing tube as his only luggage.

CHAPTER 40

Micah stopped the Cutlass sixty yards from the Savlodar residence. An idling car was a sensation that would be lost in a generation or so. Micah became very aware of the vibration in his seat and the way the engine transferred the anticipation of motion through the floorboards and into his bones. Electric cars would have their own appeal, he supposed, but there was something about rumbling at a red light that would never be replaced.

"You're either zoning out," Katelyn said, "or putting off the inevitable."

"Or having second thoughts."

"Is that all? Me, I'm already down to fourth and fifth thoughts. You need to catch up."

"He won't be home."

"So you say."

"I imagine he spends a lot of time at meetings and brunches and that sort of thing."

"You know how I met him?"

Micah turned to her.

"A group of us were at the Channel 13 studio. They were doing a piece on the sudden popularity of dancing as a viable profession, or something like that. All the dance shows on now, you know, make everybody want to get in on the action. Supposedly private lessons are even on the way up."

"I can vouch for that."

She grinned. "And you're doing extremely well, I might add."

"I credit the teacher."

"She accepts your credit. Anyway, Austin Savlodar was there that afternoon, meeting with a producer about promotions for a charity poker tournament. He does a lot of philanthropy. You'd never know he was such a slimeball."

Micah glanced back at the house. The car in the driveway matched Laci's description.

"We ended up hanging out with him for about an hour. He was a charmer, invited us all out for a night on the town at his expense. Claimed to be a big patron of the arts, but now I see that he's really a patron of . . . well, you can fill in the blank. The worst thing is that I didn't say no when he invited me over. I barely knew the man. That doesn't say much for my judgment, does it?"

"No use being hard on yourself about it now. We make mistakes and move on."

"Is that your motto?"

"No. My motto is *mind my own business.*"

"Is it? Evidently mottos change."

"Yeah. And then some." He took his foot off the brake and closed in on the house.

Chapter 41

Nirat found a cylindrical mailing container in a storage room off the kitchen. He had the house to himself, as the cleaning staff had already departed for the day, and the cook would not arrive for half an hour to begin preparing a meal for Austin and his playmate of the moment. No one was here to question his intentions or provide his description to the police. Nirat considered running upstairs and fetching a few last-minute effects—a toothbrush not the least among them—but his instincts urged a leaner travel plan. Best to cut it all away and start anew. There would be plenty of toothbrush-buying times along the way.

Yet if it was so simple, then why was he standing here in the kitchen instead of carrying himself through the Savlodar door for the final time?

As he tapped the plastic cap into the tube's end, he fended off a bit of unexpected remorse. Richard would likely be paroled next year, and his rebirth at Savlodar Corp was certain to alter the current dynamic. Forced to operate legitimately instead of cutting backstairs deals for contracts, Richard would need to exercise his famous creativity in new ways—ways that might prove both entertaining and lucrative. But Nirat would experience it only as an observer as he read the details from an Asian Internet café.

He frowned at his reflection in the microwave and got himself moving. The photo secured, he grabbed a carton of orange juice from the battleship-sized refrigerator, drank a single glass, and left the way he came. He spared the incomplete deck another glance. The fine wooden planks seemed to be waiting for him to return and unite them, and it was only with a sigh that he turned away and went to meet the cab that he heard waiting for him at the curb.

Chapter 42

"So what happens next?"

Micah wished he had an answer. Katelyn's trust in him was stunning in both its immediacy and intensity. What if he'd met her a month or a year or a lifetime ago? Had he been standing in the produce section when their paths had intersected, or waiting to pick up his cleaning, would they have ended up in this place, where faith passed as easily as conversation between them? The sensible part of him wanted to write it off to circumstance, but the sensible part was losing ground.

"You could always kick his door in again," she suggested.

"Tempting, but I thought about ringing the bell this time."

"Just to see who answers?"

"We have to start somewhere." He got out of the car.

The house was less impressive by day. In the dark it had been a Renaissance castle, as if those within were unassailable. Now it looked overblown, another inhabited monument to ego and excess.

They walked beside the lavender rows of coneflowers, closing in on the front door. Micah suspected he'd find the jamb repaired and perhaps a new deadbolt installed. His act of forced entry now seemed a distant point of light, a star too far away to have meaning.

"Micah?"

"Yeah?"

"Someone's coming."

Micah turned as the man appeared from around the corner of the house.

The stranger, seeing them, stopped so suddenly that he had to rock back on his heels to keep from stumbling. In one hand he held a long white cylinder. His eyes, vaguely Asian, revealed his surprise.

Micah searched the man's face but saw nothing familiar. But even in those first few seconds, he understood that he'd been recognized. The stranger knew him.

Micah changed course and walked toward him.

The man spun and ran.

It's him. Micah realized it a half-step too late. But then the rage let loose, beginning in his stomach and coruscating through him. Tully's killer was getting away.

Micah sprinted after him.

His legs drove him forward, his fists pumping up and down. Saliva rushed from his mouth. He cut around the corner, the anger building as he watched the man slip through an opening in a privacy fence. Micah had never run like this, pushed himself like this, and now to finally let go, balls to the wall, he wasn't about to fall behind.

He shot through the gate and closed the gap as they ran across the Mexican-pattern tiles beside a swimming pool.

The man dropped his tube, kept running.

Micah called on his muscles for more, and they responded. Adrenaline shoved him those last few feet.

He jumped.

Arms outstretched, he tackled the man from behind, wrapping him up by the knees and dragging him down. They landed violently on the hard tiles.

Micah lost control. He unlocked his arms and punched the man as hard as he could in the center of the back. A second later he drove the butt of his hand against the base of his enemy's skull, driving his face into the ground.

Weird sounds escaped him as he slid up the man's body and beat him with wild swings from both fists, one after the other. His breath was propane in his throat. Tully was dead, murdered, and this was the way to make it right, to ease his spirit, to thank him for all that he'd done—

The man twisted with such abrupt power that Micah lost his balance. Because his eyes were clenched shut in fury, he never saw the blow that landed just south of his lungs, but he felt its eruption.

"Micah!"

Coughing, he opened his eyes to see the man clawing himself to his feet. As Micah tipped backward, unable to arrest his descent, he snagged the man's ankle and pulled in the direction he was falling.

Their momentum carried them over the edge. They hit the water and went under.

The world changed. Bubbles filled Micah's ears. Sounds shifted. He clamped down on his teeth just in time to avoid a mouthful of water, but he never closed his eyes. Tully's killer, now a wavering form, lunged for the lip of the pool and pulled himself up.

Micah kicked once with both legs, propelling himself forward. He broke the surface.

Katelyn reached them and—shouting his name—dropped to her knees.

The man was almost out. Water pouring off him, he got one foot on the tiles, and then Micah grabbed a fistful of his hair. With an inarticulate cry, he yanked the man back into the water.

They went down.

Even as they sank, his fingers found a throat, and he squeezed. Arms and legs churned the water. Though Micah held his breath, his blood already called for air, his heart driving it ruthlessly through him. He forced his fingers closer together, craving the sensation of strangulation, wanting only to feel the crack of bone.

Something was wrong with his ear.

He became aware of this dimly, as if the pain were a messenger on the far side of a wall, telling him that something was wrong. When his fingers lost a tiny bit of strength, the pain surged forward, and Micah realized that his ear was being torn from his head.

He couldn't help it: he let go.

In a second he was dying.

The man was no stranger to survival. Fleeing had failed him, and so he turned his skills to killing, using the water to his advantage. He slipped behind Micah and locked his forearm around his throat.

Micah flailed. He kicked, but his feet only drummed the bottom of the pool without effect. He reached back and grabbed his assailant by the hair, but without gravity he had no leverage. And so he could only try to tear the man's arm free, and in the meantime he rapidly ran out of air.

I'm sorry.

He wasn't sure if he was talking to his father or Tully or himself, but the words were there, the only coherent thing of which he was capable. He lost strength with every second, and Tully's killer, sensing this, tightened his hold.

Something came down on top of him.

The weight pushed both men to the bottom. For a moment Micah felt the pressure relent, and he used his last reserves to wrest himself free.

He had no idea what was happening. He couldn't breathe. He pushed with both legs and fanned downward with his arms . . .

He broke through to the air above and loudly pulled down

that first breath, then another.

Katelyn appeared beside him, shaking her head and flinging water droplets, followed immediately by the man with the Asian eyes.

Just let him go.

Exhausted, Micah wanted to obey that voice. But when the man reached for the edge of the pool and pulled himself up, Micah went after him, compelled by something primitive that was not so ready to give up.

He tackled the man on the tiles and attacked him. He struck him in the head as hard and as fast as he could. Bone jittered against the ground. Blood speckled the green-and-white tile.

"Micah, stop!"

No way. He would eat this man. He would kill him and god-damn eat him.

"Micah!"

She threw herself at him. Though she wasn't heavy, her weight was sufficient to dislodge him. Lying beneath her, he stared at the mangled face only inches from his own. Blood ran from the man's nose.

"It's okay!" Katelyn said, wet hair hanging in her face. "It's okay, it's over, you got him, babe, you got him . . ."

Micah, panting, waited for the man to move. Just once. Just once and they'd go at it again.

"Easy. Easy now. Just let it go. You hear me?" She stroked his cheek. "Just let it go."

His chest lurched up and down. There didn't seem to be enough air in the world.

The man didn't move. But he was breathing.

"Let it go, okay? I'm here, and it's all over now. We win. The good guys win."

He heard little of what she said. But he was aware of her, and he trusted her, so he would have to believe that her voice would guide him back to earth.

"We need to"—she coughed—"we need to call the police."

He tried to say yes but nothing worked. His body shivered with the aftershock of the struggle.

"Is your phone in the car? In your jacket?"

He knew she was directly above him, but he couldn't focus on her face. His eyes were full of chlorine and tears. He forced himself to nod.

"I'll be back, okay? You watch him. *You watch him.*"

This time the nod came easier. Katelyn lifted herself off him, and then her hurried footfalls faded.

Micah rolled to his side and vomited. The thin stream of fluid converged with the blood beneath the man's head. Micah stared into the watery mess, hoping to find a pattern there, something that made sense before unconsciousness threw its ropes around him and pulled him down.

CHAPTER 43

I'm going to tell you a secret, Tully said.

Micah forced his eyes open as much as he could. He saw the white of a paramedic's shirt and then the black again, where Tully still lived.

You listening to me, sport?

Yeah, Tull. Say what you're going to say.

There are three kinds of people in this world.

Micah felt time passing around him. People spoke to him and he spoke back. His body moved. Maybe he was now standing and now walking and now returning to the car. When he briefly dared to focus his attention again, he saw the Cutlass. Somehow he'd gotten behind the wheel. He followed the police cruiser in front of him. For a moment he panicked and looked around for Katelyn—

She occupied the passenger's seat, a towel around her shoulder and her hair still wet.

The first kind of people, Tully said, *are the sheep.*

That's no secret, Tull. Let me guess. The second kind are wolves.

Yeah, smartass, now let me finish.

Driving toward the precinct, Micah let his friend get it out. You never knew what kind of insight you were going to get from him. And right now, having almost both murdered and been murdered in a swimming pool, Micah could use any of it he could get.

Eighty-nine percent of us are sheep. Just go along to get along. Some rich. Some weird. But sheep. Ten percent are predators or jack-offs or shitheels who don't respect other people's personal space, if you can smell what I'm shoveling.

Even in his shell-shocked state, Micah knew the numbers didn't add up. As he fought a sudden shiver—his feet frozen in wet socks—he told Tully as much.

I didn't skip the third grade, thanks for asking. That one percent are the shepherds.

Micah drifted. He was using Tully as a diversion. Without an inner dialogue, he'd fall back into that pool again, where he would have killed a man had not Katelyn intervened. Or he would have been killed himself. Even driving was no longer the medicine it once had been.

The secret, my young compadre, is that you aren't like most people. You're different.

A shepherd?

That's right. You get the rest of us where we need to go. And I'm talking about a hell of a lot more than driving that damn car.

Micah didn't want the responsibility.

You keep us safe.

He pulled into the precinct parking lot, looked at Katelyn, and wanted to say thanks but didn't know how.

Chapter 44

"You okay to drive?"

"He got us here, didn't he?" Katelyn returned. She must have tasted the acid in her words, because she quickly apologized. "Sorry about that. It's been a shitty day."

"I'll be in touch," Ling said. "Soon."

"Sure, thanks."

Micah was glad she did the talking. If only she could walk for him, as well, he'd be in much better shape.

Once they were back in the car, Katelyn said, "Those were not the best two hours of my life. I'm getting tired of police stations. They don't smell very good, for one thing."

Micah guided the key into the ignition. He needed to say something, if only to keep her from worrying. "At least we're finally dry."

"True enough. I need a shower in a major way. No, make it a bath. Now that this is over, I assume that I have time to do nothing but lay in the tub, right?"

"Anything you want." He got them moving in the direction of her apartment.

"Don't ever say *that* to me unless you mean it. After what we've been through, I could *want* a lot. Like justice. Like an explanation. Like six gallons of chocolate ice cream."

"No reason you can't have any of those things."

"I'm not so sure about the justice part. Just because that man murdered Tully doesn't mean that he can be tied to his boss.

Savlodar's a crud who deserves a punishment he won't even get unless the cops can prove he gave the order."

"It'll all work out."

"There goes your glass again, being annoyingly half full."

Micah wished that it were as full as he led her to believe. Its water level had fallen. He'd lived through the most violent encounter of his life. He would've been strangled to death had not Katelyn intervened. And moments after that she'd prevented him from killing another human being by slamming his head into the ground. Would a hot bath cure all of that?

"Kinda hard to stop thinking about it, huh?" she asked.

"To say the least."

"We kicked ass."

"Maybe so."

"*Definitely* so. You see that guy's nose?"

He'd seen it. As it turned out, the damage looked a lot worse than it was; faces tended to bleed heavily. Before taking the man in for questioning, the police had delivered him to the emergency room. Micah had overheard one of them say his nose was broken.

Katelyn twisted in her seat. "Look, I'm just as frazzled by this as you are, but I'm also glad as hell to be done with it. If it helps me to cope to say that we kicked his ass then I'm saying we kicked his ass. End of story."

"Okay, cool. We kicked his ass."

"Yes. We did." She settled back in her seat, wearing his jacket over her dried and wrinkled clothes. "And just in time."

"Just in time for what?"

"Today is Friday.

"So?"

"*So* tonight is Adelaine Haynesworth's fundraiser."

"Who?"

"Adelaine Haynesworth, probably one of the top five

choreographers in North America."

"Oh. Right."

"I told you about the party."

"I remember."

"I need to meet her and make a good impression. My biggest concern at the moment is not letting all the recent craziness show in my face."

"You'll be fine."

"So you say."

He wanted to sound more confident, but his conversational skills had yet to resurface. He hoped she was right when she said it was over, but the vibe he got from Detective Ling made him wonder. Still, he told himself to let it go. The hard part was behind him. He'd met the dragon and survived.

The drive to Katelyn's apartment—which she hadn't seen in three days—provided them with twenty minutes to discuss the relative fullness of glasses. Micah said he'd need to call Rhonda and ask about the funeral. Katelyn promised to be there. But regardless of the topic, their words built more bridges between them, so that the day's turmoil eased to more manageable elevations.

"Just pull in there behind Dezi's Mini."

"What are you going to tell her?"

"Mainly that I lived to tell the tale. I'm sticking to the basics. She doesn't need to hear the . . . the really bad stuff."

"And she has an extra phone you can use?"

"One of those pay-as-you-go things. It's not pretty but it does the job. I'll text you the number so you can call me as soon as you hear anything from Ling." She looked as if she were about to say more, but instead she just sat there staring at him, fingers on the door handle.

"Whatever it is," he told her, "I can take it."

"You sure about that?"

"I may be on the verge of acquiring post-traumatic stress disorder, but I think I can manage it. So go ahead."

"Fine." She bit her lip, then: "Do you want to be my date tonight?"

Of all the questions that might have come out of her mouth, this was one that snuck up on him. By now he shouldn't have been surprised by her ability to keep him off balance, but there it was.

"You look like I just asked to carry your love child," she said. "If you don't want to—"

"Yes." It came out before he had the chance to examine it with his usual methodology.

"Yes, you'll come?"

"It's either that or spend the night replaying everything in my head."

"Yeah, that wouldn't be the best idea. But, uh, there is *one* thing I need to warn you about." She looked worried.

"I'm afraid to ask."

"The party is, um . . . it's formal attire only. You do own a decent suit, don't you?"

He saw the grin in her eyes and delighted in it. He couldn't help but laugh, in spite of everything that had gone wrong in recent days. "I'll see what I can scrape up."

"Great." She leaned in and kissed him on the cheek. "Thanks for keeping us alive, hero."

A moment later she was out of the car and rushing up the steps to her apartment. Halfway up she looked back.

Micah held up a hand.

She waved with neither joy nor sadness but something more complicated in between, and then disappeared.

CHAPTER 45

A lone dinghy crested the surf, far beyond the memory of the shore.

The gray sea lifted and relaxed, prisoner to the invisible forces of current and tide. Out here, monsters dwelled. No laws of man projected this far. No religion purged the pagan depths. Symbiosis alone could save you, the pact between sailor and the sailed. If the ocean wanted you, it ate you in spite of which god might have created you, and so you appeased it by doing gracefully that which it desired most. You guided a boat across its beautiful vastness.

Alexander Niratpattanasai kept one hand on the tiller and the other on what felt like a Styrofoam cup of coffee. He must have been dreaming. There was no coffee out here, nothing to drink but the depleting contents of a wineskin, nothing to eat but the fish you took like a gift from below.

". . . yet as your attorney I'm obligated to tell you . . ."

His face felt on fire. Nirat supposed that the wind must have chapped his cheeks, and now the spray of salt smoldered in the wounds. That explained the throbbing. Other than this, however, he felt fine.

"Alex? Are you even listening?"

Unfortunately, he was. The man's incessant soliloquy dragged him back, and suddenly there was no succor on the sea, not even this far out.

"You can indulge in meditation another time, Alex."

Meditation? Could it be something so illusory as that?

"Look at me and tell me you're paying attention."

The sea released him. He slid back into himself with painful clarity.

"Alex?"

He saw the coffee cup. The desk. The outline of the bandage across his nose. "May I go now?"

"Not quite. I get the impression that the detectives have one more desperate gambit to make in an effort to keep you here."

Nirat closed his eyes. "Then by all means . . ." He looked inward and called to the little vessel on the waves. He anticipated its return. Yet it didn't appear. He scanned the shoreline, but he saw nothing but a black man in a bowtie, waiting for Nirat to join him in the water.

"Let us drown together," Nirat whispered to him.

"I'm sorry? Alex? What did you say?"

Nirat waited for the tide to carry him out.

Chapter 46

Micah brought the limo. No other car would suffice. Not after all they'd overcome. Katelyn deserved a gilded chariot pulled by snow-colored chargers.

Having sent a text to let her know he'd arrived, he took up a familiar position near the fender, hands clasped. Tully came back to him. His death was still so hot that Micah felt him like a fever. He'd eaten nothing since this morning, and even that small amount had happened only at Katelyn's urging. Normally standing here waiting for the belle of the ball would've been inconceivable, as his friend and part-time mentor was now gone, taken away by a man who Micah had chased and almost killed simply because he'd looked guilty and tried to run. Perhaps he wasn't even the murderer, though Micah's gut believed otherwise. Either way, Micah should have been home with the lights off. What would Tully have said if he could see him?

Got yourself an actual date with a classy broad? Then what the hell you doin' wastin' time thinkin' about me, for chrissakes?

The ghost of Tully's voice, like the man himself, never spoke in riddles.

Katelyn appeared.

The lamps along the sidewalk pushed back the night and revealed her as she approached. She wore a silk gown of midnight blue, its V-neckline and close fit complimenting her as she moved. She stopped a few feet from him, holding a clutch purse that matched her earrings. "Nice car."

"I was sent to pick you up, ma'am."

"Oh? I see. I must be going out with quite an important man."

"I don't know about that, ma'am." He opened the passenger's door.

"What, I don't get to sit in the back?"

"He thought you'd enjoy the view up front."

"To say nothing of the company."

Micah gave a quick bow of his head.

She settled herself into the seat. "You do this a lot, pick up women under the cover of darkness, whisk them away to parts unknown?"

"Actually, no. You're the first."

"Ah, I'm honored. Then let us be on our way, shall we?"

"Of course." He closed the door. As he made his way around the car, Tully spoke up again, yelling something indistinct and probably lewd. But whatever it was, it sounded encouraging. And if that was how Micah could deal with the loss without being overwhelmed by it, then he would let it play out. At least for tonight.

He settled in behind the wheel. For a moment he only sat there, turning it all over in his mind, and then he channeled some of Tully's what-the-hell bravery and looked at her. "Would you consider it forward of me, ma'am, to say that . . . that you look incredible?"

She seemed to consider it. For several seconds she stared at him without expression, then at the dashboard, then—having apparently made up her mind—back at him again. "I think I find that remark to be quite acceptable. Thank you."

"You're welcome."

"And now that you mention it, you don't look half bad yourself."

"I appreciate your saying so."

"You can call me Katelyn."

"Very well."

"And what about you? Did anyone bother giving you a proper Christian name?"

"No, ma'am. I'm just the driver." He put the car in gear and drove them away.

Chapter 47

The ice sculpture was likely the first of its kind to feature leg-warmers.

At some point in his life, Micah had seen the movie *Flashdance.* Or was it *Dirty Dancing*? Either way, the figure captured in ice—arms overhead, back arched in ecstasy—might have leapt straight from an '80s dance floor. Her transparent, pointed toes extended from leg-warmers nearly perfect in detail, backlit by candles and glimmering like crystal.

"Sir?"

He turned to find a woman in silver gloves offering him a selection of cocktails.

"No, thanks." Almost immediately he changed his mind. "Wait. On second thought, do you happen to have a water?"

"I'll bring you one right away."

Micah slipped his hands into his pockets and conducted another survey of the darkly lit room. At least three hundred people clinked glasses and reveled in their youth and traded arcane dancer lore. They wore dreadlocks and designer dresses and diamond studs in their eyebrows. Their accents hinted at Jamaica and Mexico and New York. Regardless of gender or race, each one moved with a kind of feral grace. Micah held still so as not to be noticed as an infiltrator in the ranks of the acrobatic.

His eyes found Katelyn in the crowd. She was doing her thing, holding a champagne flute in one hand and gesturing with the other as she charmed the redoubtable Adelaine Haynesworth. Micah had never met a professional choreographer before, so he wasn't sure if he should've been impressed with this fiftyish woman with the spiked black hair and fashionably frumpy shawl. But if he could have entreated her for one favor, a single boon from the theater gods, he would've asked her to give this girl a chance. Katelyn possessed in remarkable quantities what his father had called *salt.* And she looked fairly devastating in an open-back dress.

"Sir?"

Micah snapped back into himself.

"Your water."

"Oh, right. Thanks." He took the glass and set off to find a different vantage point.

Four sets of French doors opened onto balconies, two of which were occupied. Micah chose the farthest one and gathered a breath of what passed for fresh air in this city. The usual nocturnal rainbows surrounded him, great arcs of color wrapped around advertisements for jackpots and chorus lines and art-house films. The instrumental music from the room behind him made it all a bit surreal, as if his life were something he was watching unfold on a sound stage. Maybe he could blame it on his ragged mental state, but nothing felt the same anymore. His carefully hewn career of discretion and punctuality had given way to the unknown. The only thing still the same was the suit.

They'd arrived here over an hour ago. Micah had spent most of that time distracted. He shook hands whenever Katelyn introduced him and asked what he hoped were intelligent questions, but inside he was checking the seismograph. If the earth started to move, he wanted to be ready.

"Fancy meeting you here."

He didn't look at her, just leaned his forearms on the balcony rail. "Needed a break."

"Understandable. Dancers tend to be high-energy people. Not to mention emotionally fragile prima donnas who tend to trade eating for art. Yours truly excluded, of course."

"How did it go with Haynesworth?"

"She laughed at my lame jokes, if that counts."

"It's a start."

"And told me to email my résumé to her assistant."

Only now did he make eye contact. "Seriously?"

She grinned and nodded like a schoolgirl.

"Hey, all right!" He tapped his glass against hers. "Mission accomplished."

"I don't know about *that,* but at least it's something." She joined him in his contemplation of the world beyond the balcony. Even the traffic had an impressionist quality about it, as if the cars were merely blotches of paint on canvas. "Have the police happened to call you yet?"

"I'm trying not to think about it."

"That's probably working as well for you as it is for me."

"We have no proof that he's the one who did that to Tully. What's his name? Nira-something?"

She sighed. "We heard his voice on the phone."

"It was far away. It could've been anybody."

"It was *him.* You saw the look on his face when he recognized us."

"I wish that were enough. The prosecution will require a lot more than that." He scowled at himself. "Hey, I'm sorry. We were in the middle of celebrating."

"Nah, it's okay. I really wanted to meet Adelaine, but other than that I'm just going through the motions. The rest of it just seems so . . . I don't know."

"Insignificant?"

"Exactly. Which leaves me and thee out here waiting for

everything to go wrong again."

Micah wanted to reassure her, but the truth felt more appropriate. In fact, now that he considered it, the truth was the most important thing between them. They shared it the way others shared a secret.

"Looks like there's only one cure for what ails us," she said.

Micah was about to ask her to elaborate, but then he guessed. "I think the last place I should be learning to dance is within sight of basically all the best dancers in Las Vegas."

She put her glass on the rail. "Nobody's watching. Besides, who gives a damn if they are?"

There was a moment when he thought he might escape. For a second he favored the notion of using the day's events as his excuse; she would've let him off the hook if he asked. But she was looking up at him, and that was enough. He set his glass beside hers.

"They're playing our song," she said.

"We have a song?"

"No, but we have a time signature. Hear the three-count?" She stepped into him and placed her hand in his. "Do you?"

He raised his right elbow as she'd taught him and kept his back straight. "Right now I'm more concerned about not tripping over my own feet."

"I think we're past that stage, actually. We've left the foot-tripping behind."

"Maybe I'll relapse."

"I'll take my chances." She gave him a slight tug, and he flowed into her, stepping with his left foot and making the diagonal with his right. He surprised himself by executing a turn that made him almost seem as if he knew what he was doing.

After a while, she said, "So how does it feel to be getting so good at the most romantic dance of all time?"

"I thought the tango was supposed to be the most romantic."

"No, the tango might be the *sexiest,* but that's a different thing entirely."

"How so?"

"Well, the tango says, 'When this dance is over, we're jumping straight into bed.' But the waltz says, 'I don't want this dance to ever end.' "

They moved slowly across the balcony, turning, turning . . .

Chapter 48

What Nirat wanted most was the rain. Walking alone at night would've seemed more complete had the sky suddenly cracked open like black glass and turned the city into a running watercolor.

His face ached. His forehead was lacerated and his lower lip was split. It was a miracle he hadn't lost any teeth. Twenty minutes ago the police had released him instead of producing the evidence to charge him with first-degree murder, yet all Nirat could think about was his pulsating nose and his quiet longing for the rain.

He'd declined the offer of a ride from his attorney. More specifically, he'd declined the offer from Richard Savlodar's attorney, a lean courtroom beast named Cooker. Until tonight, Nirat had seen the man at various company functions, but as the plebians didn't mingle with the Roman senators, they'd never said hello. Cooker's firm represented celebrities and the scions of foreign oil interests. And now, by some crook in the universe, he was chopping heads on behalf of a convicted felon's half-breed handyman.

A car slowed as it pulled up beside him. Nirat didn't look over.

The dark window lowered. Nirat kept walking.

"Get the fuck in."

Nirat stopped, staring straight ahead and listening to the breath move noisily through his damaged nose. When he was sure that tranquility remained his, he turned, stooped, and peered into the car. "Hello, Austin."

"You planning to walk all the way to Cambodia?"

"Thailand. And no, the police insisted I don't leave. The county line is my boundary."

"Just get in the car, will you?"

Detecting an uncharacteristic weariness in the younger man's voice, Nirat did as he was asked. So much for his walk. And his peace.

Austin drove for ten minutes without speaking.

Nirat let him brood. In a wise man, the silence would shape itself into an appropriate and measured response, or perhaps—to the truly enlightened—it would even offer an epiphany. Nirat was interested in seeing how Austin made use of it.

"First it was a fiasco," Austin said at last, "and now it's a full-blown clusterfuck."

Nirat closed his eyes. There was his answer.

"You called my father?"

"I required legal counsel. Richard has made it clear that I was to notify him if I was ever in need of anything. Until tonight, I never took advantage of the offer."

"Why didn't you just call *me,* for God's sake?"

"It was my understanding that you never wanted to see me again."

Austin took both hands from the wheel, his fingers curled and tense, and then returned them with a slap. "Fine, forget it. Just tell me what happened. What did they ask you? What did you tell them?"

Nirat selected his words like a jeweler inspecting precious stones. "The sum of it is simple enough, I suppose. I was at the house, preparing to make a trip to the lumber-supply company so that I could finish work on the deck. I was chased down and assaulted by a man I've never met. Apparently the detectives believe I might know something of a homicide they're investigating, and their witnesses think my voice is similar to that of the murderer."

"Your voice?"

"They overheard the event. Apparently the victim was clever enough to place a call minutes before he died." Though Nirat didn't say as much—you never knew who was listening—he admired Tullmacher for that little bit of sleight-of-hand. Nirat had underestimated him in more ways than one. "Needless to say, a distant voice heard over a cellular network is no reason to keep a man incarcerated."

"That's all they have? Everything?"

"I'm not privy to what the investigators might or might not know. But Mr. Cooker tells me, and I quote, 'Their case isn't worth a cowboy boot full of bullshit.' "

"Eloquent." Austin didn't looked convinced. "So they have zilch as far as evidence goes? Nothing else lying around the murder scene?"

"Again, I have no idea, but it seems to me that the man they're looking for must have been very careful, very professional. Just to appease them, I willingly provided a blood sample so that my DNA might be compared to anything they possibly found near the victim."

"Was that smart?"

"An innocent man has nothing to hide, not even in his nucleotides."

"And that's it? That's all?"

"Mr. Cooker is planning on seeing that my attackers are prosecuted."

Austin grunted. "Now that's rich."

"They tried to drown me."

"Looks to me like you survived. What—did these attackers of yours have a change of heart in the middle of killing you?"

The muscles in Nirat's face tightened, and that made his nose hurt. "Mr. Cooker is looking into the most appropriate charges. I'll speak with him again in the morning."

"Sounds wonderfully ironic. Donovan gets locked up. Maybe there's some justice in this ragtag world, after all. But you forgot the most important part."

Nirat knew he was being baited, but he couldn't guess the nature of the trap. "And what might that be?"

"All of this happened at *my* goddamn house!" He stomped the accelerator. "I mean, Christ Almighty, all I want to do is *forget* about Donovan and *forget* about that whore and get on with my life, and all it takes to get that done is for you . . . to not . . . go back . . . to the house."

Nirat had no choice: he sat and tried to outlast the storm.

"*I told you to leave.* Remember that? I specifically said, *I specifically said* that you weren't to return to the house, do not stop and get your shit, do not pass Go and collect your two-hundred fucking dollars. Jesus H., you have screwed this up to operatic proportions."

Nirat pined for Richard. Richard the adult. Richard who handled the worst of problems with aplomb. Whether you were a boardroom titan or the guy who trimmed the Savlodar grass, Richard never spoke to you like that.

"I don't even know what to do," Austin said. "I just don't. You're going to bring this down on my head whether I like it or not. How am I supposed to deal with that, huh?"

Nirat stared at the man's hands. White and clean, not careworn in the least. How far would one of those fingers move independently of the others before it broke?

Austin parked at a random curb. "Just do me a favor and refrain from relaying any more of this to the grand old patriarch. We can take care of it ourselves."

"As you wish." He opened the glovebox and saw what he was

hoping to find, the five-piece screwdriver set he used two months ago to install Austin's new stereo. "I don't suppose you'd mind if I borrowed these?"

"What the hell for?" He waved it off. "Never mind. I don't give a shit. Just go."

Nirat got out of the car. Austin had brought him to a strip club.

"Go get drunk and pay for a lap dance. Piss a bit more of your life away. I mean, what difference does it make now, right?"

Nirat watched his taillights disappear.

Behind him, music pushed against the walls of the club. But he hardly noticed. Dawn was still some distance away. Between now and then lay several interesting hours.

"Let us drown together," he said, and set off walking.

CHAPTER 49

Audrey Hepburn put her finger in the dimple on Cary Grant's chin and said, "How do you shave in there?"

Katelyn giggled.

Sitting beside her on his couch, Micah smiled to himself. He'd driven them from the party with the intent of taking her home, but she requested a detour. She wasn't tired, and she hadn't enough patience to fend off her roommate's questions all night. "Dezi's already mothering me to death over the whole thing," she said, "so if it's all right with you, I'll avoid going home until I'm sure she's asleep. You have any popcorn at your place?"

As it turned out, he had a single package left in the box. While he listened to it bang away in the microwave, Katelyn found an oldie on TV. She sat with her shoes off, her feet on the coffee table, the hem of her dress at her knees.

He poured the popcorn into the biggest bowl he owned and sat beside her.

She grabbed a handful. "Have you seen this one before?"

He shook his head.

"What kind of movies do you like?"

"Short ones."

"You're not a movie person?"

"Do documentaries count?"

"What, you mean guys driving around in Africa looking at elephants?"

"Maybe. You have something against nature shows?"

"They're too sad. Somebody's always getting poached or eating someone else or going extinct or having their habitat ruined."

"If you put it *that* way . . ."

"But this"—she pointed at the TV—"good stuff."

"Seems sort of far-fetched."

"Of course it's far-fetched. But even if the plots are silly, the point is that you can still maybe identify with the characters."

"The only character I can identify with is Morgan Freeman in *Driving Miss Daisy.*"

Katelyn laughed.

Micah joined her, just because it felt good. The part of him that wasn't worrying about the shaky status quo of his life and career was marveling at the fact that he was sitting beside this woman, charming her and being charmed in return. But Tully intervened. His ghost was still too close, and Micah couldn't let himself enjoy the popcorn and the company as much as he would've liked.

Still, he did okay. They talked about the movie and famous people and what it felt like to get paid for doing something that you loved.

When the movie finally ended, Katelyn aimed the remote and killed the TV. "And they lived happily ever after."

In the absence of the television's glow, the only light was that from a shaded lamp that once, in a distant ice age, belonged to Micah's mother. She had died when he was four, so his memories of her were only those distilled in his father's photographs. Malcolm mated for life and never remarried. On most days, Micah forgot the lamp had ever belonged to her, though for some reason, tonight was not one of those times.

"It's two in the morning," Katelyn said. "I guess that means it's safe to go home."

"She won't wake up when you come in?"

"She sleeps with earplugs. Thank God. I don't think I could really explain things to her in a way she'd understand. By *things* I mean you."

"I'm not that hard to explain."

"To Dezi you would be. A suave black man bashes into a millionaire's house and drives me across the desert, where we're given a sawed-off shotgun as a door prize. We come back, and a man . . . a man dies because of us, and then we run his murderer down and almost kill him." She tapped him gently with the remote. "Yeah, *you* try explaining that."

He understood her reservations. What they shared was difficult to relate to others in a way that held any meaning. A traffic accident wasn't something so easily discussed with bystanders who hadn't felt the concussive force of impact or known the panic of almost dying. "What was that part about suave?"

"Did I say that?"

"I'm sure you did."

"It's late. I get tongue-tied when I'm tired."

"You seem plenty awake to me."

"I must have meant *strange.*"

"Birds of a feather."

"Can't argue with that."

He waited for her to say something else, to keep up the cadence they'd created. It was so easy just to sit here and trade silly commentary with her. It put all the important stuff on hold.

"I suppose I should go."

He kept himself from sighing. "I'll get the keys."

The keys dangled from a stainless steel hook near the door, just as they always did. Everything around him had its place. Yet now all of that seemed unnecessary. Sure, maybe he was brave enough to tackle a murderer, but his courage petered out with putting his keys somewhere other than on their customary hook or asking this girl to stay for another hour, just so they could talk about meaningless things.

He didn't need Tully to tell him that he was a coward.

"Would you mind terribly," she said, "if I go outside barefoot? The shoes, you know, they weren't exactly made with comfort as the guiding light."

"You know, normally it'd be an issue, but since it's dark, maybe we'll get lucky and no one will see you. I can't imagine the embarrassment. But we'll take our chances."

She raised both eyebrows. "Oh, so now he unleashes the hounds of sarcasm. You better make sure you can take it if you're going to dish it out."

"You didn't think it was funny?"

"Sorry, stud. You are many fine things, but a comedian isn't one of them."

"You haven't heard my joke about the white woman who accidentally goes to an all-black church on Sunday."

She hung her shoes over her shoulder, one finger curled through the straps. "Being the only white woman in the room, I might choose to be offended."

"No." Micah looked at her seriously. "I don't think anything offends you."

"You're right. I'm offended only by people who get easily offended."

He held the door open for her. "And I'm suave."

"I meant strange."

He followed her down the steps. The night was warm, though he couldn't see the stars.

"So what's the joke? I'm dying here."

"Oh, yeah. Well, as Tully would tell it—"

"This is a Tully joke?"

"Better believe it."

"Uh oh. I'm bracing myself."

"Anyway, there's this prissy white woman who's new in town and attends an all-black Southern Baptist church on Sunday . . ."

Chapter 50

Nirat sat in the back of the limousine.

Penetrating the long black car hadn't been as difficult as he'd feared. Twice during his employment under Richard he'd been required to enter someone else's vehicle without their knowledge. The first was to plant a package under the driver's seat; Nirat never learned the parcel's contents, nor had he asked. The second was to leave a photo of a man's nine-year-old daughter, a warning that had prompted compliance from the car's owner. But this was different. The geometry of the game he now played continued to alter shape as it progressed.

He tapped one of the screwdrivers in his hand as he watched them approach.

They laughed. The young woman—Katelyn Presley—swatted Donovan on the arm, and he feigned a shoulder injury. They were dressed as if a red carpet were not far away.

Nirat's mistake had been running. He blamed his reflexes. When he'd spotted them in the driveway of Savlodar's house, he'd assumed in that first half-second of recognition that they'd come for him. Weaponless and outnumbered, he'd given in to flight, and it had nearly gotten him killed. They could've finished him then and there.

He would never again give them the chance.

The two of them walked around the car to the passenger's side. Donovan was gesturing as he explained something, and whatever it was, it clearly amused the girl.

Nirat ignored envy whenever it presented itself. Only rarely did he ever see a man and experience that very human moment of wishful transposition, where he might swap shoes and be rich for a day or handsome or breathtakingly gifted on the tenor sax. But he knew the sour taste of it briefly as he watched them. He wondered if they were aware of what they possessed.

Donovan opened her door. "My lady."

"Why, thank you, sir knight."

Nirat didn't move. If the girl turned, would she see him? Or was the darkness too thick?

Donovan crossed to the other side and got in.

"So what about your clients?" she asked. "Are you ever going back to work?"

"I guess so. But right now . . ."

"Maybe we'll just drive up to Montana and forget the whole thing?"

He didn't reply, just started the car.

"What's up in Montana, anyway?" she wondered.

"Snow," he said.

"That's it? Hmmm. Better make it Florida instead."

"Long drive."

"You have anything better to do?"

Nirat found that he was actually curious about Donovan's response. For some reason the conversation reminded him of his sailors in their stalwart little boat.

"Right now," Donovan eventually said, "I'll just worry about getting you home."

The car carried them away. Nirat held very still and waited.

Chapter 51

". . . and if you've been driving people around for two years," Katelyn said, "then you've probably got all kinds of juicy gossip."

"None of it worth repeating."

"Oh, come on. What about Donald Trump? Have you ever had Donald Trump in here?"

"I'm sure Mr. Trump has his own driver."

"Any rock stars?"

"Haven't you heard? Everybody's a rock star in this town."

"How about hot and heavy makeout sessions?"

He shook his head. "See no evil, hear no evil."

"Well that's not very fun. Is that some kind of chauffeur code of ethics?"

"A *personal* code. And a professional one."

"Sounds to me like your personal life is just about indistinguishable from your professional one."

"You got me there. Until you came along, anyway."

"Yeah, that's me, the femme fatale." She gazed from the window. "Does it do any good to say I'm sorry again? If I hadn't accepted his invitation when he asked me over . . ."

"Then I never would've gotten to know you." He could've said more, but he let it go. What he felt most of all but wasn't about to say was that his routine had been forever altered. When had it happened? When he kicked in the door? When he found Tully dead? Or only a few hours ago on the balcony?

"I bet you say that to all the girls."

"There are no other—"

The stereo blared to life.

Micah jolted in his seat as the speakers sent a shockwave of amplified rap music through the car. Katelyn let out a startled sound. The music was so sudden and so intense that Micah took his foot off the gas and tapped the brake without realizing it.

The music stopped.

Katelyn put her hand on her chest. "That scared the crap out of me! Does that kind of thing happen often?"

Micah glanced down at the master controls as the car continued to slow down. Other than an electrical glitch, the only way the expensive sound system could be activated was either from up front or . . .

He hit the interior lights.

Something moved. Micah realized they weren't alone, but that was as far as he got before the figure in the back lunged forward, grabbing him around the head.

Katelyn screamed.

Micah jerked the wheel to the right and planted both feet on the brake, causing the tires to shriek and the shoulder harness to lock painfully against his chest. An arm encircled his neck, and in an instant he was underwater again, being strangled to death.

"Micah!"

He knew that Katelyn was fighting, but he couldn't see her. He arched his back, released the wheel, and grabbed the hair of the man behind him. It had little effect. He twisted in his seat, trying to jerk free—

A metal object touched his throat below his chin.

He released his grip and locked his fingers around the man's wrist in an effort to keep himself from being impaled. Katelyn disengaged her seatbelt and threw herself over the seat, shouting and crying at the same time. Her legs disappeared from Micah's rapidly shrinking field of vision.

The man increased the pressure, his breath falling on Micah's face. Using the seat between them for leverage, he brought his weapon an inch closer.

Micah struggled, the muscles in his neck as tight as cables. His only advantage was that he had both hands in play, and with a tribalistic yell, he forced the man's arms away.

But then his oxygen ran out. He was being choked and he had nothing left.

The blade rushed back toward his throat.

Chapter 52

Nirat had not come here to kill this man. He hadn't come to do anything permanent. He hadn't come to push himself over the ledge into the land of the irretrievable. He'd simply intended to even things up, because if there was one thing that Richard had instilled in him, it was the belief in *balance*. It was the philosophy of equal and opposite reactions.

But now, displaced from the life that defined him, he just kept pulling that screwdriver closer. Following through was all he had left.

He didn't fear pursuit. They would never find him. Austin had given him sufficient funds to secure some furtive means of getting out of the country, and there were still holes in Thailand deep enough to conceal him beyond extradition's reach.

The strength drained from Donovan's body. Suddenly, there was no resistance.

Nirat closed his eyes. Tightened his grip. And *pulled.*

Something hard jabbed against the base of his skull.

"Stop it!"

Maintaining his grip on Donovan, the screwdriver's tip half an inch from the man's bulging throat, Nirat turned his head just enough to see what the hell was going on behind him.

He stared into the barrels of a gun.

The girl held the weapon in both hands. Her hair in her face, her chest heaving, she barely kept the thing steady. *"You hurt him and I will kill you, I swear to God."*

Nirat wanted to laugh.

It was funny, really, a true gut-buster, that he was being handed his balls by a girl with smeared makeup and a wrinkled dress. She'd probably never even held a gun before tonight.

Yeah, it was a regular riot. What would Richard think of him now?

Using the thumbs of both hands, she pulled down the two hammers until they locked in place. *"Get out."*

Did he have a move to make? He ran through his options. Because his hands were entangled with Donovan, he wouldn't be able to swat the gun to the side before she squeezed at least one of the shotgun's dual triggers. With the barrels less than a foot from his face, his brain and not a small amount of his facial structure would end up on the limousine's upholstery.

But would she really do it? Would she kill him?

"Get out!"

Traffic rolled by them, horns blaring. The car had come to rest in the breakdown lane, but its extended ass end jutted partially into the street.

Then Nirat saw it in her eyes. It amazed him in the way the sunrise sometimes amazed him. It was the look of one of his unknown sailors in the dinghy, the ones whose faces he'd never quite been able to see.

He dropped the screwdriver and opened the nearest door.

She tracked him with the gun as he backed out, his eyes never leaving hers. She would not have understood had he explained to her that now he had no choice but to pursue her, and possibly to kill her, if only because she possessed something he'd always thought too ephemeral to hold. Her hands shook to such an extent that Nirat feared she might inadvertently clamp down on the trigger, and he supposed he couldn't ask for a more fitting fate than that, gunshot by his own accidental desire.

In the front seat, Donovan bent over and coughed.

Nirat put one foot on the ground. Cars slowed, blasted their horns, kept going.

"Out!"

Nirat backed fully from the car, then leaned toward her. *"Alea iacta est."*

He closed the door.

Chapter 53

Micah swallowed fire.

Every breath torched him. His throat felt as if it had collapsed during the blaze, a chimney fallen in on itself, so that now only smoke found its way to his lungs. Somehow he managed to keep both feet on the brake, holding the car in place on the side of the road.

"Micah!"

He was aware of his name but little else. Katelyn sounded very much alive, which probably meant that she'd saved him—again.

She slid over the seat and landed beside him. "He's gone, babe, he's all gone." Her arms gathered him close.

Micah knew her scent. It was the smell of dancing on balconies and falling asleep in strange hotel rooms, and it brought him back.

"Can you drive?"

He wanted his arms to stop tingling. He wanted to let her hold him until the tremors passed.

"Can you drive or not?"

He nodded. What else could he do? Driving was the only thing he knew.

"I'm calling Detective Ling."

He grabbed her wrist before she could reach for her phone. Her pulse drummed beneath his hand.

"What? That asshole just tried to *murder* you."

He held up a finger.

"Okay, I'm waiting. But hurry up. I'll get you some water."

She flew over the seat again, formal gown be damned.

Micah took his first gratifying breath just as the bottle appeared in front of his face. She guided it to his fingers. The first swallow was rough, with more running down his chin than into his mouth, but it got better after that.

Horns reverberated off the car as traffic swerved around them.

"So are we calling Ling or not?"

Micah took another sip. "After . . . after we're on the way."

"On the way to where?"

He wiped his eyes. A piston-pounding headache banged away behind them. He put the bottle between his legs, took his feet off the brake, and signaled left until he was able to merge.

"On the way to where?" she asked again.

"First my place. Then yours. Then gone."

"Gone?"

"Just wherever. Away."

"Why?"

"He knows where we live. Both of us. He had your license, remember? I need to get the money, Tully's money. We'll switch cars. Then we'll"—he took another swallow—"then we'll stop by your apartment so you can get some clothes and things."

"He won't hurt Dezi, will he?"

"I don't know."

"If the police let him go, why didn't he just count himself lucky and *stop*?"

"I don't know that, either."

"You okay? You want me to drive?"

"I can manage."

"God, I should've—I should've shot him, I should've just shot him and called it self-defense."

"Wouldn't have worked."

"Damn sure *would* have. Micah, I actually thought I was going to kill that man. I was ready to do it."

"Gun's empty."

"What?"

"We never put any shells in it."

"Oh. You're right." She put a hand over her eyes and leaned her head back. "Shit."

Micah checked the rearview but saw only blurry headlights. How long did he have to get them out of town? Could he ask for police protection? Or were they better off just laying down the miles and going to ground far beyond Savlodar's reach?

"Did you hear what he said?" Katelyn asked.

"When?"

"Right before he slammed the door. He said something."

"I guess he did. I didn't understand it."

"Me neither. But it didn't sound good."

"Kate?"

"Yeah?"

"Go ahead and call the cops."

"And why now instead of two minutes ago?"

"I needed time to think, to make sure it was the best thing to do."

The small rectangle of light from her phone was as bright as a flare in the dark car. "By the way, after we stop and get our stuff, where are we going?"

"I think the consensus was Florida."

"Will he follow us that far? If we really went there, could he find us?"

Micah had no answer for that.

Chapter 54

Nirat stared after them until their taillights vanished like closing eyes.

Cars passed.

For want of a nail, according to the proverb, the kingdom was lost. The problem with lost nails and butterflies wagging their wings to cause hurricanes was that you never saw the nail or the wing for what it was until you were well beyond them. Standing on the side of the street, Nirat wondered what tiny event was to blame. What had put these sailors out to sea?

He took out his phone, his only possession save his clothes. If he were to find them, he would need to move with alacrity. Though dawn was still hours away, the authorities wouldn't wait till sunrise if Donovan let slip those particular dogs of war. They now had attempted murder as a reason to make an arrest.

He called a cab.

As he waited for the dispatcher to pick up, he tried to anticipate their trajectory. Were they even now speeding home to barricade the door? Would they go directly to the nearest police precinct? Or did they have some dive in mind, an Old West hideout in which they hoped to weather the storm he was about to unleash?

He smirked at himself. There was no use getting overly dramatic about it. Hyperbole would serve only to distract him. He would simply run them down and kill them, though he also might have to find people they cared about and . . . damage them. The money Austin had given him would provide for his needs along the way. His first need was a taxi. His second was a two-gallon container of gasoline.

Chapter 55

The last time Malcolm Donovan had driven this car was the day he was lobotomized. Micah relived that memory with high-res clarity as he thundered the two of them away from his apartment. Though he knew that, technically, his father hadn't experienced a lobotomy, sometimes the sadness assuaged itself by exaggeration. There were a hundred words for his father's condition, some of them cruel and some more politically correct than others but none of them really worth a damn.

"This may be the dumb question of the year," Katelyn said, "but are you okay?"

"Better than I'd be if I were alone." He said it without thinking. Just threw it out there. The wires in his body hummed, and he spent as much time glancing in the mirror as watching the road. In the backseat were a bundle of personal effects and a duffel bag full of dollar bills. He was only partially aware of what came out of his own mouth. But his right hand clutched one of the gearsticks, and when she rested hers on top of it, he realized what he'd said.

"We'll be fine," she told him. "Won't we?"

"As long as we keep moving."

"No sleazy motel?"

"Only if it's a sleazy motel in Miami."

Roused from his bed, Detective Ling had instructed them to go to a friend's place and wait for him to sort it all out. "If you have reason to suspect that he's following you," Ling had said, "then pick somewhere he doesn't know about and sit tight till I call you back. Can you do that?"

"Whatever," Katelyn had replied, ending the call.

Since then they'd visited Micah's apartment, where they spent less than six minutes. He parked the limousine, transferred the shotgun and shells to the Cutlass, and then grabbed only those few things he couldn't leave behind, primarily his shaving kit and money. That done, he ignored the speed limit and guided his father's car to Katelyn's house.

He pulled in behind a Mini Cooper convertible. "Be quick."

"Are you kidding me? I plan on leaving a smoke trail through the living room."

Micah killed the headlights as she ran inside. Where would they go? With Tully gone, Micah had no one but a handful of basketball-playing guys who probably weren't close enough to call friends. Katelyn surely had plenty of artsy young acquaintances who'd be willing to put them up, but Micah wouldn't hand his trust over so easily. Not now. He had little desire to sleep on a stranger's couch and spend the night waiting for the doorknob to rattle or a window to break.

His eyes settled on the GPS unit mounted on the dash.

Tully's sister had provided them asylum once before. How would she receive them in her grief?

"Gardeners do it bent over," he whispered, remembering the sign planted in the soil of her peace lily. She'd asked if she would ever see them again. At the time, Micah had suspected the answer was no. But who was he to chart the pattern of the stars?

Katelyn appeared. Micah got out to help her with a wicker laundry basket full of clothes and random bathroom paraphernalia. He noticed a pair of small computer speakers on top of the heap. "I thought we were sticking to the basics."

"Those *are* basic. I brought my MP3 player. It's crammed

full of what we'll need, and I'm not talking about the crap like food and water but the necessities—like *music.*"

Music? Micah wanted both to growl in frustration and laugh at the moon. This was how she operated. If global warming one day flooded Nevada with the Pacific Ocean, the rescue choppers would likely find Katelyn on her rooftop, dancing carelessly as the tide touched the shingles.

"Just shut up and drive," she said.

"Yes, Ms. Daisy." He tried to infuse his voice with a levity he didn't feel. The last things he wanted were jokes and dancing lessons. Then again, he probably needed them now more than ever.

When they were back on the street, he brought the GPS to life and touched the screen.

"I take it that means we have a destination," Katelyn said.

"Interstate fifteen toward Arizona, across the desert."

"Rhonda's?"

"It's all we've got. What did you tell your roommate?"

"I didn't wake her up. I left a note stuck to her bathroom mirror. Told her that everything was kosher and that I'd call her later. Basically I lied."

"It happens."

"Not anymore it won't." Staring at the streetlights, she shook her head. "Let the word go out from the passenger's seat of this kick-ass car: I will never lie again. For no reason, big or small. I don't have time for that anymore and I damn sure don't have the heart." She turned to him. "Are you acting as my witness on this?"

"I hear you."

"I'm serious."

"I know."

"That includes white lies. So if you ever ask me if a certain pair of pants make you look fat, I'm not going to hold back."

"I understand."

"The truth shall set me free."

"Let's hope so."

"Are you *really* okay?"

He kept both hands near the top of the wheel. "No."

"Yeah." She let out a long exhalation. "Me neither."

Chapter 56

They drove across the desert, watched over by ancient starlight. Micah had read that, one day, the universe would have expanded so far and so fast that light from those distant places would no longer reach Earth. Was that true? Would a driver millions of years from now look through his windshield and see only darkness?

"Are you ever going to change out of that suit?"

He glanced at her, though he could see little of her features in the weak dashboard glow.

"Not that I mind," she continued, "because you wear the damn thing about as well as anyone, with the possible exception of James Bond, but wouldn't you rather be in something more comfortable?"

"I *am* comfortable."

"You know what I mean."

"I didn't want to waste time changing at the house."

"Uh huh. I saw the clothes you brought. How many tuxedos do you own?"

"Two jackets. Four pairs of pants. A lot of shirts."

"Quite a wardrobe."

"Carpenters wear toolbelts."

"And doctors wear white coats. I get it. Still."

"Still what?"

"I haven't ever seen you wearing anything else."

"And how long have you known me?"

"Oh, I don't know, maybe longer than you think. We were probably pals in a past life. In ancient Egypt, I was Cleopatra and you were my exotic servant from a foreign land who fanned me with a palm leaf while wearing a single-breasted tux."

"Or maybe I was King Tut and you were *my* servant."

"Possibly. But being king, you'd probably still be dressed the same way."

Micah shook his head and allowed himself a fleeting smile. "You're probably right."

According to the GPS, they were only an hour from Rhonda Tullmacher's trailer house. Time had whistled by, flowing over them effortlessly. There were no silent miles, as Katelyn kept him talking, distracting him from the thoughts that might otherwise have dragged him into the mud pit. That's how the dinosaurs died, not by comet or climate change, but rather suffocated in fear, pulled down by something too strong to resist.

Breathing, now, seemed like a gift.

"Tux or no tux," she said, "you're going to have to go back to work sooner or later."

"Maybe I'm secretly wealthy and I only chauffeur for kicks."

"Really, this isn't going to totally destroy your business or anything, is it?"

"Too early to tell. I've made arrangements for my clients with other services. When I get a call for a new one, I give them Ambassador's number."

"Who's that?"

"One of my competitors who probably thinks I'm insane for passing off all my jobs. But if you're asking how long I can hold out before it starts to hurt my professional reputation, then I've probably already taken some hits. But you know what?"

"Hmmm?"

"I'm still alive."

"And the choir sang amen."

The Cutlass crunched gravel as it turned into Rhonda's driveway. Micah had called ahead, and they found her sitting near a blue bug-light on the slightly uneven front porch. This time she didn't hold a rifle but a bottle of what had been Tully's favorite beer back in his off-the-wagon days.

Micah got out and closed his door. He and Katelyn converged in front of the hot radiator and walked to the wooden steps.

Rhonda said nothing as they approached. Her hair was pulled back, but renegade strands of mostly gray had slipped from their clasp and now hung in front of her face. She wore khaki shorts and what looked to be handmade moccasins. When she tipped the bottle back, Micah was glad to see that her eyes were clear and dry.

Katelyn was the first to speak. "Thanks for letting us come."

Rhonda lowered the beer and slowly licked the residue from her lips.

"We didn't have anywhere else to go," Katelyn said.

Rhonda blew across the bottle's mouth, producing a sound like a tugboat in the fog. "Ernie and I used to do that when we were kids. Get ourselves bottles of Orange Crush for a quarter and then blow across the top. You two ever do that?"

Micah nodded. He didn't know what else to do.

"Why the hell does it make that sound, do you think?" She did it again. "Can't get that sound from an aluminum can. Never did care for cans much."

Micah put his hands in his pants pockets.

"So which one of you is to blame for what happened to my brother?"

Micah lowered his head. This was not why he'd called her. His guilt was already stacked high enough, each brick doing its part to block out the sun. He didn't need Rhonda bringing her own load.

"What say you, missy? From what Ernie told me, Micah here

was a straight-shooter till you came along. My brother would've slit open his wrists for this young man."

Katelyn crossed her arms over her chest and looked away.

"Well?"

"Leave her alone," Micah said. "It's not her fault."

"That the case? You the one to hold accountable, then?"

"Yes. For everything."

"You think Ernie *owed* you? Owed you his life? Owed you for what happened to your dad?"

"Ma'am, nobody owes me anything."

"That your polite self talking or your secret heart?"

"I don't have any secrets."

"Everybody does."

"I'm not everybody."

She stared at him, the right side of her face tinted blue in the light. "This fellow who's chasing you, is he the one who did that to my big brother?"

"Yes, ma'am."

"Cops ain't done anything about it?"

"Not yet."

Rhonda laughed for no reason, then slammed the bottle against the edge of the porch, causing Katelyn to flinch and flicking wet droplets on Micah's shoes. Rhonda held up the bottle's neck. It was ringed with fangs of glass. "I ought to cut the both of you just to make myself feel better. Just one good slice along your cheeks or maybe across the elbows where it bleeds a lot." She touched the tip of one of the jagged teeth. "But you know what? I just don't have the energy. Not today. So you might as well come in and get something to eat. I'll warm up last night's tuna casserole." She stood up, and her knees popped. Without waiting to see if they would follow her, she entered the house, the screen door banging shut behind her.

Chapter 57

Two gallons of unleaded gasoline weighed approximately twelve pounds. Nirat had carried the red plastic container the final seven blocks, occasionally shifting it from one hand to the other. At four AM, he supposed he looked like an unlucky man on his way to refilling a car that had left him stranded. Why else would any sane person be alone at night on these flash-fire streets, waiting to get mugged by seventeen-year-olds or hassled by the police? Things happened quickly at this hour. You went from pedestrian to statistic in seconds.

He finally relinquished his load, placing it beside a fire hydrant near Donovan's apartment building.

No voices carried to him. Other than the low-key noise of light traffic and the occasional aircraft, the neighborhood was silent. Nirat remembered reading that four in the morning was the most tomb-like hour of the day, when sleep was deepest, when dawn seemed a lifetime away.

He scanned the parking spaces.

The limousine occupied an out-of-the-way area at the end of the lot, no doubt in deference to the other residents. It sat perpendicular to the painted lines, commanding three slots. The car's presence didn't necessarily indicate that Donovan was home. Hadn't he been driving a different vehicle when he and the girl had come to Austin's house?

It didn't matter. Nirat picked up the gas can and went to the car.

Richard might have understood his motives, even if Austin never would. The father was far more erudite than the son, and he—like Nirat—knew that sometimes the most important things could never be held in the hand or locked away in a vault. As Nirat set the can near the rear bumper and headed for the steps to Donovan's door, he thought about the confluence of events that had brought him here: Austin's sexual hunger, Donovan's devotion, Nirat's own blind obedience. Most important was the pivot upon which they all turned, that evanescent thing he'd seen in Katelyn Presley's eyes, the very thing that bore his precious dinghy over the waves.

He knocked on Donovan's door.

No one replied.

Nirat envisioned the two of them asleep. Or were they hiding in the dark, waiting for him to shatter the door?

He took out his phone and dialed Donovan's number. If wisdom were a scroll, its teachings illuminated with each inch unfurled, then Nirat considered his personal scroll to be nowhere near revealed. He had much to learn before reaching enlightenment's field-goal range. But he'd been smart enough, at least, to record Donovan's information before ripping his business card in half.

The phone rang. With his other ear, he listened closely at the door.

Nothing. Either the man's cell was silenced or he wasn't home.

Then someone picked up: "Driver."

Nirat hesitated. Should he say something? Make a threat? Throw out a theatrical one-liner?

"Hello?"

Nirat hung up. He decided he wasn't hip enough for one-liners. With arson, though, he was better.

Retreating down the stairs, he recalled the first time he'd set fire to something on Richard's behalf. The insurance company had suspected devilry but couldn't produce the proof. Nirat's next gas job had gone no further than the pouring: once the man had been doused in super-premium unleaded, he'd confessed everything he knew so as to avoid the match. Nirat, bearing him no ill will, had cut his ropes and let him go.

He picked up a triangular stone that comprised a portion of the landscaping trim. It was heavy and fit his hand well. And its point would focus the power of his strike in a way a larger rock would not. When he'd jimmied the limo's lock earlier that evening, it had taken him over ten minutes. He didn't have time for that now. He couldn't afford to risk drawing the attention of anyone who happened out on their balcony for a smoke. Hence the blunt object.

He stopped at the window in the center of the elongated car and drove the stone into it.

The bones in his hands buzzed, but his gloves protected him from abrasions. On his third attack, the white veins rushed across the safety glass, and the fourth turned them into a thousand capillaries and collapsed the window inward.

Nirat tossed the rock aside, grabbed the red can, and sloshed a stream through the gaping window. Then he heaved the mostly full can onto the big, J-shaped leather seat. Working quickly, he used an old matchbook from the Palomino to make a flame. It came to life like all flames do, as if eager to gorge itself, undaunted despite its small size.

This car, this elegant black car, this was Donovan's livelihood. Nirat had seen the man's exacting records and knew he had nothing else, not even any digital photos on his hard drive. If the car became a pyre, what would he have left? He seemed to be a man defined by his work, or at the very least dependent on it.

Nirat threw the burning matchbook through the window.

There was something about fire that always seemed appreciative. It made a vaporous sound, relishing its spontaneous birth, and rapidly settled down to the business of eating the car.

Nirat turned and walked away, veering from one pool of shadow to the next. Part of him wanted to be a spectator, inhaling the charcoal scent of crisping upholstery like a druid at a pagan ritual, but in moments some noble personage from the apartment complex would get himself on the news by dialing the authorities.

Nirat knew what was happening. Even as he distanced himself from the blaze he would rather have been enjoying, he understood that he was only playing his role, herding the two of them from shore, forcing them into the water and the gray unknown.

Chapter 58

Micah lay on the floor in Rhonda's old Coleman sleeping bag. Peace squatted like a gargoyle just out of reach. Every time he drew close, the creature moved its wings and stirred up Tully or Malcolm or the way that man's neck had felt when Micah was choking him. He found no rest.

Maybe it was the pillow. The feathers had settled and compacted with time, so that now the lumps were difficult to navigate. A few prickly ends poked through the worn fabric.

No, it was the darkness. His bedroom at home was never truly black. The lamps outside the apartment ensured that he never slept in a void, yet here was a void of serious intent. Was he such a city boy that he couldn't even handle nighttime the way God intended it?

A soft sound came from the direction of the couch. Katelyn lay only two feet away, and when she cried, Micah heard her.

He held very still. Though Katelyn's quiet sobs were muffled by a pillow, they transmitted their message nonetheless. Micah hated those sounds, hated them because they revealed an overwhelmed heart—and what could he possibly do to make it better? He took responsibility for her sadness. It was something for which he'd have to answer one of these days. But worse than that was the fact that it was dark. No one should have to cry alone at night.

He wiggled an arm free of the sleeping bag and reached for her.

His aim was off. He encountered the couch leg, then the edge of the cushion. He kept probing and finally found a warm shape. His own daring surprised him. He seemed to be surprised a lot lately. But he didn't alter course despite his uncertainty, and in a moment he touched her hair.

She responded. She slid her hand across his palm, sniffled loudly, and laced her fingers in his. Shifting slightly, she brought her forehead to rest against their joined hands.

Having made his offering and had it accepted, Micah relaxed and listened to her cry until her tears slowed and her respirations became even and steady. By then his arm had fallen hard asleep, the needles tingling painfully from elbow to wrist.

He didn't care. He had no intention of letting go.

Chapter 59

"Get up and piss, the world's on fire!"

Micah opened his eyes and saw the black-and-red checks of the sleeping bag's flannel lining. He'd been dreaming about—what? Even now the images separated like fallen leaves on water.

"Coffee's brewing," Rhonda said. "And if there were ever anyone who needed caffeine more than you two, I've never met 'em."

Micah pushed himself up, his back complaining only mildly about the floor.

On the couch, Katelyn sat up, her hair in her face. She stared at him silently as sleep slowly relinquished its hold, then she said, "Hey."

He almost asked how she slept or how she felt, but both questions would have come out sounding inane at best. Small talk violated their pact of speaking only the truth. "Hey."

Pans clattered in the kitchen. "How do you like your grease?" Rhonda asked as she worked. "Extra greasy or just normally greasy? We also have grease over easy or medium-rare."

Micah just kept looking at Katelyn, who finally said, "You better give us the extra greasy version. We may need it."

"I hear you there, hon."

"You take the bathroom," Micah said. "I'll wait."

"Is it always ladies first with you?"

"Blame it on my upbringing."

"Do you also stand up when a woman enters the room? They

do that in the movies, and I always thought it was cool. Quaint, but cool." She yawned and got to her feet before he could answer, then paused to make sure she had her balance. She wore shorts and ankle socks. "This is what they mean by the walking wounded." She snagged her bag and headed for the bathroom. "Smells fabulous, Rhonda."

"Grease does that. But thanks. I'm not used to cooking for company."

When it was his turn in the shower, Micah took his time. He only shut off the faucets when the water started to cool. He was nobody's clairvoyant, but he predicted that this would be a day that warranted an extended time under the stinging water.

He wiped the mist from the mirror and shaved.

Halfway through he was sorry he'd used up the hot water, but he managed to complete the task without nicking himself. That done, he slid into a T-shirt, then caught his reflection and reconsidered. There was nothing wrong with a basic cotton shirt with short sleeves and a crew neck. Such attire had been serving men on a variety of missions for decades, if not longer. Men had fought and died in these shirts, delivered babies, made babies, hung drywall, shot endless games of nine-ball, and ridden horseback through rugged country. And Micah would be escorting no clients this evening, so the black tie was optional.

But still.

Katelyn would kid him about it, but he couldn't help but feel he'd lose something without the trousers and French cuffs. As silly as it sounded to his own ears, that tie was like a charm. Maybe it wouldn't ward off bad luck or deflect a sniper's bullet, but it would make him comfortable, and there was much to be said for comfort. If he survived the day, *then* he'd worry about the psychological implications of depending on a suit to express himself. With the exception of Clark Kent, no one could really understand.

He took a seat at Rhonda's round kitchen table.

Katelyn didn't comment on his choice of clothing. She'd probably been expecting it. She was already halfway through her hash browns by the time he sat down. She'd brushed her hair but hadn't put it back. She glanced at him only once, then resumed her conversation with Rhonda. They were talking about Tully's burial.

"Mr. Wallace at the funeral home tells me that two o'clock is a good time," Rhonda said, "assuming the medical examiner releases him. His remains, I mean."

"Today?" Micah asked, pouring himself a second cup of coffee.

"Tomorrow. I've already called a few of his friends. He didn't have many. You, mainly."

"I'll be there."

"*We'll* be there," Katelyn said.

"I told Mr. Wallace that I don't want anything . . . anything *fancy*. You know what I mean? I swear, if Ernie looked down and saw a bunch of pretty flowers and things, I suspect he'd cuss a blue streak."

"Do they kick you out of heaven for that?" Katelyn asked.

Rhonda seemed to appreciate Katelyn's efforts. "I bet he's already trying to climb the pearly gates and find somewhere more interesting. They're going to have to drag him back."

Micah didn't want to think about any of this. Every time he visited his father, it was like attending a quasi-funeral, some kind of perverted ceremony that purposefully prevented closure. Yet he went anyway. The last graveside service he'd attended was his mother's, and he remembered only flashes of it, like unwanted lightning.

"What do you think?" Rhonda asked him.

He swallowed and dabbed his mouth with a paper napkin. "About the funeral arrangements?"

"Actually I was talking about breakfast. I see you're not turning green around the gills, which I'm taking as a good sign."

"Yes, it's great. Outstanding. Thank you."

She looked at Katelyn. "Is he just being well mannered?"

"He *is* annoyingly polite, isn't he?"

"Makes me sort of wonder why he ever hung around with my foul-mouthed brother."

"Men. Most of the time it's best to not try and figure them out."

"That's a big ten-four on that one, sister. Notice that I'm not sharing the old farmstead with one of them."

"A wise choice."

"Men are like mascara, hon, running at the first sign of emotion."

Katelyn seemed to understand that. As she sipped her coffee, she looked at Micah and winked.

Micah fastened his attention to his scrambled eggs so as not to give himself away. He simply enjoyed listening to them talk. They spoke real words about real feelings and real intentions. They grounded him. Otherwise he'd be in that swimming pool again, or on his knees beside the blood in Tully's flat.

"At any rate," Rhonda said, "I don't think we need to do anything special in a church. Nothing so formal. He wouldn't have wanted any kind of production. I'll just ask Mr. Wallace to plan for the cemetery. Jesus, I can't even believe I'm talking about this." She put down her fork and touched her temples with the tips of her fingers. "This is *Ernie*."

Katelyn came to her rescue, offering a hand that Rhonda accepted. "Your brother died keeping us safe. He was brave as hell."

"Brave or stubborn? It was always a close call with him."

Micah's phone hummed.

He quickly silenced it. "Sorry."

"Don't worry about it." Rhonda flicked a hand under her eyes. "I don't need to be sitting here doing the wilting daisy thing. Looks like we're about finished, anyway."

Micah checked the number.

"Who is it?" Katelyn asked.

"The police." He stood up and walked into the living room, where he was soon surrounded by African violets and devil's ivy. "Driver."

"Mr. Donovan? Detective Ling. Are you well?"

"Relatively speaking."

"And Ms. Presley?"

"Perfect."

"No unwanted visitors this morning?"

"No, sir."

"Good. Very good. Listen, here's the quick version. Your alleged attacker, Alexander Niratpattanasai, has evidently gone off the Savlodar reservation. Mr. Savlodar claims to have fired the man and has no inkling of his current whereabouts. We intend to bring him in when we locate him, but in the meantime I need the two of you to come down and give me a formal statement."

"I understand. We'll be there within—"

"Hold up, there's something else."

Micah pressed the phone closer to his ear. He didn't know what to expect. For days now, events had been impossible to predict. "What is it? What's wrong?"

"A few hours ago, Clark County Fire responded to a call at your apartment complex."

"My house?"

"Your car. It burned from the inside out. Most of it's gone."

Micah closed his eyes. He leaned his weight against the wall. Maybe he'd misheard. He'd been doing that a lot lately; they called it jumping at shadows.

Katelyn stood up, her chair legs scraping against the linoleum. "Micah?"

"Understand that this isn't the official word," Ling said, "but my money's on arson."

Arson. Certainly such a word had no place in his life. If his car was gone, how much of the rest of him had gone with it? "You . . . you're sure it's mine?"

"Mr. Donovan, it's the only limousine on the block."

"Micah, talk to me."

He wanted to tell her, but vocalizing it meant accepting it as fact. "The Chrysler. My car. He . . . he torched it."

"Holy shit."

"Needless to say," Ling continued, "we're considering this situation to be one that is evolving by the hour. I need you two in here pronto. Is that clear?"

Two years ago Micah had signed the papers on what was to become both his office and his product, the image he projected to his clients and the service he sold them. The limousine provided his income, but it had become more than that, a symbol for the fiscal decisions he'd made and the mission he'd assigned himself. In a weird way, it was an extension of his tuxedo. There had been a week or two when it had grossed two thousand dollars in six days, but even in the leaner seasons it paid his bills with change to spare.

"Mr. Donovan?"

"We're on our way." He ended the call.

Katelyn stared at him from across the floor. "It's totally gone?"

Micah supposed this was how it felt to show up for work one morning to learn that you'd been laid off. You drifted in the breeze.

"What about your apartment? Was he there? Was anyone hurt?"

Micah's fingers curled into a fist, the muscles in his arms hardening despite his efforts to relax them. "We need to go."

"I'll get my things."

Through all of this, Rhonda had said nothing. Standing at the sink, she watched him but asked no questions.

Micah silently thanked her for that. Compared to what had happened to Tully, the limo was meaningless. But its loss was one more piece of Micah's life cut away. Who would he become now?

Katelyn slid the strap of her bag over her shoulder and zipped the last pocket. "Maybe I shouldn't have stopped you when you had him in the pool."

"You had no way of knowing."

"I'm sorry, anyway."

Micah finally separated himself from the wall and gathered his scant belongings.

"Don't worry about the blankets and stuff," Rhonda told them. "I'll take care of them. You two just do what you need to do. As long as you stay safe doing it."

"I wish we could promise that," Katelyn said.

"I'll call you after I talk with Mr. Wallace. I can't think of anyone who Ernie would've wanted there more than you, myself included."

Micah was glad that Katelyn answered for him. "We'll be there."

When would it finally make sense? On the second step of the porch? Halfway to the Cutlass? Micah opened the trunk and secured their bags. Even if everything ended today and they arrested Tully's murderer, how could Micah resume his life? He wouldn't even be able to pay his bills, much less think about retiring at fifty. His entire plan had been incinerated.

"What about insurance?" Katelyn asked as they climbed into the car. "Will they cover something like this?"

Micah jabbed the key into the ignition.

"Hello?"

"Sorry."

"Don't be sorry. If I were you I'd be screaming my head off right now. Can you—I don't know—rent a car in the meantime? Use that for your clients?"

"Maybe." He backed up, shifted, and got them moving. In the rearview, Rhonda watched them go. She didn't wave.

"Well you've got to do *something.*"

"Yeah."

"Will you please stop giving me one-word answers? We've come too far for that."

He almost said, *Okay,* but caught himself in time and snagged the nearest of his scattered thoughts. "Maybe I wasn't meant to be a driver."

"Says who?"

"I don't know. Destiny, maybe."

"You're saying this is all about fate?"

"It's got to be about something. Either that or it's all just . . . random."

"So what's wrong with random? You don't agree with it?"

"For some people. But it doesn't fit my life." He turned onto the blacktop.

After a minute Katelyn said, "Do I?"

Micah couldn't bring himself to look at her. He could risk his life chasing a killer into a swimming pool, but his courage went only so far. He stared into the west, where dawn had only just begun to touch the sand.

"Never mind," she said, turning away. "Stupid girlie question."

Micah did the only thing that still felt certain.

He drove.

Chapter 60

"I've got to warn you," Ling said, "this isn't a pretty sight."

Micah, by now, had steeled himself for it. He and Katelyn had spent an hour and a half explaining the attack that had taken place in the car. The only sticky part was the shotgun. Micah hadn't described it as such, as he figured its legality to be dubious, at best. When describing Katelyn's actions, he'd referred to it simply as *a gun.* He wondered if his admiration for her was as evident in his voice as it was in his brain. At some point this morning he'd come to the very grown-up conclusion that she was the classiest woman he'd ever met. Ling, though, had seemed more concerned with the weapon. He tapped his pencil four dozen times on the desk while he considered it. But in the end he hadn't mentioned it again or asked them to hand it over, which Micah attributed to his father. Had Malcolm been killed in the line of duty, he wouldn't have cast such an emotional spell over those he left behind. But his condition bought Micah more lenience than he probably deserved.

The car looked like the target of a Mid-East pipe bomb.

As Ling escorted them through the garage, Micah observed the limousine in stages. At first he'd thought there'd been a mistake—this wasn't his vehicle—but then he realized the Chrysler 300's genteel curves remained, though it had been hollowed out, gutted, burned. Nothing remained of the leather and electronics but curled black feathers, as if it all might shake loose and drift away.

"Very basic stuff," Ling said. "Guy breaks the window, unloads an accelerant that was probably nothing more exotic than convenience-store gasoline, and throws in a match. By the time the trucks arrived, the fire had mostly burned itself out. It never reached the engine or the fuel tank."

Katelyn rested her hand in the bend of his elbow. "I'm so sorry."

Micah peered through the gaping window. It was like looking into a cave.

"Don't touch anything," Ling warned. "The boys with the tweezers and UV lights are still giving it the personal touch."

Micah wished. He never made wishes on birthday candles but he made one now. He wished for balance. That's all. When everything was being taken from you, one person and one belief at a time, the one element you missed the most was equilibrium. The only thing you could do was keep falling down.

Katelyn gave him a little tug. "Let's go. We don't need this anymore."

"We'll have a unit swing by your hotel every couple of hours," Ling said, though he'd already assured them of this twice before. "There's no way he could find you, but just in case, I want our people checking up on you until we grab him."

Micah assumed this police protection was another courtesy paid for by his father's lingering spirit. That was Malcolm for you, walking the beat even when he had far better and brighter places to be.

"Micah, come on."

He didn't want to come on. He wanted to stay here. Stay here and gaze into the ruin.

"Don't make me put you in a headlock. Grown men have cried."

Eventually Micah allowed himself to be guided away.

"I'll call you later," Ling said, "make sure you're hanging in there."

As they left the garage and stepped into the sunny world outside, Micah asked softly, "Are we hanging in there?"

"Either that or we're faking the hell out of it. I haven't decided which."

Chapter 61

Micah's tolerance, like water on the desert floor, finally turned to vapor.

He was sitting on the edge of one of two queen-sized beds when it happened, staring at an unopened Gideon's Bible. The hotel room, like those before it, pushed him farther from the handholds of his routine. He considered trolling the New Testament for answers; there were surely worse places to look. Katelyn had spent the last half-hour in the bathroom, doing whatever women did that enabled them to linger so long behind a closed door. Her absence allowed him to think without distraction, and so he observed his evaporating patience until it was gone. In its place was something like bones.

He looked from the Bible to his phone. Was he willing to make this call?

In his mind, Tully brought into question what he called Micah's stones. *As in cojones,* Tully said, *as in how long are you going to sit here and let this shithead disassemble your life?*

Micah bypassed the Bible and picked up the phone.

Maybe some other outfit in the limo biz will hire you on, Tully said, goading him, *pay you eleven bucks an hour and piss all over your dignity. Lucky for you I willed you my balls instead of my good looks.*

Micah scrolled through his call log. There, from five days ago, was Austin Savlodar's number.

Tully said nothing else.

Micah tapped his thumb against the phone. Then he pushed the callback button.

As the phone rang in his ear, Katelyn stepped from the bathroom. By the rigidity of Micah's shoulders and the hard line of his spine, he transmitted a message he couldn't conceal from her. She sat down beside him, a damp towel in her lap.

"Hello, you've reached Austin Savlodar. I'm sorry to have missed you—"

Katelyn heard the voice and recognized it. "What are you doing?"

"—then I'll ring back as soon as possible. Thanks."

In the electronic silence that followed, Micah sorted through his thoughts, each one serrated with an anger that made it dangerous to handle. He cleared his throat to jump-start himself. "This is the driver, Micah Donovan. We need to talk."

He had nothing else. He ended the call and waited for Katelyn's inevitable question.

But yet again she surprised him. "So I guess we're going after this guy."

"We can't live in hotels until the police locate him."

"Yeah, continental breakfasts can get a person only so far."

"Is that your way of saying you're okay with this?"

"Is that your way of asking me to be your partner?"

Micah clasped the phone in both hands and stared at the carpet between his knees. "This isn't about getting even. Or about settling scores. I just want it to be over."

"Uh, I don't mean to point this out, but you're sort of shaking, and it's not cold in here. If that's not about revenge then you've got me totally fooled."

He found no solace in the pattern on the rug. "Where's the gun?"

"In my overnight bag."

Micah turned the phone in his fingers, a worry stone, a crystal ball. "I guess we should load it."

"Way ahead of you on that one. I may not be Annie Oakley, but if I get that chance again, I don't want to be shooting blanks." She put her hand in her hair and looked at the ceiling. "God, I'm sitting here talking about killing a man."

"We'll just worry about finding him first."

"Before he finds us."

"If possible, yeah."

"You don't think he's running? Leaving on a jet plane and all of that?"

"Do you?"

"I was kind of hoping I was wrong."

Micah traded the phone for the remote control, bringing the widescreen TV to life. He muted the sound and watched a music video featuring a rapper and his retinue of half-clad harem girls.

Katelyn stared at the gyrating bodies. "So . . . the plan is to sit here and wait for the phone to ring? That could be hours, right?"

"I don't know what else to do. Ling said they'd do the occasional drive-by at our apartments to see if he shows up, but I'm betting they'll strike out. If we want to end this, the only shot we have is through Savlodar."

The video gave way to a commercial for garage-door openers.

Ten minutes passed. Micah used them as constructively as he could, booting up the anger-management software in all the ways they recommended, but deep breathing was overrated. The two of them sat on the edge of the bed and stared at the shifting images on the screen.

Then Katelyn sprang to her feet. "Okay, this is driving me *loco.* I can't just hang out here and perform yoga or tai chi or something like there's nothing better to do."

"I don't have anything better to offer you."

"How about traipsing off to the Venetian to win a million

bucks at blackjack?"

"I don't think I'd be very good at counting cards, and I'm not feeling lucky."

"How are you at bowling?"

"Even worse."

"Okay, scratch that. We're stuck. And I don't know about you, but personally I've always been morally opposed to being stuck." She rescued the computer speakers from her laundry basket and plugged them into an MP3 player the size of a postage stamp. "You may be able to clear your mind and meditate or whatever, but that's never worked for me."

"You pick interesting times to dance."

"I pick the *necessary* times. And I think you know that by now."

He did. She'd shown him that dancing was about more than getting your groove on. Sometimes it was the chair between you and the lion.

"Here's something I bet you couldn't guess," Katelyn said. "A wonderfully waltzable song is none other than Journey's 'Open Arms.' "

"You're right. I never would have guessed that."

"Or 'Take It to the Limit,' by the Eagles."

"If you say so."

"Would you prefer the Commodores?"

That one surprised him. "You can waltz to Lionel Richie?"

"On 'Three Times a Lady' you sure can." A moment later, the song's opening piano notes drifted from the small speakers with surprising fullness. "Up you go. It'd be stupid for us to waste all of this energy. There's no time better for dancing than when you're thinking about popping a cap in somebody."

Though she said this with her usual flippancy, her tone betrayed her. She needed this now more than ever.

Micah supposed he needed it, too. Or was there some other

reason he turned off the TV and took her hand in his? A moment later he found the proper stance. He held his right arm parallel to the floor, elbow bent, palm flush against her shoulder blade.

She looked up at him. "Waiting on your lead."

"I'm listening for the beat."

"Where I come from, we call that stalling."

Yes, there was a reason his thoughts had been clearer while she was behind a closed bathroom door. Now he could think only of the required movements and the song and the simple nearness of her.

She prompted him: "*One,* two, three, *four,* five, six . . ."

He stepped forward with his left foot on the next *one.*

Apparently she'd set the player on repeat, because the song ended only to begin again, keeping Micah's feet moving and his mind on the woman flowing around him, beside him, through him, like water over sand.

Chapter 62

Nirat pressed a strip of duct tape to the window and then struck it with his fist. The glass pane shattered but, like flies on a strip, the fragments stuck to the adhesive. He removed the mess, set it aside, and then reached through the hole and twisted the deadbolt on the other side.

"My apologies, sir." He said this to Richard, though the man himself was miles away, making license plates or whatever the hell they had you do these days when you were cloistered behind prison walls. It was bad enough that Nirat was borrowing the man's property without asking. He didn't intend on leaving broken glass lying around as well.

The office on East Tropicana was part of Savlodar's small but well-regarded Aegis Green Equipment, which leased electric vehicles to contractors. Aegis owned battery-driven trams, stock-chasers, tow tractors, forklifts, and several 48-volt flatbeds. Though the company was headquartered in Henderson, this small office handled the occasional overflow. When Nirat opened the cherrywood cabinet on the west wall, he saw only three sets of keys. He took them all and let himself through the steel door to the fenced compound in the back.

The sun murmured in waves off the hot steel. Squinting, Nirat conducted a quick inventory and decided the Phoenix would serve him best. Aegis had purchased these crewcab sport-utility trucks from a Canadian manufacturer and now used them as the face of what they hoped was seen as an environmentally compassionate company. Nirat didn't know whether or not they actually gave a damn about the planet—he assumed most firms went green merely as a matter of PR—but he considered himself lucky to have found the Phoenix, which had a hundred-mile range on a single charge. He couldn't drive the Le Mans on that, but he could at least stay mobile until tomorrow's funeral.

He wondered if he should buy a suit.

Putting Tullmacher in the ground would summon Donovan and the girl from their seclusion as surely as the moon called the tides. A few phone calls had gotten him the name of the funeral home, and one more had secured the time and location of the event. In the meantime he had preparations to make and certain pieces of gear to gather, including a box of razor blades and a gas-powered bush-cutter.

He returned to the cabinet, replaced those keys obviously not belonging to the Phoenix, and wiped away a smear his gloved hand left on the wood. It was a beautiful grain. Most office furniture was made of that pressed-board excrement, an ode to the same hucksters who created Pleather and tofu hamburgers. Nirat admired the workmanship.

The truck boasted a dutiful air-conditioner, but Nirat didn't bother with it for fear of overtaxing the battery. He pulled to the gate, and the motion sensor did the rest, cranking back the chain-link portal and permitting him to pull into the street.

What would they see, if they topped the next lead-colored wave?

Nirat thought about them again, his two sailors. He'd burned their boat but that hadn't ended their quest, whatever it might be and wherever it might take them. Nirat longed to know. It seemed unfair that he should be so curious when they themselves were probably unaware of the quiet necessity of their search.

He adjusted the rearview mirror. Briefly he caught a glimpse of himself, a recent bleach-blonde in a ball cap proclaiming him a KARAOKE KROONER. He'd bought the hat and the bottle of peroxide shortly after sunrise. It was surprising what a small makeover could do. Maybe the disguise wouldn't get him past any facial-recognition devices but, like the Phoenix, it would serve his short-term purpose. Beyond tomorrow, nothing mattered.

With the motor emitting little more than an insectoid hum, he drove toward Super Pawn on Boulder Highway, looking to make a deal.

Chapter 63

Micah turned toward her just as Katelyn jumped.

This time he managed to get his hands on either side of her waist without ending up colliding with the hotel nightstand. He guided her momentum upward as she'd taught him, but the ceiling prevented him from fully extending his arms. He held her in place for a three-count, his biceps straining, before lowering her less than gracefully to the floor.

"Hey, not bad!" She clapped three times. "Much better!"

"I think leaps are a little above my pay grade as a dancer."

"They're called *lifts,* and you're totally wrong. You're good at this. Admit it."

"I admit only that I'm tired of hearing that song."

"What? Thirty-three times too many for you?" She smiled and killed the music.

Micah sat down on the bed. Was he so out of shape that a simple waltz was winding him? Then again, it had progressed beyond a mere box step. Now Katelyn was throwing trapeze acts at him.

She snagged a water from the mini-fridge, tossed one to him, and plopped down on the floor. "The earth is flat, you know."

By now Micah should've been ready for her. Her wild words. Her suddenness. But this was one he couldn't figure out. He took a few breaths. "Okay. So the earth is flat."

"No, seriously. Why didn't people way back in the day do any long-distance traveling?"

"Is this a trick question?"

"All those sailors before Columbus, that's who I'm talking about. They had the ships, but they were afraid that if they sailed too far from home, they'd fall off the edge of the world."

"So?"

"So nothing's changed."

Micah set his bottle aside and leaned back on his hands. Katelyn was about to make a point, and she was a point-maker not to be denied. "Okay. Lay it on me, then."

"It's like this. Everyone's afraid. Don't you think? People are afraid of the weird guy who lives in the upstairs apartment. White people are afraid of black kids in baggy pants. Americans are afraid of the Spanish language. Muslims are afraid of Americans. China's afraid of the Dalai Lama."

Micah successfully tamped down his smile. He enjoyed listening to her rants, her fist-shakings, her fledgling philosophies. He wanted to be more like her. Bolder.

"And so nobody goes anywhere," she said. "Not really. We might travel someplace physically, sure, but we always leave our hearts behind, locked up somewhere safe. Like leaving our cars under the awning at the airport."

"And that makes the earth flat?"

"Don't you see it? Terrorists are blowing people up. But do we ever bother to go over there and ask them what we're doing to piss them off in the first place? No. Because we're afraid that if we go too far from what's familiar, we'll fall off the edge."

"You want me to play devil's advocate for a minute?"

"You don't agree with what I'm saying?"

"Actually, I do. But what if it isn't about fear at all?"

"Okay." She shifted so that she was sitting cross-legged. "Enlighten me, dancer man."

"That weird guy who lives upstairs? Maybe I'm not afraid of him. Maybe I've just got too much going on to worry about meeting him. And those brothers in the baggy pants? Maybe I just assume I've got nothing in common with them, so why bother? Same thing for Christians and Muslims. We're not afraid of each other. We're just busy."

"So you're telling me that people aren't afraid. They're just self-absorbed."

"Look around. Makes sense to me."

Katelyn pondered it, staring at him with one of her eyebrows raised just enough to let him know that she appreciated his argument but wasn't so ready to accept it.

Micah's phone vibrated.

Things changed. Katelyn went from intrigued to worried. Micah forgot about debating with her—inside he asked himself if they were flirting—and snatched the phone from the top of the TV.

"Driver."

In his ear, Austin Savlodar said, "I can only assume you called to set up some kind of meeting of the minds to discuss our mutual problem, in which case I agree. I'll be waiting at my house. But if you kick in my door again, friend, I'll fucking kill you."

The line went dead.

Chapter 64

"I don't want to sound like a potty-mouthed sissy," Katelyn said as they turned onto Soaring Court, "but this worries the shit out of me."

Micah slowed, then stopped the car in the middle of the street. Keeping his foot on the brake, he looked at her and hoped she sensed the meaning of his words because he wasn't altogether certain of it himself. "If you want me to turn around and drive, and I mean *drive,* then I will, no questions, no debate."

She regarded him carefully. "Drive, like . . . where?"

"*Any*where."

"I'm not sure what you're saying."

"I think you are."

She glanced down at her hands. "You don't know how tempting that sounds."

"Maybe I do." He tapped his finger on the GPS. "See this?"

She looked up.

"A beach in South Carolina. A forest in Idaho. A wheat field in Oklahoma."

She seemed to be imagining those places. "You're serious about this?"

"In case you haven't noticed, all I've got left is serious."

She touched his leg. "I really, really want to give you an answer, but yonder asshole is watching us."

Micah looked toward Savlodar's house. The man stood in his

yard near the flowers, hands riding the pockets of his pressed trousers. His shirt was as white as a beacon.

Micah wished he had the spirit to swear. Just let out a real Tully-worthy expletive to inform the world how unfair it could be, how cruel its timing. But that had never been his style, not even now when he was *in extremis.* And that was when you needed your style the most.

He pulled to the curb and shut off the engine.

Katelyn disengaged her seatbelt. "Right out here in the open, huh?"

"Does that make you feel a little better?"

"Hardly. This douchebag almost raped me."

"That's why we're leaving the gun under the seat. Avoiding temptation." He got out and faced the man.

The street and its grand houses seemed too normal, all things considered. Cacti grew artfully from curbside containers of polished rock. The sunlight minted every piece of metal, turning it to gold.

Savlodar stood in his yard, its grass as fine as that on a putting green. "Hell of a nice day, isn't it?"

Katelyn walked around the car and joined Micah as he took a few steps closer.

"Leg's healing sportingly," Savlodar said. "Thanks for asking."

Katelyn flipped him off.

Savlodar seemed pleased. "That's more like it."

Micah stopped when he was ten feet away. The majestic homes along the street stood quiet and nonjudgmental, like unconcerned nobility. The date palms pushed their evening shadows across the yard. The only sound was that of a distant water sprinkler.

"Forgive me if I don't invite you in for a cup of Earl Grey."

Quietly Katelyn said, "Can I just kick this guy in the nuts

and get it over with?"

Micah clasped his hands in front of him, hoping that Savlodar hadn't already noticed he was shaking. "My friend was murdered. My car was burned. That's why we're here."

"I had nothing to do with either of those events, I assure you."

"Maybe. But you know who did."

"And so too do our dear friends with the police department. I've officially cut ties with Mr. Niratpattanasai. As the detectives will tell you, I gave the man his severance pay and sent him on his way. Since then, I've learned that he killed someone and tried to do the same to you. He's bringing as much grief to me as he is to you fine folks."

"I doubt that."

"Your doubt is irrelevant. What matters is ending this."

"Where is he?"

"What will you do if you find him?"

"We're not here to play games," Micah said, feeling the sweat form along his hairline. Though he knew his rage would be at least partially misplaced if he planted it here, there was no way to avoid it; its seeds were too many. "Tell me where he is, and you'll never see us again."

Savlodar stooped suddenly and reached for something lying among the coneflowers.

Micah moved. He stepped in front of Katelyn, shielding her, and then backed them toward the car.

"Whoa, whoa!" Savlodar waved at them. "Easy does it, folks." From the flowers he extracted a cardboard mailing tube.

Micah stopped, his body humming. Katelyn gripped the inside of his elbow and peered around him. She was so close to him that Micah felt the rise and fall of her chest against his back.

"Something I thought you should see," Savlodar said. "This

is what he came back for. It led to your little tussle in my swimming pool. God only knows why he wanted it. But I'm damn sure not hanging it back up."

Micah hesitated, waiting for the net to fall from the palm fronds or the poison darts to fly. What kind of trick was this? Who did Savlodar have skulking in the wings to ambush them?

Savlodar used the tube like a cane and supported his weight on it. "The both of you are being a bit skittish, don't you think?"

"You can eat shit and die," Katelyn said. "Dontcha think?"

Savlodar sneered. He hefted the tube and threw it toward them.

It hit the grass and rolled toward Micah's feet. There was a time when he would've wondered what was inside and how it could possibly pertain to the events at hand, but now he honestly didn't care. He stopped it with his foot. "You know how to find him, don't you?"

Savlodar shifted his weight, clearly favoring his injured leg. "I wouldn't have agreed to this little tête-à-tête if I didn't think it could end our mutual angst. What is it you propose?"

"Call him. Tell him where I'm going to be tomorrow night."

"Interesting. But you presume both that he carries a phone and that I have his number."

Katelyn squeezed Micah's arm. Keeping her voice low, she said, "If that's true, then why didn't he just give the number to the police so they could use it to track the guy? Can't they just call him up and trace his location?"

"I don't think he wants the man to be arrested. Leaves too many loose ends."

"For the sake of conjecture," Savlodar said, "what is tomorrow night's mystery locale?"

"I'll let you know. You just make sure he shows up. Tell him you found out where we're hiding. I'll take care of whatever happens after that."

"Will you, now?"

"I guess we'll see."

"I must say, Mr. Donovan, confidence becomes you."

Micah picked up the tube and backed to the car.

"Don't ever return here," Savlodar said. "The next time we speak shall be the last."

Micah got behind the wheel just as Katelyn slammed her door. He reversed into the neighbor's driveway, feeling Savlodar's eyes on him.

As he turned onto the tree-lined Eagle Hills Drive, Katelyn said, "God, I wanted you to just go over there and clobber that guy."

"I'm sorry."

"Don't be. Probably wouldn't have been the most fabulous of ideas. But damn."

"Yeah."

She held the tube in her lap. "Dare I open this?"

"Go ahead."

She removed one of the white plastic caps. "One more question."

"The answer is I'm working on it."

"Working on what? How do you know what I was going to say?"

"You were going to ask about tomorrow night after the funeral. Where we're going to be."

"Okay, mind-reader, where *are* we going to be? Oh, wait, you're working on it. Any ideas at all?"

"Not yet. But something tells me I'll know it when I see it."

Chapter 65

Katelyn shifted closer to him on the bed.

Micah sat with his back against the headboard, legs extended, a poster unfurled in his lap. The image was perhaps two feet long and eighteen inches wide, printed on photo-quality paper. The scene was a monochrome vista of the sea at a moment of indecision: would the waves topple the small boat, or would its sailors reach their unnamed destination?

Crossing her legs, Katelyn said, "It sort of makes me sad."

Micah looked for sadness in the picture. He'd never spent much time analyzing art.

"They look lonely." She sipped her complimentary hotel coffee. "Or lost."

Did they? Micah wasn't so sure. But contemplating it was better than thinking about tomorrow's funeral. And about what might happen when it was over.

"Or maybe it just looks gloomy because it's done in black and white. What do you think?"

"This boat . . . it reminds me of something. You want to hear a funny story?"

"If you have one up your sleeve, I think we could both use it about now."

Micah had forgotten about that afternoon with the bicycle until now. He summoned the memories. "About six months after the accident, I went over to check on Tully, but he wasn't home. This was way before I was driving the limo, and my car was in the shop. I used to drive this high-mileage Ford Tempo that was jacked up about six inches too tall, with these crazy chrome rims. Dumb kid stuff, you know."

"I used to dot my *i*'s with little hearts. I am definitely familiar with dumb kid stuff."

"Yeah. So I was riding my old ten-speed bike. I certainly never considered using the Cutlass. It was still too soon, and this was back when I knew—I *just knew*—that Dad was going to wake up and ask me how the Rams were doing. I kept thinking how mad he'd be when I told him he'd missed the whole season."

Since when had he decided to throw himself wide open like this? How long had he known this person? What right did she have to hear any of it?

"I found Tully drunk outside the bowling alley at the Silver Nugget. Every day was a fight. Every day I expected to find him with his wrists slit or an empty pill bottle beside his bed. But he wasn't going to kill himself. He told me that it was hell. That he'd died in another life and that this was hell. He said to me once, and I'll never forget it, 'Suicide is another name for death by despair, and what I got ain't goddamn despair.' It was guilt. And every morning of his life he tried to hold it off with booze."

"Uh, I thought this was supposed to be a funny story."

"Bear with me."

"Bearing."

"So I tracked him down at the bowling alley, and he was still breathing, which relieved me just like it always did. He had this . . . this scent about him that day that I've never smelled since. It was like . . . an overheated sidewalk in the middle of the afternoon. Anyway, I got him on his feet, but then I realized I had no way to get him home."

"So . . . you put him on the bike?"

"I didn't have any money for a cab, and there was nobody I

could call, at least not anyone convenient. So yeah, somehow I got him on the bike. Man, if ever there was someone in need of a good set of training wheels . . ."

Katelyn smiled.

"He swayed like crazy. It took me three times to get him upright, and he swerved at buildings and parked cars . . . it was a miracle he didn't break his neck. I don't know how long it had been since he'd ridden a bike, but if he could do it mostly drunk, then I guess it's true when they say you don't ever forget."

Katelyn watched him as he related his bit of history. Micah didn't look at her for fear of the blueness in her eyes.

"Anyway, I set off walking. I was going to head home and then pick up the bike later on. But I hadn't made it even a hundred feet when I heard all these horns coming from behind me. I thought I'd probably gotten him killed with my dumb idea."

"But he was okay?"

"Oh, he was all right. But a car had swerved to miss him and it ended up running into a truck that was hauling a boat. The boat was knocked off the trailer. I remember running around the corner, and the first thing I see is this fishing boat sitting in the middle of the street. For a second I couldn't figure out what was going on. I was like, 'Why is there a boat here in the center of Hunkins Drive?' And Tully was just standing there, straddling the bike, looking at it all like he'd planned the whole thing."

"So what happened?"

"I ran up and said something like, 'Tull, you hurt?' And he turns his head really slowly and looks at me as he points at the boat. He says, 'Hey, man. You wanna go fishing?' "

"Nice!" Katelyn laughed.

"I don't know why it was so funny to me at the time, but I just busted up. I couldn't stop. I guess it was the first time I'd laughed since the accident. Pretty soon Tully was laughing, too."

"It sounds to me like you were really good to him. After what happened, most people in your position would've hated him, and they certainly wouldn't have looked after him like that."

"I tried hating him. I really gave it a shot. Still do, sometimes at night."

"But?"

"But it doesn't fit. It's not what my dad would've wanted and, more importantly, holding a grudge just isn't the way I roll."

She thought about that for a moment. "You know, the world would be better off if more people rolled like you."

"I don't know about *that* . . ."

She poked him on the leg. "No need for modesty. You've got it goin' on."

"Kate, I may kill a man tomorrow."

"Not if I see him first. And I like that, by the way."

"Like what?"

She gave him a little roll of her eyes and slid off the bed. "Nothing. I better just shut up and go brush my teeth. It's late."

She closed the bathroom door.

Micah looked back at the seascape on his lap but didn't see much of it. His vision was internal, as it too often was. After a few minutes, he forced himself back to the present tense, rolled the poster, and returned it to its cylinder. He turned off the muted television and did the same for one of the room's two bedside lamps, then stretched out on top of the blankets of the bed he'd staked out—the one nearest the door. He couldn't say why, but he sensed somehow that this was the most strategic position.

He drifted. Why did humans generally choose to bury their

dead? What purpose was there in interring the leftovers after all the vital stuff had fled? Cremation seemed more logical. He'd heard of the old custom of burning bodies on public pyres. Was that the Vikings or the American Indians? Either way, Tully would've liked that. Everyone could have stood around the bonfire and sent his smoke into the sky. Knowing Tully, he would have wanted folks to roast bratwurst on the flames, make a picnic out of the event, and don't forget the beer bottles of iced tea.

The opening door nudged him from his reverie. With his arms crossed behind his head, he stared at the ceiling and didn't look over as Katelyn slid into her bed and doused the light.

He suddenly wanted to be funny again. What could he say here in the dark to get her laughing?

"Just got a text from Dezi," she said. "Everything's fine. No sign of any stalkers, no heavy breathing on the phone."

"That's good."

"You think he's been by there, looking for us?"

"Probably."

"And there's no chance he's going to find us here, right?"

"There's a chance of anything, I guess."

She said nothing more.

Micah paid attention to his eyes adjusting, compensating, taking in details where before there had been only darkness. It was amazing, really, how that worked. If he had bigger eyes, could he see even better at night? He didn't know the science behind it. But he wondered how human interaction would be different if people could see in the dark.

Katelyn sighed.

She didn't sound very tired. Maybe they should've danced a bit more. Though Micah offered his token resistance whenever the subject came up, now that he was lying here, he didn't bother trying to ignore the truth. There was something about moving with her like that, the synchronicity of their steps while the world imploded around them . . .

The air conditioner hummed.

He remembered the first time he'd seen her. She'd sat just behind the limo's front seat. How could he have known then, days ago, that he would soon be on his back on a hotel bed, his business destroyed and his best friend dead, and all he could think about was the way it felt to put his hands around her waist and lift her skyward?

He ventured a few words: "You asleep?"

She shifted but made no other sound.

He turned his head so that he was looking at her. By now his vision had recalibrated, and he saw that she'd moved only her arm, reaching for him across the gulf between their beds.

Micah grasped her hand.

She squeezed tightly.

When they released, she rolled over, pulling the blankets around her head.

Micah lay there and listened to her breathe.

CHAPTER 66

Half an hour after midnight, Nirat approached the graveyard.

A tidy fence of white and black encircled Woodlawn Cemetery, where death had been neutered in the typical American way. Nirat was as guilty as the rest of them, forgetting that the bones beneath those plots were crumbling, the veins shriveling like strings, the eyeballs hardened and shrunken in their sockets. This was the same society that, since the bloodfest of Vietnam, had portrayed war as painless surgery and forbidden photos of flag-draped caskets returning home.

"Get off it already," he said to himself. He'd never been one to mount a soapbox, and this was certainly no time to begin.

He entered the cemetery grounds and conducted recon.

Tomorrow morning at ten o'clock, the world would witness what type of man Ernest Tullmacher had been. How many friends would gather? How many former lovers, orphaned children, and jilted creditors?

Nirat studied the fence.

He remembered being at a party once, two decades ago, when someone had asked him who he'd most like to meet, if he possessed that oft-mentioned time machine. His answer then was the same as it was now. He wanted to know the name of the first man who'd ever erected a fence. How had this ancient builder conceived of such a thing without precedent? And what type of beast had he been hoping to contain? Musk ox? Mammoth? Or man?

Nirat left the fence and walked among the stones, an interesting tour at night. Last rites were different in Thailand. They celebrated your life for five nights, with the monks attending on the final evening to receive alms and generally make everyone feel better simply by exerting their stoic presence throughout the room. The funeral chambers held a bounty of incense and flowers, with everyone performing a *wai* or two at some type of ceremonial centerpiece. Nirat wasn't clear on the details. But he knew that the only thing that decayed were the corpses, because the spirit—like energy itself—was conserved. It never left. And when he met Tullmacher again, under a different sky and different circumstances, how would Nirat comport himself while he was being murdered to right the scales?

He stopped with his feet in the low grass and looked around. This, then, was where the next circle would begin, as well as where it would end.

Chapter 67

The morning sun, much brighter than the stuff of his dreams, warmed Micah's cheek.

He opened his eyes, blinking against the glare. Someone had thrown back the drapes.

"Does this look okay?"

Micah rolled over. At the moment, *nothing* looked okay. His sleep had been gouged by knives that only now were dissolving.

"It's the one thing I brought that might be appropriate. For a funeral, I mean."

He pushed himself halfway up, pinched the grit from his eyes, and looked at her as best he could. She wore straight black pants and a white shirt with a modest neckline. Her hair was hidden in the turban of a bath towel.

"I like the hat the best," he said. "Tully would dig it."

"From the neck down, funny man."

"From the neck down is fine." He settled back onto the bed.

"Did you even look?"

He laughed before he could stop himself.

"What is it now?" she demanded. "What did I say? I don't recall you being so punchy in the morning."

He shut his mouth before it further betrayed him. Yes, he had looked. Yes, her curves in that outfit looked fine. Yes, even though his eyes were shut, he could still see her.

"You better get in the shower," she told him. "We don't want to be late. And you still have to make that call to the dirtball."

A moment passed before Micah made sense of this. Right. He needed to phone Savlodar and have him set up an ambush disguised as a meeting.

The hair dryer wouldn't let him return to his dreams. He shoved himself to his feet and headed for the bathroom.

Katelyn shut off the dryer and intercepted him. "Seriously. Does this look okay?"

"Why do women ask that when they already know the answer?"

"Why don't men just shut up and humor us?"

Perhaps because he was still half grounded in sleep, he was brazen enough to touch a few strands of her damp hair. "Haven't you heard? Men are stupid sometimes."

"That's what's called preaching to the choir."

"You look great. As always."

"Thanks." She gave him a partial grin. "I guess I don't have to ask what you're wearing today."

"So I'm predictable."

"Not all the time you're not."

He smiled, wanting to say more, but instead chose to close the bathroom door behind him.

CHAPTER 68

". . . but that is not why we've congregated here today, and it's not why we weep for our fallen colleague, brother, and friend."

Two dozen men and women stood under a sky so clear it seemed to be painted glass.

"Instead," said the minister in the dark suit, "we shed those tears because we know that our world is no longer *his* world, that his memory abides within us, but his spirit, the true essence of him, seeks the mysteries of a new and wondrous place."

Micah knew few of these faces. The casket rested three feet away from him, and when he gazed around it, he saw mostly strangers. Detective Ling was here, along with a handful of other vets who'd known Tully before everything had disintegrated and he'd quit the force. They wore their uniforms and stood with their hands held in front of their crotches, the very pose that Micah assumed when waiting for a client beside the limousine door. He vowed never to stand that way again.

"We take heart when we think of him, and this is all the legacy any man can ask."

Immediately to his right, Rhonda remained safe behind her sunglasses. Her dress hung from narrow shoulders. She'd barely spoken since meeting him at the gate. Though she and her older brother hadn't been as close as other siblings, the loss had carved a ravine in her. Micah saw it in her stance and the way she walked like a cancer victim.

"And so we have met here on this spot under this sun not

only to remember our friend, but to thank him, for our lives are better because of him."

Standing on the other side of Rhonda was Tully's second sister, Ruby, whom Micah had met briefly before the service started. Though Tully had claimed she was overweight, apparently he hadn't seen her in many years, because Ruby was proportioned quite normally. She'd lost the weight, but the resemblance to her siblings remained in her eyes and the way she set her jaw when trying to withhold her emotions.

". . . and I'm sure that Ernest would have been delighted to see you all on such a warm and vibrant morning."

You shittin' me? Tully said so that only Micah could hear. *Tell all these fair-weather wankers to get back to work and let the guy with the shovel do his job.*

Micah managed to sublimate his smile.

"At this time, I would like to welcome anyone who wishes to say a few words."

No one moved. Other than the cops, also in attendance were several members of Tully's clan from AA, as well as his landlady and the elderly Asian gentleman who owned the liquor store where Tully still stopped to smell the roses even if he didn't allow himself a bouquet. They kept their eyes straight ahead, staring at the burnished box or the grass or at some meaningless point in their minds, averting their gaze in hopes of being ignored. In the last decade the police officers had lost touch with Tully and understandably had nothing to say. His landlady was known as the Gorgon in Tully's vernacular, so it was no surprise that she didn't choose to utter a parable or two on his behalf. Which left only the wine merchant and Micah.

Katelyn slipped her hand in his.

Her message transmitted through their fingertips and, as she intended, prompted him to clear his throat.

Heads turned. Eyes shifted toward him.

The minister or officiate or whatever he was—Micah assumed he was just a rent-a-reverend—nodded his encouragement and assumed his own version of the limousine stance.

Katelyn held on tightly.

Micah felt like the first man on the moon. He didn't want their stares and their expectations, nor their thanks for speaking up and absolving them of the responsibility. He didn't, in fact, want to say anything at all, but only to observe this torpedo-smooth container and think of the man who'd finally been given the chance to die for him. It might not have roused Malcolm from his catatonia, but Tully had been waiting to make this trade since that night so long ago in the dark.

Katelyn traced her thumb along the back of his hand. She inscribed a rune there, a magic pictogram of strength.

"Tully would call this a swap meet," Micah said. His voice sounded odd to his own ears, just the way your voice likely sounded inside your helmet when you stood on the moon. "He took me to one a few years ago. He bought a cardboard box of old vinyl records for three dollars and change."

He didn't look at any of them, but focused on a grave marker just beyond their downcast heads. Across the top of the granite slab, someone had left three die-cast hot rods—Matchbox cars placed there by a child or perhaps by a mother for the boy she'd lost.

"He'd call it a swap meet because we're all here to barter something, I think. Or at least that's how it feels to me. Some of you are here"—he took a breath, steadied himself—"some of you are here to trade your sadness for closure. Maybe some came to trade bad memories for good ones. Personally I'm looking to pick up some of Tully's endurance. To use his own term, he had a shitload."

Smiles flickered across faces.

"All the things he had to put up with . . . they eventually

broke him. We know that. I saw him go down. But then I also saw him get up. He just kept getting up, every morning, and that's not something I think I could do. Some days I can barely do it now."

Katelyn took a half-step toward him and held his hand with both of her own.

"So, Tull, if you're not using it anymore . . ." He blinked several times, sensing the tears. "If you're not using it anymore, I'm taking some of that stamina, because I think real soon I'm going to need it."

He never looked away from the metal cars, casting their tiny shadows in the sun. But he knew that Ling was watching him.

After a silent moment, the minister said, "Amen to that."

He was met with several muttered *Amens.*

"Let us pray."

Though other heads bowed and other eyes closed, Micah didn't move. The warmth of his hand pressed between both of hers was all the stamina he was going to get, as Tully had no doubt taken the full store of his to whatever trouble might be found in need of fixing on the other side.

The prayer ended. Feet shifted uncertainly until the minister released them. "I want to thank you all for attending. On behalf of the family, we hope you go with God."

They dispersed.

Micah waited until they separated, moved away, faded. Rhonda remained, her hand resting on her brother's box.

The minister looked at the three of them. "Is there anything else I can do? If any of you would like to talk—"

"Don't worry about it," Micah said. "Thanks."

A minute later, the minister too had faded away.

Micah didn't want to leave. It felt like abandonment. Once he fled this place, the last of what passed for his family would be gone. And his friends? His only real one was holding his hand.

"You know none of this is your fault," Rhonda said.

"Maybe not."

"You two seem to have a hell of a good thing going for you, and Ernie wouldn't want you taking a seat on his account. No sitting down, got it? You keep on moving. You keep on *moving.*"

Micah nodded. Cosmetics seemed to have aged Rhonda's face, as the eye shadow and rouge were not subtle enough to conceal but only to emphasize the narrow cheeks and filigree of lines around her mouth and eyes.

At the edge of the cemetery, a groundskeeper brought a hedge-trimmer to life.

"I have something for you," Micah said.

Any curiosity she might have expressed wasn't sharp enough to pierce her grief.

"It's in the car. I'll be right back." Though he was afraid that releasing Katelyn's hand might cause him to drift away in this low lunar atmosphere, he managed to stay on his feet. His shoes, polished this morning, whispered across the grass.

He unlocked the passenger's door of the Cutlass, tipped the seat forward, and grabbed the duffel bag from the back. Then he shut the door gently and made his way back to the mound of earth that was covered with green cloth in an effort to camouflage the hundred and forty cubic feet of dirt that would soon rest atop Tully's body.

Micah cradled the canvas gym bag in both arms and presented it to Rhonda. "I don't know how much is here. Nowhere near a fortune. But it was meant to be his."

She studied him, a few strands of graying hair in her face.

"Please," he said.

"You don't have to do this."

"I do."

"It's not mine."

"It is now."

A few seconds slipped away, then she moved her arm through the straps. "I'm not entirely sure that my brother deserved you, Mr. Donovan."

"I'm nobody special."

"That so? I think if I called for a show of hands, you'd be outvoted on that one."

Katelyn slipped her arm through his. "Hear, hear."

Rhonda gave the casket another glance, moving her tongue behind her cheek. "You know, I think I'm going to take the money and run. Just like the song says. A nice lunch of greasy mall food sounds just about right. Maybe I'll have a cold beer for my brother."

"Will you call me?" Micah asked. "If you need anything. Please."

She pulled her eyes from the box for what Micah suspected was the last time. "You're some kind of heartbreaker, you know that?" To Katelyn she said, "Keep a lookout for this one, honey. Don't let the desert wind blow him out of sight."

Katelyn smiled tightly. "I'll do what I can."

Rhonda walked away.

Micah waited to feel normal again. Or a sense of relief. Wasn't something supposed to happen after a funeral, a sensation that you'd made it over the splice in the wires and that your juice could start flowing again?

"What happens next?" Katelyn asked, so quietly he almost didn't hear her.

"I was wondering the same thing."

"Can you eat?"

"I don't know."

"And that phone call?"

"We'll talk about it." He hoped that she'd lead him away

from this place so that the workers could go about the business of zipping Tully into the ground. But Katelyn left it up to him. "Let's go."

They passed the marker with its rows of little cars. The last time he'd played with such things, his father had been a force, a laughing, snoring, storytelling storm of a man whose favorite thing in the world was to put his fingertips on the seams of a football and tell his son the magic words: *Go deep.*

"It was nice," Katelyn said. "The service."

"More people there than I expected."

"Police solidarity, huh?"

Micah had parked off the street, as near to the fence as he could. He wanted to be out of the way and out of sight—by-products of his recent paranoia. The only person around was a groundskeeper in safety goggles, noisily pruning the hedgerow.

Micah held open Katelyn's door. As she got in, their eyes met, and Micah realized that he didn't have to make that call to Savlodar. There were better things to do. Better places to see. More than anything he just wanted to get in this car with her and do what he did: drive.

He closed her door.

The walk around the car was no better. Part of him anticipated putting those double barrels against the side of a man's head. Another part was too busy being amazed that someone so beautiful and self-possessed was sitting in his old man's ride, waiting for him.

He reached his door and shoved the key in the slot.

What happened next made no sense. As he had done so many times before, he gripped the door's handle as he turned the key, tugging at the same time as he worked the lock. The Cutlass had a rectangular handle that was activated by lifting it up. Thinking about the first night she'd taught him to dance, Micah hooked his fingers into the space on the handle's underside, and as he pulled, a concealed razor sliced deeply into the flesh of his index and middle fingers.

The pain came from such an unexpected source that, for a moment, it was delayed, hung up in his nervous system. His first thought was that a wasp had taken refuge in the dark gap beneath the handle, but a second later, it firebombed his fingers.

As the car door swung open, Micah cried out and snatched his hand away. Blood streamed like running watercolors down his arm.

The groundskeeper ran toward him. As he neared, he hoisted the churning trimmer as if it were an axe.

Micah staggered backward. His mind was still busy processing his injury, trying to make sense of just what was happening, and the charging assailant cleared fifteen feet before Micah realized it was all a trap.

He made a fist of his left hand in an effort to shut off the flow of blood.

The man in the goggles swung his weapon, the gas-powered blades growling.

Micah dropped to a crouch, avoiding the trimmer's slashing teeth. He lost his balance and braced himself with his uninjured hand, then leapt sideways as the trimmer came down again. It struck the street with a kiss of sparks.

"Micah!" Katelyn threw herself from the car.

"In the trunk!" He didn't know what else to do but send her after the gun. His intended plan to lure this man to his death had been preempted, and now Micah could do nothing but try to avoid being ripped open. He jumped back as the blades cut an arc through the air a few inches in front of his chest.

Katelyn sprinted around the car and tore the key from where it was still seated in the door.

The blades came in again, forcing Micah into an awkward half-turn to his left. The gasoline fumes stung his eyes. He weighed his chances of hurling himself at the man, but he wouldn't be able to get inside the reach of the blades without being gutted by them.

The man kept coming, making a figure-eight with his weapon, driving Micah back.

He lost sight of Katelyn. He kept his eyes on the center of the man's mass, synchronizing his movements, dancing with him, timing each step so that the two of them performed their own kind of waltz, the motorized knives flowing between them. Blood dripped from his closed fist.

Micah stopped thinking. There was a time during his most recent dance with Katelyn that he'd let himself go, his mind finding a peaceful place and his body quickly following. He'd moved differently when that happened, as if finally he understood, at least in an outsider's clumsy way, why Katelyn had chosen this sublime thing as her profession. Bending his body to avoid being cut, pivoting from side to side, he went there again, where the only activity holding him together was motion.

Katelyn fired the shotgun.

The sound threw Micah off his rhythm. His next step faltered. At the same time, his attacker let out a startled cry as several steel pellets shredded his sleeve and embedded themselves in his arm. He released the hedge-trimmer, which shut off automatically even before it hit the ground.

He spun and—screaming—ran at Katelyn.

Micah may have been guided by reflex, but he was still playing defense and thus fell a half-move behind his enemy. Katelyn had been standing at the trunk when she pulled the trigger, and the gun's shortened barrel spread the buckshot so wide that she hit her target but failed to disable him.

The man swatted the gun to the side as she discharged the second shell, sending the shot into the car's fender. With animal swiftness he punched her in the side of the head, spinning her into the Cutlass as if she were weightless. She fell.

The man tore the gun from her hand, then leapt over her and ran, his injured arm flailing like a fractured wing.

"Kate!" Micah collapsed to his knees beside her, cradling her as she sank to the ground. "Kate, look at me!"

Already a red contour rose along her cheek and jaw. Her eyelids fluttered.

"Katelyn."

"I missed him. I'm sorry. I tried but I missed him . . ."

He gasped down a breath.

"I can't really feel my face . . ."

He caught her hand before she could touch it. "You're going to be fine."

"He's getting away."

"Can you sit up?"

Clearly in pain, she leaned against the car, eyes closed. "Didn't you hear what I said?"

"Just don't move, all right?" He kissed her on the forehead and set out after the man.

By the time Micah found his stride, Tully's murderer had reached the far side of East Owens Avenue. A car had stopped in the middle of the intersection, its driver watching the chase with his phone against his ear. Micah's pulse struggled against the noose his tie had become. The black fabric of his jacket strained at the shoulders as he ran.

He hit the street and barely checked for traffic. The horns were no more than distant smears of sound, making little impression on him. On the north side of Owens lay a residential labyrinth, and by the time Micah reached the first pair of driveways, the apparition he chased had vanished into the maze.

Micah jumped a fallen bicycle and ran between the houses.

Any of these privacy fences could have provided concealment. Though the yards were not exceptionally vast, they sported enough trees, lawn furniture, and oversized barbecue grills to offer unlimited cover. He knew his search had ended only seconds after it began.

He broke from the line of houses, crossed East Webb, and charged through the gap between garages. Sweat drew a line along his face and touched the corner of his mouth, salting his lip. He looked from right to left, hoping to catch of glimpse, a fragment of a fleeing man, anything.

The Cutlass met him on Stanley Avenue.

Katelyn honked as she braked, the car skating a few feet to the side as the tires locked against the asphalt. She threw open her door. "Do you see him?"

Micah was breathing too hard to respond. He shook his head and veered toward her.

"Get in. We'll circle the block."

He fell into the passenger's seat, shaking as if in the throes of a fever.

Katelyn got them moving down the street. "I'm sorry I missed him, babe, I tried, I really thought I had him—"

Micah waved a hand. He didn't have the breath to tell her not to worry about it. He was simply thankful she was alive.

She wiped away a rogue tear and then put both hands on the wheel as she turned. "I thought you were dead. I really thought he was going to kill you . . ."

Micah watched the shadows between the houses. He was in there. Somewhere.

"You're fine, right?" she asked. "He didn't get you with that damn thing?"

"I ducked."

"Yeah, sweet. You ducked. Glad to hear it." She squeezed the wheel so tightly that the veins stood out in the backs of her hands. "Holy *shit,* that scared the hell out of me."

"Where's the gun?"

"He took it from me."

Micah saw an elderly man bent over a rose bush and two co-eds in bikini tops heading for a Jeep full of frat boys.

"We've lost him, haven't we?" Katelyn asked.

Micah didn't want to say it. If he admitted that the man had gotten away, then he'd also be forced to confess that his desire to run him down had also diminished considerably in the last minute. Suddenly he simply wanted to leave everyone alone—the entire city and the continent on which it stood—and go somewhere that knew nothing of regret.

"You want me to try the next street up?"

Micah scanned the trees, the parked cars, the fence lines.

"I'm pretty sure somebody's called the cops by now," Katelyn said.

"I hear you."

"And?"

"And you're right. Let's just go."

"I know it sucks. We had him. And now we don't. Is your hand okay? You're going to need stitches, aren't you?"

"I said let's go."

Katelyn was looking at him; he felt it without turning around. But she didn't press him.

He studied the sidewalks, letting his heartbeat settle, letting his sweat dry.

"Uh, I hate to mention this," she said, "but there's one more thing."

Micah wanted no more burdens. "Whatever it is, just say it."

"I think I may have shot your car."

He pulled his eyes from the window and offered her the best smile he could muster. "I'll have the body shop send you the bill."

"Won't work. I don't think I have a permanent address these days."

"Hey."

"Yeah?"

"We better make a detour to the emergency room. The bleeding's not going to stop."

"I'm on it." She drew her shoulder harness across her chest and rammed it home.

CHAPTER 69

Motels these days, even the lowballers with stains on the shower curtains, required ID. Nirat avoided them. He couldn't risk his name being fed to the wrong computer. His freedom was now measured in hours, and he wouldn't facilitate its depletion by showing his driver's license to a flophouse jockey.

And so he'd driven the electric truck across town and returned here, to the Savlodar pool house, to pluck the steel bearings from his arm.

The girl had only winged him, and most of the buckshot seemed to have flown wide. Still, it felt as if thumbtacks were lodged beneath his skin, rendering his arm mostly useless. He counted four distinct points of impact, blood leaking from each. So far he'd managed to dig two of the bastards out, using the cheap pair of tweezers from the pool's first-aid supplies. Removing them hurt more than leaving them in.

A car pulled into the driveway.

Nirat paused with a cotton ball poised above the third entry wound. No one had seen him steal across the property and let himself in, and he had no intention of being caught back here playing paramedic. He waited until he was certain that one of the maids wasn't approaching from around the pool, then resumed his work.

After cleaning the area with rubbing alcohol, he began the grisly business of excavation. Clenching his jaws helped a little, his body pushing back against the pain by tightening the muscles in his face and upper body. His fingernails were dark with his own blood.

He pinched the small sphere and pulled it out. Slickened with gore, it shot from the tweezers and lost itself somewhere in the corner near the chlorine supplies.

The pain rose and set in his arm, a tiny sun.

Six minutes later, he extracted the last pellet, then wrapped himself in more layers of gauze than he probably needed, using his teeth in cave-dweller fashion to hold, pull, and tear. Finally, it was done.

No more. No more taping up shotgun attacks. No more wild pursuit. Maybe this near miss was what he needed to shake him from this jihad he'd initiated. Let them have their dinghy and the ineffable secrets of the sea. He would never be able to capture whatever they'd found, and destroying them no longer compelled him. He would leave and never return.

He exited the pool house, saw Austin's car in the driveway, and changed his mind.

Chapter 70

"You sure you want to do this?"

Katelyn didn't immediately respond. Hands on her hips, she surveyed her room.

They'd come here to her apartment from the hospital, where Micah had received two stitches in each of the first two fingers of his left hand. The intern had bound them so thickly that he couldn't bend them, but they no longer throbbed. The tetanus toxoid had hurt much more.

"We leave and let them catch him," she finally said, heading toward the closet. "Personally it just seems a lot less stressful that way. I don't want to be expecting a car bomb every time we fire it up."

Micah leaned against the wall, his jacket off, his French cuffs rolled up his forearms. Katelyn's room, unlike the woman herself, was not surprising. Famed dancers hung on the walls, including an autographed shot of Katelyn arm in arm with someone Micah didn't recognize but assumed was famous.

"For all we know," she said as she claimed several pairs of shoes, "he's circling the block this very instant. And the thought of him just waiting out there somewhere is kind of making me sick. So yeah, we're leaving. I'm *definitely* sure."

Micah wished he could say the same. He dreaded the idea of being unemployed and adrift. Every time he thought of the destroyed limo, shadows tugged at his spirit. He was scared of having to dip too deeply into the well of his savings. But at the same time, if he was being honest with himself, he admitted that the idea of driving away with Katelyn Presley held a small spark of appeal.

"You're not saying anything," she observed.

"Thinking."

"About?"

You, he thought. "About where we're supposed to go."

"It doesn't have to be some kind of major road trip. It's not like we're driving to Fort Lauderdale for spring break. How about Reno? Actually I don't really care, as long as I can sit down at lunch and not have to worry about the waiter not being who he appears to be. This guy is a psycho, Micah. We need to get out of here."

"Yeah."

"Don't sound so enthused. I realize the prospect of being shackled to my side for the next couple of days could be considered torture, but you're tough. You can handle it. And don't think you're getting out of dancing, by the way."

Her buoyancy again amazed him. He wanted to say as much but wasn't sure how.

"Is two bags too many?" she asked.

"As long as they fit in the car."

"Let me check the bathroom, see what I'm about to forget." She carried one of the open suitcases through a door bearing a sign that read ¿CÓMO SE DICE "BAÑO"?

Micah considered sitting down on the bed, then opted to remain where he was, just in case he needed to move quickly. Had Katelyn not been around, would he have found it so easy to put this morning's encounter behind him? Sure, he was shaken up and likely would be for days, but his second face-off with a man intent on killing him didn't resonate quite so potently with Katelyn in the room.

"Can we swing by the bank on the way?" she asked. "I don't

have my debit card anymore, so I'll need to make an old-fashioned withdrawal. Oh, and I'm starving. Just so you know."

"We'll stop." He knew she was trying to keep the conversation clipping along, because that was her particular brand of magic: move your feet, talk a lot, and forget the trauma until late at night when you couldn't elude it any longer. He hated to hear her cry in the dark.

She came out with her case snapped shut. "I think that's everything. Except my aquarium in the kitchen. I don't suppose we need a dozen goldfish and a betta named Baryshnikov as partners in crime."

"Probably safer for them to stay."

"Yeah, they'd just slosh water all over your car."

A door closed somewhere in the adjacent room. "K, you home?"

"It's Dezi." She shouted, "In here!"

"Girl, I didn't expect to see you for"—Dezirae rounded the corner and stopped a foot away from Micah—"oh, wow. Hi."

"Hello."

"You're the guy? I mean, *the* guy? The one K's been—"

"He's the one," Katelyn said, intervening. "Micah, this is—"

"Her BFF," Dezi said, showing him a smile of perfect teeth. "Dezirae Landon."

Micah introduced himself and offered his hand. Dezirae looked as he'd expected, with blond highlights in her hair and a T-shirt sized precisely for flashing glimpses of her midriff when she moved.

"Before you ask," Katelyn told her, "we can't stay. We're in the process of skedaddling, so I'm sorry but we're going to have to take a raincheck on lunch or whatever you're about to suggest." She handed Micah one of her bags. "I'll call you soon, I swear." She headed out of the room.

"Just like that?" Dezirae chased after her. "You just introduce me and leave?"

Micah, sighing, followed them.

"Things have changed," Katelyn said.

"Things like what?"

"Like me." She bent over and planted a kiss on the aquarium—"Hold the fort, guys"—then left the apartment.

"What's that supposed to mean? I know you saw some scary things but—"

"Not just *saw,* my dear, but *did.*"

"So you're running away? You've known this guy for how long?" She turned and walked backward. "I didn't mean anything by that, really."

"No problem," Micah assured her.

She spun back around in time to see Katelyn put her bag in the car's open trunk. "Look at all that stuff, K, how long are you planning on being gone?"

"When's rent due again? Can I mail you a check?"

"I'm being serious."

"Then I *seriously* don't know. We might decide to fly off to Jamaica and smoke pot all night with Bob Marley serenading us in the background."

"That kind of answer doesn't help at all."

"Maybe it's a nice way of asking you to, you know . . ."

"You're telling me to mind my own business?"

Micah added the second suitcase to the trunk. At this point he just wanted to avoid the anti-aircraft fire the two were exchanging. He may have made some questionable choices in the last few days, but he was wise enough to know when to pretend to be invisible. Malcolm Donovan didn't raise no fool.

"I'll call you," Katelyn said. "On the hour, every hour. Give or take."

"I thought you said the trouble was over."

"Do I look like I'm in trouble? Micah, do I look like that to you?"

Micah quickly got in the car, hoping it was a rhetorical question.

"The cops have been here," Dezirae said. "They told me they were just making sure I was all right. And that means you *are* in trouble. You're kind of scaring me here, K."

Katelyn opened her door. "I'm in good hands. He hasn't let anything happen to me yet."

"Yet?"

"Oh, shut up, girl, and let me hug you."

Micah stared at himself in the wing mirror because it made him feel as if he were giving them a modicum of privacy. He didn't want to hear what they said between them, so he was glad they kept their voices low.

Katelyn got in and slammed the door. "How are your fingers?"

"Fine. How's your friend?"

"Mother hen will be perfectly all right. Let's just get a move on before she throws herself in front of the car."

Micah asked nothing else. He got them headed down the street.

"She's not, by the way," Katelyn said.

"Not what?"

"My BFF. I don't think I've had one of those for quite a while."

Micah's reply was interrupted by his phone. Twice already today he'd taken calls from potential clients who were now happily giving their money to other transportation services. All of that income slipping away . . .

He recognized Savlodar's number.

"It's him, isn't it?" She must have seen it in his face.

Keeping one hand on the wheel, Micah pressed the Accept

button, though Ignore had a strong appeal. "Driver."

For a moment there was only silence, then: "Mr. Donovan?"

"I'm here."

"You . . . you said that you were going to telephone with a . . . a location." Savlodar sounded uncertain about the prospect, as if perhaps he was reconsidering. "I was wondering . . . if that was still your intention."

"He tried to kill me today."

"I'm sorry to hear that. Like you, I, uh . . . hope to be rid of him."

Micah used his thumb to increase the phone's volume. "Look, I'm not sure if—"

"I know where he's at."

"Hold on." He put the phone against his chest. "He says he knows where to find him. What do you think?"

Katelyn shook her head. "I'm tired of messing with this guy. I think he deserves to die as painful a death as possible, but . . . are you still up to killing him?"

"I just want it over."

"Then make it be over."

Micah nodded and went back to the phone. "Okay, here's how it's going down. You listening?"

"I hang on every word, Mr. Donovan."

"You tell us where he is, and we'll find him and end it."

"Glad to hear you say it. Are you familiar with Henderson?"

"I'm the driver," Micah said with more than a little impatience. "I know the lay of the land."

"Yes, I'm certain you do. My company has an office suite there, currently unoccupied. You'll find it at the corner of Sunridge Heights and Eastern. The door is marked 'Savlodar Financial.' Your man has gone to ground there."

"You're sure?"

"He called my father for assistance, and my father, in turn, called me. It seems that we're all being dragged into the mud by the same liability. I'm supposed to meet him there at midnight. I suggest you show up a bit earlier than that and deal with him, Mr. Donovan. Permanently."

He hung up.

Micah dropped the phone in his lap.

"So we're going there?" Katelyn asked. "We're going after him?"

Micah drummed his fingers twice. "No."

"Okay . . . so what're we doing?"

Micah came to a decision and picked up the phone again. "I'm calling Ling. Let the cops have him. There's been enough murdering for now."

"End of story?"

"Hope so."

"Just like that?"

"Are you prepared to try and sneak up on him and shoot him while he's sleeping?"

"Well, if you put it *that* way . . ."

"I want to get this over with. Just like you do."

"You want that more than you want revenge?"

"I don't know. I better not think about it or I'll change my mind." He scrolled through his call log and dialed Ling's cell. After he explained the full conversation twice, the detective was finally satisfied, promising to make contact as soon as they had him.

The Cutlass rolled for a silent mile, then two.

After mile number three, Katelyn said, "I guess if this is going to be over tonight, we won't need to take quite as long a vacation as we thought. We might have packed too much."

Micah wasn't so ready to believe that. "We'll see."

CHAPTER 71

Nirat dropped Austin's phone into the garbage disposal.

The machine stalled for only an instant, its steel maw wedged against the compact device, then the motor overcame the momentary resistance. Plastic splintered. The racket of the components being pulverized filled the kitchen.

Nirat hit the shut-off switch. "Damn noisy thing, isn't it?"

Austin stared at him from the chair in which Nirat had ordered him to sit. The shotgun—a brutal, shortened thing that had nearly killed him—rested on the marble-topped counter. Though the shells in its barrels were empty, Nirat had let Austin assume otherwise.

"Why are you still here?" Austin asked, his fingers white against the armrests. "Why don't you just get out, leave the goddamn country? God knows I gave you enough money . . ."

Nirat saw no use in trying to explain himself to this younger, paler version of the Savlodar patriarch, especially when he'd failed to adequately explain it to himself. There was a longing there, a yearning for the way things had been and—through the photo of the sailors—a desire to be lost in the majesty of the moment, but these concepts were nebulous, at best. And certainly not worth killing for.

Yet here he was.

He took a seat with the gun in his lap. "Until our rendezvous with Jack and Jill, let us pass the time with moronic entertainment." He pointed the remote at the TV and decided that anyone who kept a television in the kitchen deserved whatever fate the coming night would bring.

CHAPTER 72

"On the road again," Katelyn sang, "going places I ain't never been . . ."

Micah, having now sat through two verses of Willie Nelson, wasn't sure if Katelyn's singing ability quite matched that of her dancing.

"Seein' things that I may never see again . . ."

He suppressed the urge to join in.

"I just can't wait to get on . . . the road . . . again!"

Micah waved a hand. "Okay, okay, I surrender."

She punched him in the arm. "It wasn't that bad." She wrinkled her nose. "Was it?"

"Didn't you say you were hungry? We can stop."

"Was it?"

"It was fine."

"Hey, every road trip needs at least a few miles of singing."

"I said it was fine."

"Then why are you trying so hard not to grin? Look at your face. Your jaw is almost shaking."

He could stand it no longer. He smiled and laughed.

"See!" She punched him again.

"What can I say? I'm just thrilled to be alive." The truth was that he needed that laughter, needed it to make the rest a little easier to manage.

"You're lucky I like you." She turned away, fighting a smile of her own.

"I won't argue one bit with that."

The drive south through the Eldorado Valley to the border town of Laughlin was supposed to be no longer than an hour and a half, but Micah saw no reason to rush. Though he was taking nothing for granted, it looked as if Detective Ling would be able to drop the hammer on Tully's murderer tonight, assuming that Savlodar's information was accurate. Tomorrow, then, Micah would need to commence reassembling his life, and that meant talking with the insurance company about the car and probably renting a replacement for the interim. There were clients to call, contacts to reestablish . . . but none of that mattered now, hence his light touch on the accelerator. Nothing sounded more appealing at the moment than listening to Katelyn sing classic country.

"So this town," she said, "Laughlin . . ."

"Sits on the Colorado River. Great view. It's a mini Vegas, in a way, but a bit more geared toward the family, sort of the gateway for anyone driving in from Arizona, so it sees a ton of tourist traffic. Clean, safe, fun—all those things I find myself valuing more than I used to. Guess that means I'm getting old."

"Considering these last few days, I'm valuing them an awful lot myself."

"We have a room reserved at the Edgewater. Hopefully this will all be over tonight, but in the meantime we can distract ourselves."

"A little bit of R and R, huh?"

"You don't think we deserve it?"

"Are you kidding me? We deserve medals and a ticker-tape parade. *And* a few minutes on at least two or three talk shows. Maybe even our own website."

Micah didn't disagree. They needed *something.* He just couldn't quite say what.

Laughlin dazzled in the sun. The river bore the secrets it had carried since the high realm of the Rockies, delivering them to the desert but not revealing them. Shoreline casinos stood over the water, the windows of the resorts flashing like facets in jewels.

When Katelyn stepped from the car at the Edgewater, she said, "So you do this all the time, right? Bring wayward women to fancy hotels?"

"I think by now you know otherwise. And it's not so fancy."

"Says who? Is there room service?"

"I honestly don't know."

"If there's room service then it's fancy. You know I'm a sucker for bellboys bearing cinnamon bagels."

They ate stuffed mushrooms and pasta for dinner, trading stories that moved between silly and sad with an easy rhythm. He told her more about his dad and about his sophomore year in high school when he knew he was destined to be a rap star, and she admitted to a bad spell with weight-loss pills and followed this with a guided tour of My Worst Date Ever, which started with her noticing a giant deodorant stain on her shirt and ended with her second-favorite skirt getting caught in a car door.

"If I could go back and do that night again," she said, "I would've been more careful with the roll-on and less inclined to fake like I was paying attention. We went to a movie, but I can't remember what it was, only that it was long."

"I take it that you didn't go out with him a second time."

"He didn't call. He had about as thrilling a time as I did. He was boring but he wasn't dumb."

"Remind me to keep my boringness to a minimum."

"Uh, I think you and I could use a bit more boring in our lives. And fewer shotguns."

Between the slot machines and the blackjack tables, they lost forty-two dollars, which was a record for Micah, who rarely gambled. He was a man whose clinical eye simply wouldn't let him compete against those kind of odds. But tonight he needed the release. And besides, he enjoyed listening to Katelyn sweet-talk the slots when the dials were spinning.

"Come on, you beautiful thing, come on, I love you and your generous robot heart . . ."

The robot hearts took more than they gave, and eventually Micah decided he'd had enough. Katelyn agreed. She took her shoes off in the elevator, and when the door slid open, Micah led her down the carpeted hallway to their room.

Chapter 73

"It's time."

Nirat waved the gun like a wand. He'd spent the last several hours sitting in another man's kitchen, watching another man's TV, and drinking another man's expensive spring water. Outside, night folded its wings over the city.

Austin stood up. He put weight on his bad leg. He grimaced but didn't fall over.

"You drive," Nirat said. "I brought the electric truck, and my faith in the battery leaves a bit to be desired, as they say. So we'll take yours."

Austin made no reply. He'd kept his mouth shut through the evening. Nirat could almost hear him calculating the odds.

As he settled into the passenger's seat of the Lexus, the shotgun in his lap, Nirat tried to anticipate Donovan's strategy. Certainly he would've found another gun in the last few hours. Perhaps the girl would also be armed. Nirat suspected that their need to avenge Tullmacher compelled them just as forcefully as his own need to . . . to what? He still wasn't able to define what he wanted, just as he couldn't quite describe the needfulness of those sailors alone on their ambiguous sea. But he wanted it, and if he couldn't carry it home in a box then he'd content himself with destroying it. And there was also the fact that he was pissed at himself for so far failing to finish the job. They had almost drowned him and almost shot him, and thank God that Richard wasn't around to witness any of this embarrassing shit.

"Where are we going?" Austin asked. His voice was that of a condemned man. And maybe he was. Nirat had yet to decide.

"You already know the answer to that. You're the one who set up the meeting."

"Want to know something? I'm sorry I started all of this."

"A little late for regrets, I should think."

"I'm not kidding around here, Alex. You went too far. I never wanted anyone to get killed. It's not too late to—"

"It *is* too late. If you had half your father's instincts you'd know this."

He expected Austin to argue, but to the man's credit, he kept his mouth shut and drove.

When they were a block and a half from the rendezvous point, Nirat instructed him to pull over. They sat in the semi-dark beneath the street lamps. "Kill the lights."

Austin complied.

Because Nirat had so recently brought up the subject of instincts, he wasn't about to ignore his own. Donovan wouldn't walk into a trap. Was he hiding in a wedge of shadow between two cars?

"Unroll the windows. All of them."

Austin touched the controls, and the windows hummed.

Nirat listened.

One night eight years ago he broke a pimp's clavicle with a pair of eight-inch, slip-joint pliers. He'd always enjoyed working with tools. Though Richard had never dabbled in the prostitution trade—not even the legal variety in Nye County—the pimp had borrowed heavily from one of the Savlodar lending firms and hadn't been lucky enough at the tables to keep up his payments. Nirat experienced a small amount of difficulty when trying to grab the man's clavicle with the pliers, but eventually he applied enough force that the steel teeth were able to get a solid bite. Breaking the bone required a surprising amount of pressure. But the main lesson he learned that night was that a silent neighborhood generally wasn't a good omen. The man's screams had been so loud that when Nirat emerged from the apartment, he found the street deserted. Everyone in a three-building radius had heard the man's cries and, like transgressors of old fearing the Inquisition, they darkened their windows or just plain got the hell out of the area.

Eight years later, Nirat found this street to be the same.

"What do you want me to do?" Austin asked. He no longer sounded petulant. He sounded exhausted and afraid.

"Drive to the next corner. Turn left."

As the car drew closer to the office complex, Nirat poured his eyes into the background, as if it were a painting whose less important places held secrets to a greater meaning. The cars against the curb might have been revelations waiting to happen. Though he saw no vans, the traditional Trojan horses of police surveillance, he noted at least four SUVs with darkened windows. Only two people were in sight, a man and woman sharing a cigarette at the crosswalk.

Nirat watched the light. "Go left here."

The Lexus slowed. The light flashed WALK. The couple with the cigarette didn't move.

Fighting a sudden ache in his jaw, he slammed the shotgun on the dash. "It's a set-up."

"How do you know?"

He swung the gun around and pushed the barrels against Austin's head. *"The cops are waiting for us."*

"I don't know anything about it!"

"You were taking me right to them."

"I've been with you the whole goddamn afternoon!"

"Then why are they here? How did they know?"

"He must have told them! Donovan! He set it all up. I had nothing to do with it, all right? I thought you two were going to shoot it out, but I guess he had other plans."

Nirat wished for a moment that the gun was stuffed full of twelve-gauge buckshot so that he could paint the window red. Donovan was yet again eluding him.

He brought the gun down on the dashboard a second time, cratering the leather-covered plastic. The act was not as cathartic as he'd hoped, but only further enflamed him. If he'd had Donovan here with him now, if he'd had the man here he would—

Austin breathed noisily. "Where do you want me to go?"

Nirat pinched his eyes shut. His heartbeat seemed to originate from inside his bones, so that he shook with each stroke. "The highway. Get on the highway."

"Which . . ."

"*West.* Take 160 west." How long would it take them to find an empty place? By the time they reached the wilderness, would he still want to kill this man beside him as much as he did now? In the absence of Donovan, would a surrogate suffice? "I'm sorry," he said through his teeth.

"What? You're goddamn *apologizing*?"

Nirat didn't explain himself. Yes, he was apologizing, but not to Austin. He wanted to ask Richard to forgive him for what he was about to do.

CHAPTER 74

Micah sat on the edge of the bed, listening to the sink behind the bathroom door.

He did that a lot lately. It seemed that he'd gone from being a driver to being Rodin's *The Thinker,* perched on a hotel mattress while a hundred-and-fifteen-pound dynamo powdered her nose. Except Katelyn didn't do that. She depended very little on makeup and had no patience for pretension.

He realized his foot was tapping. He put a hand on his knee and stilled himself.

That worked for less than a minute. He stood up and removed his jacket.

The hotel hangers were heavy and wooden, the best kind. You never hung a suit on wire, otherwise you risked stains and discoloration. Back in his previous life, before a certain passenger had asked his name, he'd owned two dozen walnut hangers of the highest quality. The crossbars sported a rubber ridge to hold the trousers in place without creasing them. Luxury had nothing to do with it. He simply wanted to maximize the life of his tuxedos. The hangers were a kind of investment.

The last few days had not been good on his apparel. Sweat stains, dirt, blood . . .

Katelyn swung open the door. "Guess what I just did?"

Micah observed her, and in doing so also observed himself. She'd changed into sweatpants and a tank top, her face was freshly washed, and what she might have done in the bathroom was incalculable. Standing in the doorway, blond hair touching her shoulders, she was, Micah admitted, magnetic. Now that it seemed as if their troubles were finally settling down, his thoughts kept returning to her, no matter how much he busied himself with walnut suit hangers.

"You're not guessing," she said.

"I don't think it would do any good."

"You're right. I just prayed."

"You what?"

"Prayed. As in 'Now I lay me down to sleep, I pray the Lord my soul to keep.' "

"That was your prayer?"

"You don't think God listens to prayers like that? They're not good enough for Her?"

"Your god's a her?"

"Why can't She be?"

"If it's all the same to you, I'll take a pass on the religious debate."

"You have anything else to do?"

"Anything would be better. Even dancing."

She smiled. "I was hoping you'd say that." She crossed the room to her MP3 player and plugged it into the speakers.

Micah stood there wondering if he'd just been suckered.

Katelyn scrolled through her playlists. "I have only one more song that I know is in three-four time. They're kind of rare these days."

Micah pushed off his shoes. He usually took the time to sit and untie them, but like the rest of his routine, that part was left on the rocks of a shore he might not ever see again.

"Can you shove one of the beds against the wall?" she asked.

Micah did her one better. After pushing the first of the two queen-sized beds out of the way, he did the same with the other, butting it against the air-conditioning unit below the window.

He wondered what his father would've said had he known his son could waltz. What would Malcolm have thought of this woman?

Micah knew the answer to that. Without a doubt, Malcolm Donovan would have taken his son by both shoulders and said, *"My boy, I think you may have found the one woman in the whole world, black or white, who is too good for you."*

Malcolm spoke those words as a compliment. He'd always told Micah that girls wouldn't be able to live up to him, but with Katelyn in the room . . .

"This is it," she said. "The last one. It's a little before my time, but I downloaded it after hearing it at a competition last summer. It's a killer."

Micah rolled up his sleeves. He was warm, despite the cool air pushing from the vents behind him.

"Ready?"

Micah thought it was a question that could be interpreted in a variety of ways.

A moment later, Jim Croce's voice rose clear and wistful from the speakers. Katelyn adjusted the volume while Jim speculated on what he would do if he could save time in a bottle.

Micah put his hands in his pockets and watched her.

Katelyn turned toward him, a dervish waiting to whirl.

They met in the center of the room. By now Micah had mastered the placement of his hands and the level plane of his right arm. He'd been swatted on the elbow enough times to get it right without thinking. Her back was warm beneath his palm.

"I guess we'll be heading back home in the morning," he said quietly.

"Yeah."

"Hopefully Ling will give us a call pretty soon and let us know."

"Hopefully."

"And we can get back home and sort things out."

"This is the point where I tell you to shut up and dance."

"Right." He took a breath, then stepped forward with his left foot.

She glided backward, mirroring his movements as he completed the six-step box. He no longer had to watch his feet, which was both good and bad, because now he had no excuse for not looking into her eyes. For her part, Katelyn seemed to have no difficulty staring up at him, which proved to Micah who owned the courage in the room.

He varied their pattern as she'd taught him, curving through the space between the beds.

A minute into the song, he realized that the distance between them had diminished. When they turned, her body sometimes brushed his. He became aware of her in a way that threatened to distract him and bungle his steps. His thoughts fired randomly in self-defense. His pants needed pressed. He would have to purchase another limousine. The hotel breakfast menu had looked promising. His phone could probably use a charge . . .

Katelyn relaxed the fingers of her right hand, then reaffirmed her grip while being mindful of his bandaged fingers. She hadn't held on this tightly before. In fact, Micah unmistakably recalled her instructing him to keep things loose and light in order to dance more naturally.

In front of the dark television screen, he spun her, caught her, kept moving.

She would not stop looking up at him. By now Jim Croce was starting over again, his second go-round with making days last forever and wishes come true. It was a damn good song, Micah decided. They needed more like it on the radio today. A moment later he admitted to himself that the fiber-optic lines of his nerves had never felt more overloaded. He needed to get some distance and recover.

They cornered around the bed. Katelyn remained mostly on her toes, as light as a fey creature in a forest.

Micah arched his arm, and she stepped under it smoothly. Then she melted back into him, closer still, her face only inches from his. Maybe it all was worth it. He would've brought Tully back to life if he had the power, but the rest of it . . . the rest of it was a path he'd walk again if it led to this place and this dance and this woman so near him that he felt the rise and fall of her chest. He wanted to laugh for the sheer simplicity of it. He was nobody, a chauffeur who days ago had valued only discretion and financial security, and now he was pressed against a woman who could save the world with her perfume.

"What are you thinking?" She spoke so softly that he wouldn't have heard her had they been farther apart.

He smiled. "I better plead the Fifth."

She let him get away with it. They angled toward the wall, then spun away before making contact. "You're cool as hell," she said. "You know that, don't you?"

"I'm just doing my thing."

"Yeah? Well, your thing is seriously turning me on."

He would receive no better invitation than that. Still, though, he hesitated.

Then he stopped hesitating and kissed her.

She rose up to meet him but never stopped moving. They slid through a box step without breaking contact. Micah delighted in her mouth.

She pulled away, smiling. "You're a very good dancer."

"Thanks. You could use a little work yourself."

She laughed and kissed him again, harder this time.

Micah wanted everything. The desire overcame him, having been dormant for so long that now, spreading through his blood, it emptied him out. Whatever she needed from him, he would give her, if only to fill himself up in return.

She whispered, "Don't you ever take off that damn tie?"

Micah released his hold but kept moving. Katelyn put her arms around his neck, and their dance continued as Micah tugged the corner of the black silk and pulled it free of his collar.

"Feel better?" she asked.

"Not yet." Though his steps were not as smooth as before, Micah continued to dance at the same time as he passed the tie behind her and brought its ends together at her throat. His hands were clumsy with anticipation, but this was a task he'd performed a thousand times and one he could have completed under a variety of debilitating conditions; Tully used to say that it was his only skill. Though the motions were reversed when tying it around someone else's neck, it was no different than working with a mirror, and in seconds he finished the bow. "*Now* I feel better."

He took her hands again and they swept across the room and he kissed her mouth and chin and down the pale curve of her neck.

She pushed her body closer to his. He pulled tighter with the hand against her back.

They bumped the wall.

"Sorry," he said.

"Shut up." She let go and pulled his shirttails from his pants.

He tried to keep them moving. She worked the buttons of his formerly pressed shirt with its rolled-up sleeves and wing-tipped collar, somehow also managing her footwork. Micah's pulse beat in his temples and his chest, and he thought at any moment he'd trip and shatter it all.

But they held. She pushed the shirt from his shoulders. He dropped his arms long enough to let it fall away, and in that second Katelyn skinned away her tank top and then he enfolded her again. They danced through another verse, eyes on eyes. The strap of her bra lay beneath Micah's right hand, and as the song progressed, he pinched the fabric and worked it between his fingers. On the fourth attempt the latch parted.

He lost all concept of the room's geography. He danced them into the nightstand and the writing desk. They bumped wood and glass and never stopped moving until he spun her and—instead of rolling back into him—she released his hand and in a single motion pushed her sweatpants and panties to the floor. She stepped out of them and, wearing only his tie, leapt at him.

He caught her, and her arms and legs encircled him. Holding her, kissing her, he completed his steps as she'd taught him—*one,* two, three, *four,* five, six—and repeated the move twice before breaking rhythm and putting her against the wall.

As she held on, he worked the black metal buckle on his belt, and when he resumed his steps moments later, there was nothing between them but a thread of sweat that had already formed where their stomachs met.

She relaxed her legs and let them slide down his until her feet found the floor and she blended with his steps, her arms still locked around his neck. He tasted her in each breath and wanted more, but the river of the waltz carried them in its current, drawing them near the bed but not stopping there.

A minute more was too much. Micah swung her upward, fell to his knees with her in his arms, and pinned her to the floor with the full weight of his body. She closed her eyes as he explored her, seeking out the hollows of her with his hands and then his tongue. He lingered here and there, enjoying her flavors, while she breathed through her teeth and sank her fingertips into his shoulders.

Then she made a noise he'd never heard before and spun, rolling him onto his back.

Looking up at her, his tie a black brushstroke against her

skin, he found himself laughing out of nothing but a new and simple joy.

"What is it?" she asked, hair in her face.

"I think I might be falling in love with you."

She smiled, her eyes luminous. "What do you mean *might*?" She bent down and kissed him, her tongue in his mouth, then guided him into herself as she rocked back.

Chapter 75

Nirat bent the man's finger until it snapped and touched the back of his hand.

Austin's cry carried across the sand to nowhere.

"Your father never had a problem keeping his cock in his pants," Nirat said, turning his back on the man and strolling a few feet away, his eyes on the blurry stars over the hills. They looked like pictures sent back from the Hubble.

Behind him, Austin swayed back and forth and hissed in pain.

"True, he had his own dumbass moments," Nirat continued, "like the time he went apeshit at that private baccarat game with the investors from Santa Barbara. Remember them? The ones who thought they could push him? Damn, but I thought we'd never get the glass out of that poor bastard's hair."

He turned back around. Austin's coat lay on the ground and he was missing a shoe. During their three-hour drive from the city, Nirat had paid out his patience until the rope had entirely slipped from his grasp. Perhaps this was why Richard had kept him around, because he always knew what Nirat himself was only learning, that his own sanity was as amorphous as the swirling Milky Way overhead. The truth was that he missed the old man. Missed him and had no rudder without him.

He retrieved the shotgun from the ground and squatted in front of Austin—a man who'd become more of a symbol than an actual pain in the ass. "Ever wonder what's waiting on the other side?"

Austin cradled his hand. "You want money, is that it? I can get you more."

"You think that's why I hang around, building decks and weeding flowerbeds?"

"My father thought that—"

"Your *father* treated me more like a son than he did *you.* Who was about town running his business interests and who was standing beside him when he intentionally hit the fan with shit when the blades were spinning? You're the former, but you never were much of the latter."

Austin ran his tongue over dry lips. "He won't approve of this, when he hears."

"You've got me on that one, my friend." He hit him with the gun.

Austin toppled, clutching his ear and the side of his head.

Nirat stood up. He walked a circle around the man. The night was cool, the desert ground having given up the heat baked in it by the day.

He ran through his agenda. After he finished here, he would return to the city and see if he could catch Donovan at the girl's apartment. Maybe they'd gone there for the night. After that he'd head to Soaring Court and conduct an experiment in fire-department response times.

And then?

"Do what I should've done the first time," he said. "Slit the vegetable's throat."

He turned back to Austin. "Sit up, for God's sake."

Austin pushed himself up, blood spidering down his face.

Nirat put the barrels against his forehead.

Austin held up his hands. "Jesus, no . . ."

"No? Why do you think we took this little joy ride?"

"Alex, *please*!"

"You never answered me. I asked if you ever think about what's out there."

"Out where?"

Nirat shrugged with one shoulder. "Anywhere. Over the waves. In that part of the ocean we can't ever see."

"I'm sorry, Alex, but I honestly don't know what you're *talking* about."

Nirat thumbed back both triggers.

Austin wept. Eyes pinched shut, shoulders shaking, he wailed with surprising intensity.

Nirat studied him. This was genuine dread, the unadulterated kind that came only with the fear of dying. It was cowardly and weak, the currency of beggars and bullies.

"Have you pissed yourself yet?" he asked.

Austin doubled over, stammering his pleas as he cried.

Nirat, annoyed by how embarrassed he was on Richard's behalf, clubbed the man in the back of the skull.

Austin slumped forward to the dirt.

Nirat walked away. He had ahead of him a drive of several hours in which to contemplate those questions that Austin had failed to answer. Perhaps he'd call the prison and see if he could leave a message for Richard, though he didn't know how to put in words what he could barely put in thought. All he knew for certain was that, at some point before he visited the nursing home, he'd need to procure a knife. And probably some ammunition for the gun.

The moon rose behind him, pushing his gray shadow across the ground.

Chapter 76

Micah opened his eyes.

He was a blind man. In his half-sleeping state, he pretended that he'd lost his vision. His other senses, then, pulled the night-time world toward him.

The hair in his face smelled of coconut shampoo and distantly of sweat. Her body was curved into his, her back against his chest, his folded knees form-fitting into hers. What seemed more important than anything was square inches; the more he had of his touching hers, the better. His arm was curled around her, and in her sleep she held his hand against her breast.

He still tasted her on his tongue.

Tiny sore spots flashed in his abdominals and calves. Over the last few days, he'd called upon his body to perform feats far beyond waxing the limo and playing pickup basketball on Sunday afternoons. Tonight was the culmination of that, when unused muscles found themselves pushing, flexing, stretching for just a little bit more closeness. He'd spent so much of his adult life maintaining a certain separation from everyone else that now his desire for the opposite surprised him with its strength.

At some point when they were entangled in each other, he'd laughed. Laughed for the simple ease of it all, laughed because he'd tumbled so completely through the rigid margins of his routine. Maybe they'd move to a lake and open a bait shop. Or buy an eighteen-wheeler and drive as a team, hauling machine parts from Vegas down to Shreveport, just east of the Texas line. Neither of those choices sounded very conducive to maintaining his obsessive-compulsive lifestyle, which was why they made him so giddy.

Giddy? He tried to recall the last time such a word had applied to him, and lying there in the darkness he almost laughed again.

Morning was sure to bring decisions. Over breakfast he'd throw a thousand and one options at her and see which she preferred, where she'd like to go, what sights she wanted to see before the two of them burned out in a proverbial but very cinematic blaze of glory and lived forever as paragons in the hearts of the young. Or maybe, melodrama aside, she'd simply opt to stay in bed.

Micah would be happy either way.

Chapter 77

After pulling in behind a convertible Mini, Nirat shut off the car but didn't bother with any kind of disguise. At four in the morning, the neighborhood lay encased in the ice of sleep, like an ancient village trapped when the glaciers came. No one would see or hear. Besides, there was little use in worrying about being identified. He'd already triangulated the position of his fate and knew it couldn't be moved.

Donovan's car wasn't around. Unsurprising. Nirat didn't really expect to find them here, this Bonnie and Clyde duo that had so far eluded him. But he'd be remiss if he didn't take a look. You never knew what you'd find at this time of the morning. The world's clocks ticked differently at this hour, even here in Vegas. *Especially* here.

He rang the bell.

A moment passed. He pressed it again, then three more times in quick succession, followed by a few clubs from the butt of his hand.

Light appeared in a window.

Richard had depended on him not to plan, not to overanalyze, not to waste time with needless strategy when simple impulse would suffice. So when the voice said "Who are you?" from beyond the closed door, Nirat prepared to throw his shoulder into it as he said, "I have information about Katelyn Ann Presley, and I think she might be in danger."

The lock slid back. The door opened three inches, a gold

chain connecting it to the jamb.

The girl on the other side looked so young that, for a moment, Nirat was taken aback. The sleep in her eyes turned the twenty-five-year-old into a little girl, one with her hair crazy on her head and worry in her endless eyes. Nirat wondered why he'd never had the chance to run into someone like this, who defied time by simply hugging her robe to herself and looking so uncertain.

"Is K all right?" she asked.

Nirat banished his thoughts and heaved himself against the door.

The chain's brass moorings ripped from the jamb. The door blasted inward, striking the girl in the face. She stumbled backward as momentum carried Nirat into the house. He slammed the door as she fell. Her head drummed against the floor, she made a small sound, and her eyes closed.

He knelt beside her. Blood issued from her nose and ran in matching tributaries down either cheek. Nirat could tell it was broken. "No time for napping, I'm afraid." He slapped her.

Her eyes opened and cleared. She tried to roll, but her movements were groggy, like someone trapped underwater.

Nirat grabbed her by the hair, his knuckles close to her scalp. She cried out.

"Are you listening?" he asked.

She said something that might have been *please,* but her ruined nose made it sound more like *bees,* which Nirat found inexplicably humorous. Bees. That was damned funny. He frowned at himself and lifted her to her feet by her hair.

She yelped and grabbed his wrist in both hands in an effort to keep her hair from being torn out. Tears mixed with blood on her face, turning it pink.

"Where does she sleep?" he asked.

She wept loudly and breathed as if headed toward hyperventilation.

"Show me."

She pointed.

Nirat dragged her that direction.

The room provided no answers. Tugging the girl behind him as if she were not a living thing at all, Nirat glanced in the bathroom. One of the drawers was open and mostly empty. Were they already gone? Had they truly moved beyond the farthest waves and left him alone on the shore?

He pulled her back into the bedroom and held her at arm's length, his fingers still knotted in her hair. "Were they here?"

Sobbing almost uncontrollably and clutching his wrist, she nodded.

"And now?"

She said something unintelligible, the bottom half of her face smeared with blood.

He shook her. "Where are they?"

"Gone, I don't know, they left!"

"Left for where?"

She was having trouble speaking. *"Away!"* Between the tears, the shattered nose, and the general histrionics, it was impressive that she even managed that single word.

"Correct me if I'm wrong," he said, "but I'm inferring that they aren't coming back."

She blurted out nonsense.

"I don't suppose you know if they collected Donovan's invalid father before they left? I was rather hoping to meet him one more time."

She dug her fingernails into his wrist, now crying beyond all coherence.

Nirat would get nothing else from her. In that moment he hated her for what she was, for her naiveté and her senselessness and her saltwater tears. Riding the sudden upswing of rage, he bunched the muscles in his back and arm, spun the girl in a circle, and released his hold so that inertia hurled her into the wall.

He marched from the room, pulling strands of hair from his fingers.

Chapter 78

"Micah, wake up."

The words stung him in his dreams. He lunged to the side and rolled out of bed, flaring instantly awake and preparing to face their attacker. Naked, his feet tangled in the sheet, he blinked against the glow of the bedside lamp, hands held in front of him.

"Wait, it's okay, he's not here!" On her knees on the bed, Katelyn waved him down. She wore nothing but his tie, and she held her phone in both hands. "It's Dezi."

He dashed a hand over his face, trying to wipe away the sleep. "What's wrong? What's the matter?"

"He was there, he just left, he *hurt her.*"

Micah's brain, weary from days of running and fighting and surviving, computed this with maddening slowness.

"She called the ambulance," Katelyn said, her words pressed together in alarm. "He hit her in the face and I've never heard anyone so scared . . ."

"Is he gone?"

She nodded. "What do we do?"

"He was looking for us?"

"She said he asked about me and then you and then—"

"What?"

"Your father."

Micah bent over and put his hands on his knees.

"We need to call Ling," she said. "Right *now.*"

Micah found it somewhat astounding how quickly he moved from love to hate. Hours ago he had no thoughts but of running off to the Louisiana bayou with this woman and saying to hell with everything else. He wanted it in the way that a soldier wanted home. He could work on a shrimp boat or whatever they did down there, so long as he could go home every night to her arms. And now, as he stood here with his fingers hardening like talons, he wanted only to rip out a man's eyes.

"Hey," she said.

"We need to get to my dad." He looked up. "We leave in thirty seconds."

She required no more prompting than that. The two of them exploded into motion, throwing on clothes, snatching the car keys from the desk, and running down the hotel hall toward the elevator. When the doors closed, Micah saw his reflection in them and realized he was wearing an untucked white undershirt and tuxedo pants. He'd left the rest of his usual wardrobe in a pile on the floor.

Chapter 79

Nirat let himself into the Savlodar house through the back door and placed the first of the five-gallon gas cans near the sink. Once again he felt the need to apologize to Richard. It seemed he was doing that a lot lately, sending mental vibes to an incarcerated man. Perhaps in the next life he'd find forgiveness. Until then, he had only fire.

He stepped back outside and brought in the second can. Until Austin had so foolishly tried his hand at rape, Nirat had used this fuel for the lawnmower. Now it would become his accelerant. Strange, the way things changed form. Under the right conditions, even the most innocent items left behind their normal tasks and cast a shadow with sharper edges than before.

He closed the kitchen door and drew a glass of ice water from the fridge. He took his time with it. He'd always liked the feeling of cold water moving down his throat. When the glass was empty, he placed it upside-down in the sink and headed upstairs.

The master bedroom remained sealed. Austin slept at the opposite end of the house, as far from his father's lingering spirit as he could. This chamber, then, was something of a time capsule, awaiting the return of a traveler from the past. Nirat drove his foot against the door four times before it finally capitulated.

Everything within was covered in white.

Sheets draped the furniture, so there was little to see of the man whose presence once filled this place. Nirat found this to be a blessing. He didn't want to become spellbound by Richard's personal effects or hypnotized by memories of him giving orders with a glass of cognac in his hand while a black-eyed beauty half his age lay waiting in the sheets behind him. Matters would've turned out so differently had Richard been here to engage them like a matador with a bull. He could have told Nirat where to direct the spears so that the damn thing died and everyone could get on with their lives.

Nirat went to the closet. It was as spacious as a ship's cargo hold.

What he was looking for would not be easily found. The sheer volume of random items would thwart him. With the police searching for him, Nirat knew that he could be interrupted at any moment by officers at the door. So far he'd managed to avoid human contact, and even if Austin crawled his way out of the desert and reported him, there was still time to do this last thing that needed doing.

He searched.

Nearly thirty minutes later, he found the scuffed mahogany coffer that Austin had brought back from South Africa. Lifting the lid, he saw a clutch of photographs, a custom key fob made from rhinoceros scrotum, a nimble-bladed carving knife, and a half-full box of twelve-gauge shells.

Avoiding the pictures—he didn't want to see the old man looking so virile—he removed the knife and ammunition, then left the closet open and returned to the kitchen. He retrieved the stunted shotgun that had caused this ache in his arm and broke open the double barrels. After he discarded the empty shells, those barrels were cold and long and empty, just two pipes waiting to be filled with fire. Nirat slid a fresh red shell into each, then snapped it shut.

He removed his belt, slid the sheath onto it, then put it back on, seating the knife firmly at his hip. He wondered what creatures Richard had skinned with it and whether or not it was true that a good knife could taste the blood of those it cut.

He took his time with the gas.

Everything had to be right to ensure a full-on inferno. He went through the house systematically, preparing evenly spaced burn points that, when lit, would create multiple fires at particularly vulnerable places. He wanted to be saddened by it, this loss, this sending away of so many memories, but when he looked around inside himself, he saw only one prominent event, and it wasn't a happy one: Richard had bequeathed him a shit-for-brains son.

When it was finally done, he took a luxuriant piss, left the lid up, and went in search of matches.

CHAPTER 80

Malcolm Donovan's black Cutlass/Hurst, bought new off the lot in the summer of 1983, took on speed along US 95 North.

"Isn't it about time we called the cops?" Katelyn asked. "If your dad's in trouble—"

"He isn't in any trouble. Not anymore. There's nothing anyone can do to him."

She touched his leg. "You know what I mean."

"Yeah. But I don't want to call Ling."

"You sure? From what Dezi said, that monster may be on his way there right now."

"I have a better idea."

"Consider me a captive audience."

"I'm going to call the nursing home and talk to Laci."

"Who?"

"Nurse's aide." He scrolled through his contacts, dividing his attention with the highway. "I'm going to tell her to keep an eye down the hall and wait for someone to head for Dad's room. If she sees anyone, she needs to call the cops first, then me."

He pressed the green phone button and waited.

The speedometer touched eighty.

"Why not just have the police there already? Why wait for him to show up?"

"Because we're not sure if he will. Apparently they missed him last night. Savlodar gave me bad information, and I gave it to Ling. I don't want to be wrong again."

"Horizons Health Care, this is Dorothy, how may I help you?"

"This is Micah Donovan. Is Laci Gueterez available?"

"Hold, please."

Katelyn applied pressure to his leg. "That's not the only reason you want to get there before the police."

Micah didn't feel it necessary to reply. He threw her a grin. "You blew my mind last night, by the way."

She smiled in that radiant way she had. "You're a smooth talker when you intentionally change the subject."

"I don't want to lose you."

"I'm not going anywhere."

"Things have changed. My bills are suddenly not getting paid."

"Doesn't scare me in the least. You've sort of made me fearless."

"Wish I could say the same thing for myself."

Laci came on the line, and Micah gave her instructions as his foot inched toward the floorboard, asking his dad's car for just a little bit more.

CHAPTER 81

They drove in silence for over half an hour, holding hands between the seats.

"There's a light in the trunk," Micah said.

"A light?"

"The kind that goes on top of the car. Truckers call it a cherry."

"A police light?"

"It's been in there for years, wrapped up in a golf towel."

"Your father used it?"

"Occasionally. I don't think cops do that anymore. It was a long time ago."

"Do you want to pull over and get it?"

"Thought about it. But I don't think the Highway Patrol would understand."

Without looking over, he felt her studying him. "We're going to get there in time," she said. "It's going to be all right. He's not going to hurt your father."

"Hope you're right."

"What happened to that half-full glass?"

"Just wish I could drive a bit faster, that's all."

"It's fast enough. It always is, even if just barely. I doubt you've ever been late for anything in your life. For what it's worth, you're the most punctual person I know." She gave his fingers a squeeze. "You're always right on time, Micah."

"Maybe." He slipped his hand from hers to get both of them on the wheel. "But the day's not over yet."

Chapter 82

From the end of the block, Nirat watched the smoke blacken the windows. He'd worked methodically so as to ensure a comprehensive burn. It had taken an hour to create the conditions for an optimum temperature. When the fire settled in and started stroking, it would advance in such a way that nothing would remain when it was through. Like Chernobyl, the only choice would be to encase the ruins in lead.

"Or bulldoze it, at the very least," he said to himself.

Flame appeared on the second floor. He'd disabled the alarms, so until a neighbor noticed, no one would come. Orange hands waved behind the glass of the master bedroom. Nirat had opened every third window, turned on all the ceiling fans, and throttled up the air conditioner so as to give the beast the breath of life.

A few weeks ago he'd fixed the balustrade on the east staircase. He imagined the fire painting it as if flowing from a pail. The fine woodwork would never again tell the story of all the hands that had rested on it. How many hours had Nirat spent on its repair?

Smoke suddenly roiled from a guest-room window. It was so thick and so black that it seemed to be a solid funnel affixed to the side of the house.

Across the street, a man ran out of his garage, phone against his ear.

Time to go.

Nirat took his foot off the brake. He'd wasted nearly two hours here already, but why was he reluctant to leave? The house was his tether, it seemed, and now that it was dissolving, he had no connection to Richard Savlodar other than his son's blood on his shoe.

He shifted the sheath on his belt; now that he was seated, the knife handle jabbed him uncomfortably. He ended up slipping it free and letting it rest on the passenger's seat. What African beasts had Richard field-dressed with it, or had he carried it just for show? Nirat planned to bury it in the desert once he was finished with it this morning. Perhaps in a millennium or so, archaeologists visiting from the domed cities on Mars would unearth it and wonder what strange purpose it had served.

He raised his eyebrows at himself in the mirror. Normally his thoughts were less inclined toward the fantastic. But then again, considering the last few hours, it appeared that being prosaic no longer served him.

During his drive across the city to the senior Donovan's care facility, he'd waited for paranoia to poison him. Yet he remained calm. Why wasn't he worried about a squad car suddenly jumping the median and giving chase? Of course, they weren't looking for a silver Lexus, and with the exception of the girl's roommate, he'd tactfully avoided interacting with anyone or even crossing their line of sight. He warred with himself over the causes for his lack of suspicion, then unrolled the window and let the wind absolve him of whatever bit of responsibility that might have otherwise impaired him.

Twelve minutes later he pulled into the quiet parking lot and received a gift.

Micah Donovan's car occupied a slot beside the handicap places near the door.

Nirat braked too quickly. His seatbelt locked against him. He recognized the vehicle from the cemetery, its rear fender bearing a star pattern of tiny holes.

Nirat opened his mouth but made no sound. He didn't have the right word for this mash-up of fate and symmetry and the dharma of completing the path he'd been given. But this being Vegas, maybe Donovan's presence here was none of those lofty things but instead just common lowball luck.

He parked directly behind the black car, leaving less than two inches between their bumpers. If Donovan ran this time, he'd do it on foot.

Nirat sheathed the knife, wrapped the shotgun in a coat, and got out. The engine of Donovan's car still radiated considerable heat. Nirat guessed that he'd been here less than fifteen minutes. Briefly he considered running his key across the hood like some kind of juvenile punk, and though the act would've offered some baseline satisfaction, he kept walking.

The sun watched him through the desert willows, flashing through the fronds.

He glanced back. Other than a young woman pushing a middle-aged man in a wheelchair, he saw no one.

He went inside.

Luck seemed to be hanging around, because the foyer was crowded, and crowds meant camouflage. A variety of paralyzed, crippled, and otherwise incapacitated patients of all ages had been wheeled out to enjoy the television and the natural light streaming in through the wide bay windows. They were victims of Lou Gehrig's disease and car wrecks and nervous system disorders. Nirat moved through them without making eye contact, irrationally afraid, like a man whistling on his way through a graveyard.

He turned left at the hallway, kept going.

Assuming Donovan and the girl were alone, Nirat knew he'd have no trouble. His knife would prove agile enough, and of course there was always the backup of the gun. As soon as it was done, he'd retrace his entry route, drive the Lexus to the Savlodar Financial Group construction site west of the city, and exchange vehicles before leaving this place forever. The efficiency of the plan excited him. Richard would have approved.

He slowed as he neared the room, holding his bundled coat so as to cover the knife at his belt. The prattle issuing through the door was distinctly that of morning sportscasters commenting on yesterday's games. Though Nirat saw little point in providing a TV for a human marionette, he supposed it made the family feel a bit better to know that, should their loved one suddenly come back to life, he would be greeted by the snarky anchormen of ESPN.

Pulling in a nervous breath, he looked around the corner.

With one exception, nothing had changed since his previous visit. The room was bright and clean. Its occupant sat in his mechanical seat and faced the window. But now the Presley girl was here, legs drawn up in her chair and blanket tucked in around her. The seat beside her was vacant, and from behind the closed restroom door came the sound of the shower.

Go.

Nirat heard Richard's voice and obeyed. He closed the door behind him as he moved, kicking the stopper that held it open. He crossed the tiled floor quickly. Sliding the knife free, he walked toward the girl, knowing he had to sever her vocal cords before she had the chance to scream.

The men on the TV kept up their inane repartee. Between them and the shower, Nirat's advance was soundless.

Presley opened her eyes.

Nirat stopped, three feet away.

"Micah wanted me to tell you something," she said.

He tightened his grip on the knife. "And what might that be?"

She looked at him through strands of unbrushed hair. "I'm

the designated decoy."

Behind him, the brain-dead cop stood up from his chair.

Startled, Nirat spun, and even before he got fully around, he realized his mistake. Micah Donovan had taken his father's place.

"Fuck me," Nirat said, and then Donovan slammed into him.

CHAPTER 83

The hardest part had been sitting still.

Micah had told his dad the plan as he'd wheeled him into the bathroom. If the old man were listening somewhere deep in his abyss, he surely approved. Micah had never been able to convince himself that Malcolm would've been satisfied with his son's career as a chauffeur. But these last few days, when he seared the paint from the sky and danced at the edge of the world, he felt the change. He'd never wanted his dad to wake up more than now. It was one thing to take care of your father when he needed you, but it was entirely another to show him the scars of honorable combat and the blue-eyed beauty on your arm.

I'm the designated decoy, Katelyn said.

Micah rose from the chair he'd borrowed from the room next door. He had no weapon, but he saw two within reach, both in the hands of Tully's killer.

He stepped forward with his left foot as she'd taught him, crossed diagonally with his right, and drove his shoulder into the man's chest.

The impact carried them over Katelyn's chair. Micah caught a wrist in each hand as they went down on the other side, using his body as a jackhammer when they struck the floor.

Air discharged from the man's lungs in a single burst.

In the tiny gap of time that followed, when his enemy was without oxygen, Micah tried to shake the weapons free. The shotgun, the heavier of the two, spun across the floor and slid under the bed. But the knife remained.

Katelyn went for the gun.

A sudden inhale gave the man life again, and his furious strength returned.

It wasn't enough. Lying on top of him, Micah headbutted him in the face.

Tully had once told him that the skull was the hardest part of the human body. Micah believed him then and he believed him now, feeling the man's already injured nose further crumple beneath his forehead. He did it again, the concussive force vibrating down his spine.

The man brought up a knee, but Micah flowed with him, twisting away so that the kick delivered little energy when it made contact. He maintained his grip, feeling a pulse beneath each palm. The two of them lay more like lovers than combatants. Each time the man tried to wrest himself free, Micah didn't resist, but instead followed the direction of the movement so that they rippled together but didn't come apart.

He dropped another bomb with his head, crushing an eye.

"Micah, get back!"

Katelyn's words came from beyond the dance floor and made little sense. Here in this dire syncopation, Micah understood only the rhythm as he reacted to every attempt to disrupt their embrace. Farther out were other voices, nurses shouting in the hall.

He attacked again with his head, this time connecting with the man's temple. The violent bone-on-bone contact sent motes of darkness across his field of vision but didn't impair him. He curled his body into every strained attempt at escape, riding their shared momentum.

"I have the gun!"

The next time the man spasmed for release, Micah rolled

with him all the way, exchanging positions with him and putting his own back against the floor.

Katelyn fired.

Most of the steel bearings struck the wall, blasting away paint and plaster. But at least two of the pellets carved ravines along the cheek of Tully's murderer, with one of them blowing out flakes of teeth as it left his mouth.

The gunfire turned the cries in the hall into screams.

Making a manic, gurgling sound, the man—dripping blood—used the advantage of his superior position to force the knife toward Micah's throat.

Micah relaxed and let it come. He twisted to the side just before it reached his throat, causing the blade to strike the floor and skid. For a moment the strength evaporated from the man's buckling wrist.

Micah turned that wrist around and forced it up at the same time that he shifted his pliancy into leverage and pulled the man down.

The blade slipped easily between two ribs.

The face hanging above Micah's transformed. The jowls tightened. The lips peeled back over blood-smeared teeth.

Micah rolled. As he freed himself, Tully's killer fell forward, pawing at the knife in his chest. But his own body weight now trapped it against the floor. He flopped onto his side and made a buzzing noise—red bubbles popping on his lips—as he worked his fingers around the knife handle. He made no attempt to withdraw it as blood flowed around the steel. He stared at nothing. His legs shook, but his hands remained almost placid on the knife. His eyes focused, but Micah couldn't see whatever it was he watched with such acute fascination.

He exhaled one last time and closed his eyes.

Micah, gasping so hard it hurt, let his head fall back against the floor. He wanted to do nothing but remember how to breathe normally again, how to take a breath without his lungs catching fire, and how to dance without almost the possibility of getting killed.

Epilogue

The limousine, as white as the desert moon, turned away from the lights of the Strip and sought the darkness of a backstage door. Yet even here, night was thwarted by a string of bulbs along the porte cochere, reflecting off the car's waxed steel. The Lincoln idled in the colored glow.

The door swung open, and the driver emerged.

His shoes were blacker even than the car's windows. His tuxedo fit him comfortably, though he spent a moment tugging on his shirt cuffs so that the proper amount of white was exposed, vibrant against his jacket and the coffee color of his skin.

That done, he assumed his post near the door.

There was a time when he would have stood with his hands clasped at his crotch. But the planets had shifted since then, and he'd vowed to avoid that posture. Instead, he slid his hands into his pockets and leaned back. The casualness of such a stance no longer bothered him.

The stage door opened.

Dancers came out, laughing, congratulating one another on the show. They were lean and vital and wore too much makeup—the better to be seen throughout the theater. The driver watched them, and when a few of them waved, he tipped his head back in return. The show had been running for nine weeks, and they knew him by now, though only one of them approached.

Katelyn said goodnight to the others and peeled away from them, her hair sprinkled with glitter, her bag hanging on her arm. She stopped in front of him. "Hey, handsome. You don't think I'm spoiled, do you, riding home in a shiny new limo every evening?"

"It's not my place to say, ma'am."

"Ooh, so I'm getting the *ma'am* tonight. What's the occasion?"

The driver motioned toward the car's rear door.

"What, I'm riding in the back? Are you hiding a box of chocolates on the front seat?"

The driver said nothing, only walked to the back and held the door for her.

Katelyn grinned. "Okay. I'll sprawl in the back like an heiress. Just don't tell anyone that you're turning me into a total diva."

He closed the door after her and got behind the wheel.

Seconds later they were moving.

Her voice came from the intercom: "Uh, where are we going?"

"I'm afraid that information is on a need-to-know basis only."

"Ah, like in the spy movies. I'm cool with that. Hey, you at least want to lower the divider?"

"No, thank you."

"What do you mean *no, thank you*? This is the love of your life back here, and she wants to smell your cologne."

The driver smiled to himself. "We're almost there, ma'am."

They crossed the Strip and stopped near the service entrance at the Hilton, among the laundry trucks and delivery vans. A valet jogged toward the car as the driver got out.

"Yo, man," the valet said. "Right on time."

The driver handed him the keys. "I'll call you when we're done."

"Dude, take your time. I'm a sucker for true romance, know what I'm sayin'?"

As the valet slid into the car, the driver opened Katelyn's door. "Ma'am."

She bounded out and looked around. "So who do we know at the Hilton?"

"A valet and a custodian, as it turns out."

"You're letting him take the car?"

"He's parking it."

"Yeah, but you've had the thing for over two months now, and I've never seen you let anyone else drive it."

"There's been no need." He held out his arm.

Smiling, she slid her hand into the angle of his elbow.

He led her through a pair of loading doors that were propped open with commercial-sized soup cans. Moments later they were intercepted by a janitor who led them to a key-operated elevator. He touched a button not found in the lifts accessible by hotel guests.

"Micah, where are we going?"

Now it was his turn to smile. "You'll see."

He watched the elevator doors close, loving the sound of his own name.

Micah had encountered only minor difficulties when reestablishing his client base. He'd been forced to crack the dam of his savings but was on his way to repairing the damage. His momentary celebrity status had helped, but after a few days even the local bloggers had moved on to more topical heroes. Micah's mortal matchup on the nursing-home floor had provided a little career traction, but in this town, maintaining fame was as tricky as rolling the hard six.

"How high does this thing go?" Katelyn asked.

"The moon."

"Hmmm. One of *those* elevators. Is this the part where it

conveniently breaks down and we have to depend on shared bodily warmth in order to make it through the night until we're rescued?"

"That wasn't exactly my plan."

"What *is* the plan?"

"Patience."

"Patience sucks."

Austin Savlodar had survived. At first the authorities had presumed him dead in the house fire, though no evidence of his body had been discovered. A day later, a family driving down from Oregon had found him unconscious beside Route 95. He was broken by abuse and seared by the sun, but alive. Detective Ling had called a month ago to say that Savlodar had relocated his corporate HQ to San Jose.

Micah thought of him more often than he wanted. In a peculiar way, Micah owed everything to him. If not for Savlodar, this woman would not be riding in this elevator with him now. She would not be sharing his bed and his shower and his life.

The doors opened.

"Uh, I don't mean to sound unimpressed or anything, but all I see is an empty hall."

"Come on." Micah took her hand and led her to the stairs marked ROOF ACCESS.

"The roof? Okay, I take it back. I'm officially intrigued."

Though the door was normally locked, Micah had made arrangements, one of the benefits of fraternizing with the city's servant class. They ascended the metal steps and then stepped out onto the hotel roof, the sordid artistry of Las Vegas spreading in every direction around them.

"Wow." Katelyn raised a hand and waved. "Hello, world!"

Standing on the roof under the night sky was like being on the deck of a ship. On one side lay a golf course like a dark sea, while on the other was unchecked civilization, a continent outlined by the Strip. Thirty stories up, Micah felt at least somewhat removed from it all. There was even a whisper of a breeze at this elevation, passing its hands through Katelyn's hair.

Micah left her standing on the edge, a beautiful figurehead on the prow of a ship. He went to the portable stereo whose batteries he'd replaced this morning. Beside it rested an ice chest.

"Is that a boom box I see?" Katelyn called across the open expanse of the roof.

"I don't think anybody calls them that anymore."

"What can I say? I'm old school."

It wasn't true. She was new *everything.* Each morning, Micah shook his head at some new piece of her she revealed.

She made her way over as he inserted a CD. She picked up the case and held it up to read it in the faint light. "*Favorite Ballroom Waltzes.*" She put the case against her face and stared at him over the edge, only her eyes visible. "If I didn't know better, sir, I'd think you were getting ready to ask me to dance."

He held out a hand. His father remained a silent pharaoh in the sarcophagus of his own body, and here was Micah, offering his hand to a woman he would've loved to introduce to Malcolm Donovan. He suspected this particular brand of pain would be with him for all time, but he also suspected that he could manage it. "Please," he said.

"No, thanks. I've always been more of a wallflower girl."

He nodded his understanding. "Doesn't surprise me."

"Too shy."

"And two left feet?"

"Definitely."

He pushed PLAY and stepped toward her. "I think all you need is a little practice."

"I guess I never really had the right teacher."

"I can show you the steps. If you trust me."

She closed her hand in his and looked up at him. "You know what I'm most thankful for in the whole world?"

"What's that?"

"That somebody lost that earring in your car and you came back to see if it was mine."

Micah revealed nothing with his expression. "Me, too." He'd told the truth to only one person, and his dad knew how to keep a secret; he was the true master of discretion. "Here we go."

She smiled. "Lead on."

Micah stepped forward with his left foot, and followed it with his right.

ABOUT THE AUTHOR

Lance Hawvermale has waited tables, fought grass fires, won the Cub Scout Pinewood Derby, protested the death penalty, touched the Rosetta Stone, and received a personal letter from Ray Bradbury. He is currently Assistant Professor of English at Ranger College.

He is the author of the Five Star Mystery *The Tongue Merchant* (2008).

Under the pseudonym of Erin O'Rourke, Lance published the thrillers *Seeing Pink* (2003) and *Fugitive Shoes* (2006). His poetry and fiction have garnered numerous awards. He is an alumnus of AmeriCorps and continues to believe in the power of giving.